Tr

Brian Battison

Truths
Not Told

For my sister-in-law
NORMA BOWKER
with thanks for the critiques

This edition published in Great Britain in 1999 by
Allison & Busby Limited
114 New Cavendish Street
London W1M 7FD
http://www.allisonandbusby.ltd.uk

First published 1996 by
Constable and Company Ltd

A catalogue record for this book is available
from the British Library

ISBN 0 7490 0366 9

Printed and bound by Biddles Limited,
Guildford, Surrey.

Prologue

The wound bore no resemblance to those so favoured by Hollywood directors; there was no neat black hole, no thin red line of blood travelling gracefully from it. Half the victim's face had been torn away where the bullet had entered the forehead; congealed blood and powder burns obscured his eyes, obliterated the bridge of his nose; and dried brain matter together with sharp fragments of skull were splattered on the back of the armchair in which his body was slumped.

Heavy velvet drapes drawn across the windows allowed in little light to penetrate the gloom. And an eerie silence, broken only by an occasional buzzing of newly hatched blowflies, hung over the elegantly furnished room like an invisible sinister mist.

Chapter 1

Chief Inspector Jim Ashworth skipped down the front steps of his home in Bridgetown. Gravel crunched beneath his size twelve shoes, while a light early-summer breeze ruffled his thick dark hair which showed signs of greying.

A boyish excitement gripped him as he slipped his key into the lock of the new Ford Scorpio. The car was police issue, and Ashworth had taken delivery of it only the previous week. As the door swung open on well-oiled hinges, he savoured the new-upholstery smell before climbing into the driver's seat and activating the engine, taking his eyes off the dashboard just long enough to wave briefly to his wife, Sarah, who watched from the lounge window.

He slipped a cassette into the slender tape deck and entered into a duet with Sinatra as he carefully drove to the police station.

In the CID office, high up on the fourth floor of Bridgetown station, Detective Sergeant Holly Bedford was studying her reflection in the glass wall.

'Do you think I'm putting on too much weight?'

'No,' was the monosyllabic reply from Detective Constable Josh Abraham, who continued to scrutinise his computer screen as he spoke.

'You can tell me the truth,' she said, her large green, almost hypnotic, eyes glued to her image.

Josh swivelled round to face her.

'Holly, I've worked with you for two years now,' he said, hardly concealing his impatience, 'and for all that time you've been trying to put on weight. Now you have, you're complaining about it. Believe me, you look great.'

'What's the matter with you, Abraham? You're being nice.'

Josh laughed. During their time together, they had developed a good-natured, sometimes outrageous form of banter in which flattery played little part.

'You look fantastic,' he insisted.

'Good enough to convert you?' she asked with mock allurement.

He turned away abruptly, and a puzzled Holly studied his profile.

'You all right, Josh?'

'Do you think people change?' he asked, suddenly earnest

'Don't get heavy with me, Abraham,' she laughed. 'Look, I'm always saying I'll take you to bed and convert you. I don't mean anything by it.'

'I wouldn't be offended by anything you said. I know you've got a sick mind.'

She giggled. 'Yes, haven't I just?'

'No, it's just that, well, when I said do you think people change …' He hesitated. 'Well, the thing is, three years ago I was with someone – Greg Albrine. For me it was the real thing, but he was putting it about.' He glanced at her shyly, unused to confiding. 'This was up north. When we split, I moved down here. But now Greg's turned up again – he came down to chase a job in Rutley, and he looked me up.'

'Ah, and are you two … ?'

'No, no,' Josh said, shaking his head vigorously, 'but he's staying at my place, and I just wondered if people do change, get things out of their systems.'

'God, that's a hell of a question to ask somebody like me.'

Holly's own love life was deeply complicated. After the death of her husband five years ago, she had shunned any form of emotional involvement; but her highly charged libido had finally refused to be denied and in recent years she had become rather promiscuous.

'You don't think they do then?' Josh said, despondent.

'I'm saying, I don't know. The way I see it, in love you have to weigh things up and decide if you want to take the chance.'

'I suppose so.' Suddenly, he brightened. 'Would you like to come over for a meal tonight and meet Greg?'

'Thanks – yes, I would.'

'About eight, then?'

'Okay, I'll look forward to it.'

With reluctance, she turned her attention back to her desk.

'As nothing's come in, I suppose we should catch up on some paperwork,' she said, picking up a file with fervent apathy.

But what Police Constable Alan Bennett – Gordon, to his friends – was about to discover would ensure that CID paperwork would remain largely untouched for the remainder of the day.

Yawning widely, he braked his panda car to a halt at a junction. The call had come in at the end of a long night on duty, during which he had been abused and spat at when the pubs turned out, and punched on the cheek whilst attending a domestic dispute in the early hours. His immediate future held nothing but the promise of recriminations from his wife for not arriving home in time to look after their baby daughter while she took their son to school. And this call would delay his arrival home still further.

Driving slowly along the tree-lined avenue, he searched for number twenty-three, easing the car to a stop when he caught sight of it. The house was similar to the others in the avenue: a large detached with six bedrooms, standing in its own grounds behind a high stone wall.

PC Bennett approached its wrought-iron gates and let

himself in. How the other half lives, he thought enviously. Close up, the house was even more impressive. Bennett mounted wide steps flanked by stone lions, entered the porch and knocked briskly on the door, shuffling his feet impatiently while he waited for someone to answer. Presently, the door swung open to reveal a middle-aged man in a smart grey suit. In his hand was a bone china cup containing coffee.

'Bridgetown police, sir,' Bennett announced. 'I believe you called us.'

'Ah, yes,' the man answered in a clipped Oxford accent. He placed the cup carefully on the hall table, and said, 'It's about Reggie Carter.'

'What about him, sir?'

'He lives next door,' the man said, pushing past the young constable to stand on the steps where he pointed to his left. Bennett looked in that direction and tried to appear interested, but his wife was still very much on his mind.

'Goes away a lot on business,' the man informed him, 'but he always leaves the curtains open, and the lights on a timer switch.'

'Yes, sir?'

'But this time the curtains have been drawn for three days, and when I went past last evening, I believe the morning paper was still in the letter box. Couldn't be sure at that distance, but that's what it looked like.'

'Right, sir, thank you, I'll go and check.'

Bennett was hurrying down the steps when the man called, 'There's something else.'

Suppressing a sigh, the constable turned back. 'Yes, sir?'

'Late Saturday evening, we heard something which sounded like a car backfiring ... Well, call it paranoia if you like, but one reads such terrible things in the newspapers, and after all, the cars in this district are too well tuned to backfire.'

'Are you saying it could have been a gunshot, sir?'

'Yes, it could have been, although I didn't think anything of it at the time.'

'You haven't checked yourself, sir, knocked on the front door or anything?'

'No, I hardly know the chap. I thought it better to ring you people.'

'Thank you, sir.'

Starting back along the drive, he glanced at his watch and groaned. 'She'll bloody kill me.'

PC Bennett's irritation was growing steadily as he trudged up the driveway to number twenty-five. Finally, he stopped in front of the house.

'Odd,' he said aloud as he surveyed its eight large windows, all of which had curtains drawn across. 'Very odd.'

He made for the front door, where one of the free weekly newspapers was indeed protruding from its letter box, and rang the bell. When there was no reply, he banged hard on the highly polished oak. Still there was silence, so he knelt down, pushed the newspaper into the hall, and peered through the flap.

'Police,' he called.

There was no movement, no sound apart from the quizzical buzzing of a fly intrigued by the sudden shaft of light.

Bennett walked round to the side of the house. Beyond the integral garage was a side gate which was not locked. He opened it a few inches and glanced into the garden, his nose wrinkling at an odious smell drifting up from the drains. Before going any further, he backtracked to the garage and peered through its side window.

'A Merc – wouldn't you know it? But all tucked up in bed.' He glanced back towards the gate. 'And when people go away, they usually lock everything up.'

His wife was temporarily forgotten as Bennett made his way round to the rear. Passing the drain, he saw the reason for the smell: a black plastic sack had blown into it, stopping the water from draining away. Bennett skirted round the soapy puddle, and went on into the garden proper; it was huge, with vast lawns and borders.

Hurrying towards the kitchen door, he spoke urgently into the radio pinned to his lapel. 'Sarge, it's Bennett.'

Static crackled. 'Okay, Gordon, go ahead.'

'I'm at the rear of twenty-five Lilac Avenue, sarge. Can't raise anybody inside, and there's signs of forced entry to the kitchen door.'

'You haven't been in?'

'No, sarge, I'd like some back-up. It's got a funny feel to it.'

'All right, Gordon, wait there.'

'Make it snappy, sarge.'

'Yes, I know, the missus. Don't worry, I've phoned her. You'll still get your cocoa when you get home, son.'

Ashworth left the Scorpio at the rear of the car-park and headed for the station building, walking backwards and thinking how rich the midnight-blue paintwork looked compared with the garish red of Holly's Micra and the subtle silver-grey of Josh's Nissan Sunny as he set the remote alarm.

He bounded up the steps, his immaculate dark blue suit showing off to good effect his strong and supple frame. For a man in his middle fifties he was remarkably fit, and only his heavily lined face betrayed his age. His facial expression rarely showed emotion, but his large brown eyes were truly the windows of his soul: often they would glower with hostility or anger, but for the present they twinkled with good humour.

Front reception was empty but for Sergeant Martin Dutton busy at the front desk.

'Good morning, Martin,' Ashworth called heartily.

Dutton's smile was warm. 'Morning, Jim.'

The sergeant was of the same age as Ashworth, but for him time had not been so kind: beneath the blue uniform his middle had spread, and his hair had long since departed.

'How's the car?'

'Sweet as a nut, Martin, sweet as a nut.'

'It's all right for some,' Dutton grumbled.

The chief inspector was well used to Dutton's good-natured moans, so he merely smiled and was waiting for the sergeant to recount the details of his latest drama when Holly's high heels clicked on the stairs.

'Gordon Bennett, guv –'

'Language, Holly,' Ashworth warned, with a smile.

'That's the mood we're in, is it?' she muttered under her breath. Then, approaching the desk, 'Gordon Bennett's answered a call at twenty-five Lilac Avenue. The neighbours haven't seen the occupant for some time. There's evidence of a break-in, and Gordon's requested back-up.'

'So why are they telling us?'

'Because there're no mobiles available.'

'Why is it, whenever anything happens, there aren't any mobiles available?' Ashworth asked heavily.

'No idea, guv,' Holly sighed.

'All right, you and Josh come with me to Lilac Avenue.'

'On our way, guv.'

It was early May, and the trees from which Lilac Avenue derived its name were not yet in full blossom. Ashworth had left the Scorpio behind Bennett's patrol car, and was scanning the avenue with irritation because Holly's Micra had not yet appeared.

He opened the iron gates and walked slowly towards the house, making a mental note to rebuke his detective sergeant when she did finally arrive with Josh. But half-way there, he relented. Ashworth was a man who prided himself on his ability to miss very little, and his guess was that Holly had entered into one of her 'good girl' phases, when she strove to control her amorous nature, and deny herself the pleasures of the flesh. These times lasted for anything up to six weeks, during which Holly could become extremely touchy, and in view of this, he decided not to force a confrontation over such a minor misdemeanour.

Josh, on the other hand, seemed almost uplifted of late, with just the occasional flicker of doubt showing in his eyes. The romantic in Ashworth assumed that his detective constable was in love and at that stage in a relationship when niggling insecurities forced their way through the euphoria. He was pleased for Josh, but did however push from his mind the realities of physical love for a man such as he.

When he reached the house, Ashworth was greeted by a somewhat disgruntled PC Bennett.

'Good morning, sir,' the constable said, clicking his heels.

'Relax, Gordon, skip the formalities when we're away from the station. What have we got?'

As Bennett explained, Ashworth glanced at the windows. 'I see,' he mused, 'and the break-in's round the back?'

'That's right,' Bennett said, leading the way. 'Kitchen door.'

They had inspected the damage and were back in the front garden before Ashworth's two detectives could be seen heading along the drive. Holly's whole demeanour suggested that today her fuse was very short, and Ashworth smiled to himself as snatches of their conversation reached his ears.

Holly was snapping at Josh, 'You're saying I can't

13

drive a bloody car.'

'No, I'm not, I just said the guy was in the right. You should have slowed down at the roundabout.'

'He had plenty of time to brake when I pulled out,' Holly huffed.

'But he didn't,' Josh insisted. 'You came out of nowhere.'

'Good morning, team,' Ashworth called with a sunny smile from the top of the front steps.

'What are you doing, guv?' Josh asked, glad of a respite from Holly's sharp tongue.

'The lock on the kitchen door's buckled. We can't get in that way, so I'm going to smash the glass and get in here.' He held out his hand for Bennett's truncheon.

His first blow to the side panel of the front door caused fissures to run all ways across the toughened pane, and the second was accompanied by the tinkling of glass. With great care, Ashworth put his hand through the hole and felt for the lock. Soon his fingers touched cold metal and he turned the catch.

'Try the door now.'

'It's open, guv,' Holly said.

'There's a mortise lock, but only the Yale's been used,' Ashworth remarked, carefully withdrawing his hand.

They entered the house, exchanging glances as their shoes sank into the expensive carpet. The fragrance of furniture polish hung in the air, together with the scent of stale flowers.

And there was a third smell, slightly stronger. They had all noticed it, were all aware of its significance. Something was wrong.

Chapter 2

Lenny Spencer paced the floor, every so often stopping at the table to scrutinise the morning paper.

'Surely they've found it by now,' he muttered, hurriedly flicking through the pages.

His smart appearance was in sharp contrast to the dingy two-roomed flat in Rutley, a major city, fifty miles from Bridgetown.

He stopped by the window and looked out at the wretched view: disused factory chimneys and old terraced houses converted into flats, endless rows of neglected gardens and drab outbuildings.

Lenny was almost thirty years old and, for the first time in his life, was experiencing real fear. His palms were clammy, his head ached, and his eyes were sore from lack of sleep; and despite the foul taste in his mouth, he would stub out one cigarette and immediately light another.

He was desperate to leave this place, to go as far away as the money would take him. But until the body in Bridgetown was discovered, he had to stay.

Yet again his mind travelled back to Friday, the day before the murder. How he wished it was still Friday.

Ashworth gripped the handle of the dining-room door, and eased it open. From the threshold, his first impression was one of oak panelling, which adorned every bit of wall space. He advanced into the vast room, immediately picking up the faint scent of food

'An empty plate and a wineglass were set on a mahogany table. Ashworth examined them, noting the dried steak fat pushed aside on the plate, the wine dregs in the glass. Six empty chairs stood around the table.

He stopped to count the downstairs rooms on his

fingers – sitting-room, lounge, dining-room, study, kitchen – and was ready to assume that the ground floor was clear when he spotted an oak-coloured door almost concealed in the panelling.

Taking a deep breath, he strode towards it and turned the handle sharply. The room beyond was large, with heavy velvet curtains pulled across the windows, but through the gloom, Ashworth could see that the walls were lined with floor-to-ceiling bookcases, all crammed with books. In the centre of the room, with its back to the door, was a dark red leather chair. Beside it stood a small table holding a whisky glass and decanter.

All seemed quite normal, apart from the dozens of bluebottles buzzing around the chair, some hovering, others diving out of sight. Ashworth caught his breath and approached the chair.

The man was dressed in a plum-coloured dressing-gown and leather slippers. A book lay open on his lap, and half his face had been blown away. Ashworth had to turn his back when a number of flies emerged from the wound.

He returned to the dining-room, and although he was shaken, his voice was firm and resonant as he called into the hall, 'Body in the library. Gunshot wounds.'

He knew he need not say more. PC Bennett was already calling Central Control, requesting the attendance of the police surgeon, the pathologist, and the forensic team.

Ashworth felt sick.

That feeling of nausea was still with him when the police surgeon arrived to make the obvious but necessary statement that life was extinct. While the forensic team began their work, the pathologist, Dr Alex Ferguson, examined the body.

'Okay, as the surgeon said, he's dead, and I've got another surprise for you – he was shot,' he said, displaying a rare flash of dry humour.

Ashworth could not manage a smile. 'When?'

The pathologist's serious face beneath thinning blond hair was a mask of concentration. 'Rigor mortis has left the body, but there's no staining to the flank or abdomen, which means he's been dead for more than thirty-six hours, but less than forty-eight. So, time of death was probably Saturday evening.'

'Yes, that fits in with the steak dinner, the wine and the scotch, not to mention the drawn curtains.'

Ferguson nodded agreement and loudly snapped shut his black bag. 'Now, if you'll excuse me, I'll arrange for the post-mortem.'

Ashworth caught his arm. 'Before you go, what do you think happened?'

'Not my province, guesswork,' he answered crisply.

It has been said that a policeman and a pathologist need to view at least a dozen bodies together before a rapport can develop; this was only their second case, and so far that old adage was proving to be correct. Ashworth felt that the doctor was far too stiff and formal.

'Lighten up, Alex,' he ventured. 'I'm asking your opinion because I value it.'

Flattery worked well on the doctor, as with most people, and he relaxed slightly.

'Since you've asked, I think that whoever did this came here with the intention of committing murder.'

'Not a burglary gone wrong?'

'No, it doesn't fit. The break-in was at the rear, and one could go all over the ground floor of this house and miss the library.'

Ashworth agreed; it was only by chance that he had noticed the door, which blended so well into the oak panelling. 'I think you're right,' he said, 'I think the murderer was heading for this room.'

Ferguson, warming to his new role of detective, went on, 'The assailant came in through the back, along the

17

passage to the dining-room, and let himself into the library. Now, at that point, the victim must have been asleep – a combination of rich food and alcohol.'

'How do you know he was asleep?' Ashworth asked, amused by the doctor's enthusiasm.

'I don't, of course, but he was either asleep or so drunk, he'd passed out. It's obvious. He didn't move, didn't stand up and try to defend himself, didn't run. The photographs will bear that out. I mean, the book was open on his lap, it hadn't been dislodged and it would have been if he'd tried to get up. I believe the body was in more or less the same position as it was prior to the shooting.'

'Very clever. So what do you think happened?'

Ferguson removed his spectacles, saying, 'I believe the murderer came into the room …'

Ashworth stood enthralled as the doctor began to act out the scene, gripping his spectacles as if they were a gun.

'Now, all he could see was what we see – the back of the leather chair,' he said, advancing towards it. 'The gun's already in his hand, and he comes round to the side of the chair but he doesn't shoot his victim, or panic and run. Quite calmly, he walks to the front of it and blasts off one shot, dead centre.'

Looking now at Ashworth, he stood facing the body, his spectacles in both hands; then he took aim, lifting his arms to simulate the recoil from a pistol shot.

'An execution,' Ashworth ventured, as he joined the doctor and looked down at the corpse.

'A calculated, cold-blooded murder, I'd say. Sex or money – aren't they the main motives for murder?'

'Or revenge,' Ashworth said.

'Ah, yes, he could have been an errant spouse. Or perhaps he stole money from someone.'

'Tell me, Alex, can you make a guess at his age? It might help for immediate identification.'

Ferguson thought for a moment, then said, 'Going by

the lines on his face, or what's left of it, and the skin on his hands …' He paused. 'I'd say fifties, back end. Oh, and this might help – the hair's dyed. It's a professional job, but it's just too uniform black for a man of his age.'

'Thanks,' Ashworth said, smiling. 'You should have been a policeman.'

The doctor returned the smile and made a face as he retrieved his bag.

'Thanks for coming in, Alex.'

The chief inspector waved him off as sounds drifted through from the hall. Holly could be heard loudly issuing orders in a strident voice. Ashworth shook his head despairingly and withdrew into the dining-room.

Holly bristled in, and it was obvious that her mood had deteriorated as the morning progressed. She stopped in front of Ashworth, her face grim.

'Right, guv,' she said, consulting her notebook, 'we've interviewed those neighbours we found in, and the owner of the house is a man by the name of Reginald Carter, aged somewhere in his fifties. Pleasant enough man, but keeps himself to himself, rarely says more than hello. Because of his lifestyle it's assumed he's in business, but nobody seems to know what he does. He drives a Mercedes –'

'I know, it's in the garage.'

'It's an L reg,' Holly continued as if he hadn't spoken.

'Hold on, Holly, L reg, you say?'

'Yes.'

'But the one in the garage is an M.'

She looked again at her notebook. 'Perhaps he traded it in.'

'Perhaps, but people don't usually trade in a Mercedes every twelve months. What else have you got?'

'That's about it, guv, apart from the woman at number sixteen thinks Carter dyes his hair black.'

'Right, then I think we can safely assume, Holly, that the body in there is Reginald Carter.'

The postmortem was performed that afternoon, and almost immediately Alex Ferguson telephoned the results through to Ashworth. The findings, however, revealed little more than they already knew: death was due to a single bullet fired into the brain, and time of death was around nine o'clock, Saturday evening.

The chief inspector was sitting at his desk, watching intently while Josh harassed Forensic for any information they might have gleaned.

'That's all you've got? You may not have had long, but the message from my guv'nor is, he wants this like yesterday.' He listened for a moment, glancing at Ashworth briefly, then laughed. 'No, I definitely couldn't tell him to go and do that to himself. Do your best then, eh?'

He replaced the receiver. 'Not much, guv. Some fibres were found on the glass in the kitchen door. They think they're from woollen gloves. There're fingerprints all over the place, but because of the gloves they're not too hopeful on that score. And they've dug a .38 bullet from the back of the chair.'

'That's all?' Ashworth asked. 'Not much, is it?'

'Uniformed are going over the gardens with a fine-tooth comb but, so far, nothing.'

Ashworth turned to Holly at her desk. 'You've handled the press?'

'Yes, guv, the usual. We haven't named the victim, but we're treating the death as suspicious. That's got to bring people forward who can identify the body, and hopefully tell us about Carter.'

Ashworth was about to respond when a knock came on the door and Superintendent John Newton strode in, resplendent in his crease-free uniform, its silver buttons shining in the arc of sunlight slanting through the glass walls of CID.

'The murder in Lilac Avenue, chief inspector – everything under control?'

'Yes, sir, no problems whatsoever.'

'Good,' Newton replied curtly.

The superintendent was relatively new to the job and although hardly compatible with Ashworth, he had, after a few initial skirmishes, developed a healthy respect for the craggy-faced chief inspector.

'I'll wish you goodnight then.'

'Goodnight, sir.'

The door was closed quietly, and for a few moments, Ashworth sat looking at it.

'No problems at all,' he said scathingly, 'apart from the fact that we've no idea who did it, why it was done, or anything else, for that matter.'

He let out an impatient breath and studied his watch. 'If the good superintendent's going home, that means it must be five o'clock, so why don't you two push off? Tomorrow could be a busy day.'

They needed little coaxing, and when he was alone, Ashworth sat drumming his hands on the desk while he gazed out over the town. Paradoxically, the office was one of his most favoured places on earth. Yes, he hated the building, which was ninety per cent glass, but he adored the view it afforded him of Bridgetown. From such a high vantage point it was possible to make out the original Midlands town, which was now little more than the main high street; and although most of the cottages had been converted into shops, they still retained a rustic appearance with their thatched roofs and timbered wall supports. But in recent years, much to Ashworth's disgust, the town had spread, as more and more green fertile land vanished beneath bricks, mortar and tarmac. Indeed, the town was now of a size that could qualify for city status, and Ashworth could put a date on each of the estates by their very designs. But for now he focused upon the nucleus of the sprawling mass, and set his mind to work.

'What do I know about you, Reginald Carter?' he

thought aloud, enjoying the solitude. 'Quite a lot. I know you were a dealer in antiques and fine art. There were just too many pieces and original paintings in that house for you to be a collector. So, you used your home as a warehouse; as you sold one piece, you replaced it. Your bookshelves told me you liked Shakespeare and the classics. Your CDs were all opera, and you drank Macallan malt whisky. Yes, you had taste.'

Suddenly, he stabbed a finger as if the corpse had come to life and was standing before him. 'But there's one thing that doesn't fit: there's not an alarm system at the house. Mortise locks on the doors, security locks on the windows – enough to deter the opportunist thief who's after the television and microwave, but not the real pro. That means you knew you weren't likely to be burgled and that suggests power, the ability to inspire fear in others, but it doesn't fit the rest of the picture. Still, if you were powerful you must have made enemies, so revenge is a likely motive for your murder.'

So engrossed was he in his deliberations that Ashworth was unaware that the door had opened and a cleaner was hovering in the doorway. She glanced around the room, puzzled to find the chief inspector alone.

'Sorry, sir,' she stammered. 'I didn't know you were in here.'

'It's all right,' Ashworth smiled. 'Just give me a minute.'

The cleaner withdrew hastily, and he muttered, 'I must stop talking to myself.'

Lenny Spencer studied the newspaper headlines. He felt calmer now that the body had been discovered. It was time to leave. He went over every detail again, eager to cover his trail as effectively as possible. They would find out where he had gone, he knew that. All he could hope for was time, time to buy a forged passport and get out of the country. They would follow, of course, so he would need to change his identity again on arrival at his destination. Temporarily, he pushed from his mind the thought that for as long as he lived they would be trying to track him down. He would be forever looking over his shoulder.

His job as a night-club bouncer was on a week-to-week basis, so he would not be missed there. Girlfriends were many and varied, so it should take a while for him to be missed in that department. He knew only too well that eventually his very absence would point the finger at him, but if it could only be delayed for a couple of weeks …

He took the snub-nosed .38 pistol from his waistband, crossed to the bed and concealed it between shirts and underwear in his leather suitcase. Then, hesitating slightly, he reached for his black executive bag and opened it up to gaze once more at the banknotes filling its confines. Snapping it shut, he wandered across to the window and peered cautiously around the dirty curtains. In the street below, a man paused to light a cigarette, his head bowed, his hands cupping the lighter, and for a second he looked up as smoke trailed from his mouth. Lenny sank back against the wall, the breath held fast in his lungs. After a count of ten, he gingerly pulled back the curtain, and exhaled thankfully as he watched the man walking off into the distance. Then, very quickly, he picked up his cases and left the flat.

The meal at Josh's was not a disaster exactly, but it came pretty close to it.

Holly's sexual frustration was reaching a peak; and to be in the company of two gorgeous males with whom she was absolutely safe did little to relieve her tension. Greg was tall, with broad shoulders and an unruly shock of blond hair. His horn-rimmed glasses lent a studious air to his handsome features and, as far as Holly was concerned, only served to make him more desirable.

Dinner was a vegetable lasagne, prepared by Josh, and they ate it in his tiny living-room. Greg seemed only politely interested while they discussed the case, and slightly revolted by the mention of blood.

Holly tried to make appreciative noises about the food, but they sounded false. She supposed that she resented Greg's presence which obviously inhibited Josh, making their usual suggestive repartee impossible. Eventually, after what seemed like an age, the meal was over, and she could offer her thanks and leave.

'The train now standing at platform two is the ten fifteen to London Euston ...'

Lenny Spencer listened to the announcer's voice filtering around Rutley railway station, as he leant against the wall of platform two. The night was mild, but he wore an overcoat with the collar turned up to conceal his face.

Footsteps sounded loudly on the stairs leading down to the platform, and instinctively, Lenny held his breath as a man glanced in his direction, seeming to look him over before strolling off to a carriage at the front of the train. Although aware that his imagination was in overdrive, Lenny was powerless to dispel the knot of fear in the pit of his stomach. He warily watched the British Rail worker busily closing all doors to the train then, seconds before its departure, Lenny raced forward and entered the nearest compartment.

With the train edging out of the station, he heaved a sigh of relief, and sat at the back of the empty carriage, suitcase between his legs, executive bag held firmly on his lap.

Chapter 3

'I'd say she didn't like me,' Greg remarked from the kitchen doorway, while he watched Josh washing the dinner things.

'You're too sensitive.'

'I think she fancies you, and I think she resents me being here.'

Josh put down the washing-up mop and stood with his back to the sink. 'Look, Greg, she knows I'm gay. She's a good friend, nothing more.'

'Do coppers always talk about finding people with half their faces blown off during dinner?'

'When you see something like that, it does tend to stay with you for the rest of the day,' Josh snapped.

'Sorry.'

Greg watched Josh's stiff back for a few moments, then joined him at the sink, and picked up the tea towel.

'I found it interesting really,' he said, half-heartedly polishing a plate. 'Tell me about this Reginald Carter. Have you found out why anybody would want to kill him?'

Josh shrugged. 'We've found out very little about him yet. All we know is what the post-mortem revealed.'

'And what was that?'

'That he was shot,' Josh said, snatching back the tea towel.

Greg lit a cigarette. 'That's all?'

'Yes. Why the interest?'

'Oh, I don't know,' he said, wandering back to the door. 'I just need something to take my mind off things, I suppose.'

Josh put down the saucepan he was drying and stood looking at him. 'What's wrong?' he said. 'You're not how I remember you.'

'How do you remember me?'

'With a lot of pain,' Josh answered with rancour. 'No, bitter/sweet really. I mean, things were great until you started messing around.' He turned back to the sink, adding quietly, 'You hurt me so much, Greg.'

'I regret messing about, I really do.'

'Why have you come here?' Josh asked softly.

'Can we talk?'

'We are talking.'

'I don't mean like this, standing in the kitchen. Josh, can we sit down and talk?'

'Okay, let's go through to the other room.'

The macabre happenings at number twenty-five Lilac Avenue were very much on the mind of Police Constable Bobby Adams as he sat in his panda car outside the house.

Bobby had been with the force for two years, and for most of that time he was considered too lacking in authority for the beat patrols, so had been confined to duties behind the reception desk. Then, as his confidence grew, he was thrown into the hurly-burly of police life. But the fact that he had drawn all-night guard duty outside the murder house because no one else wanted it indicated that he still had some way to go to earn the respect of his peers.

The eastern sky was fast turning a pale grey, and Bobby flicked on the interior light to glance at his watch. At the same time, car headlights curved along the drive, dazzling him momentarily as the full beams shone directly into his eyes. Quickly he killed the light.

'Dip 'em, mate,' he muttered.

But instead of moving on to the house, the car reversed back into the road, its powerful engine roaring away into the night, and Bobby admonished himself for not concentrating fully. He had closed the iron gates at the start of his shift, so the driver of the car had obviously opened them.

But why race off at the sight of a police vehicle?

Bobby reached for the radio handset.

Chief Inspector Jim Ashworth was enjoying the sleep of a man with a clear conscience and a tired mind and body … until the telephone rang.

He reached for the receiver, and growled, 'Hello,' as he squinted at the digital numbers on the alarm clock.

'I'm not disturbing you, am I, Jim?' It was the cheerful voice of Sergeant Bert Ward.

'It's half-past four in the morning,' Ashworth barked. 'This had better be good, Bert.'

'Sorry, but I had to call. There's been a development on the Lilac Avenue case.

Holding the telephone between ear and shoulder, Ashworth climbed out of bed and listened while pulling on the clean socks Sarah had left out the night before.

'All right, Bert, I'm on my way.' Then, slamming down the receiver, 'What the hell's happening now?'

Sarah stirred behind him. 'What's the matter, dear?'

'Something's come up at the station,' he told her flatly. 'I've got to go.'

She lay back and listened as he stumbled about in the dark for his clothes, cursing softly and repeatedly when he stubbed his toe on the dressing-table.

Eventually, he whispered, 'I'm off, love.'

'Yes, dear,' she said, propping herself up on an elbow. 'Be careful, and do try to control your temper.'

'My temper? Oh yes.' His smile was rueful. 'I'd forgotten for the moment – like you do when you're called out at half four in the morning on the word of someone who may well be a nutter.'

Josh would have welcomed anything that could have kept his mind occupied during the long, sleepless night.

Greg was snoring noisily in the next bedroom, the

sounds reverberating through the thin plasterboard wall; and as he listened, Josh again went over their earlier talk. His first reaction had been one of shock, but that had quickly dispersed when the enormity of the problem became clear. And that in turn led to the gnawing, aching worry which now robbed him of his sleep.

Dawn was breaking, morning birdsong had begun, and the pale light of a new day bathed Bridgetown in its beautiful balm. But it failed to soothe Ashworth, who stomped aggressively into the station.

He marched towards the desk where Sergeant Ward, fresh from the canteen, was cradling a steaming mug of tea. Like many others, Ward found it easy to be flippant with the chief inspector on the end of a telephone, but when faced with the man in bullish mood, caution dictated a more diplomatic approach.

'I'm sorry, Jim, I talked to him but he wouldn't budge. I had to call you.'

'I know, Bert.' He eyed the mug of tea. 'May I?' he asked. 'I didn't get time to make a pot before I left.'

'Yes,' Ward said grudgingly, handing it across.

Ashworth downed half in one swallow, then asked, 'Where is he then?'

'Interview room one. He's screaming blue murder, but I didn't know where else to put him.'

'If he starts screaming at me, he'll get a kick up the backside,' Ashworth said, handing back the mug. 'Good cup of tea that, Bert. You would've enjoyed it.'

Then, with a wicked smile at the sergeant, he headed for the interview rooms. The station was deserted as he strode along the corridor, scratching at the irritating stubble on his chin. Reaching interview room number one, he paused briefly, then pushed open the door. The man sitting at the table looked up. He was tall, slim-built, with a hawk-like nose and black hair parted on the left-hand side.

'And who, may I ask, are you?' he demanded, the cultured voice matching the well-tailored suit.

I'm Chief Inspector Ashworth. But, more to the point, sir, who are you?'

'I'm Reginald Carter,' he said, getting slowly to his feet. 'And I demand to know what's happening at my house.'

Holly knew he was Michael Douglas, even though the man swore he was not. Throughout the party he was most attentive, ignoring the rich and famous, and showering her with compliments.

After a time, they left the glittering affair, and went back to her place. There her certainty deepened. He *was* Michael Douglas. He was even acting out a scene from *Fatal Attraction*, pinning her down by the sink in a passionate embrace, his hot lips on hers, his tongue probing her mouth.

When their lips parted he pulled back his head, that famous smile flashing across his face, and his hands slipped easily on to her buttocks, rotating, caressing her firm flesh.

He's incognito, she decided, because he doesn't want his wife to find out.

Her skirt was pulled up roughly, and she gasped when his strong hands ran along the exposed flesh above the tops of her stockings.

He must be over here for a film, she pondered, as her pants were pulled down. Then it all became too much, and with frenzied movements she helped him to remove them. Cries of longing caught in her throat, then tumbled from her lips. His face was contorted with passion, and pure desire overtook him. Somewhere in the background, the telephone rang.

'Leave it,' he growled.

And then he was forcing her back, lifting her on to the edge of the sink, prising her legs open. She was fumbling with the zipper on his trousers, her urgent fingers hindering. Finally the zip gave, and above their cries of mutual excitement, she heard it slide down. Reaching out, her hand closed around the firm object …

And then she threw it on to the bedside table.

'Shit,' she muttered. 'Double shit.'

Opening her eyes, Holly glared at the telephone receiver and sighed as the familiar voice poured from it. Still cursing she reached out and picked it up.

'Hello,' she snapped.

'Holly, it's Ashworth.' There was a pause. 'Are you all right?'

'No, guv, I'm not all right. You've just chased Michael Douglas out of my life.'

'I've … ?'

'Just a dream,' she said, glancing at the time. 'Guv, it's only six o'clock.'

'I know. I'm at the station with Reginald Carter. I want to interview him, Holly, so I need another detective present.'

'And I've won the prize, great. Hold on – Carter? Wasn't he dead the last time we saw him?'

'It's a long story, Holly. Can you come down to the station?'

'I'm on my way.'

She threw the receiver in the general direction of the telephone and climbed out of bed, stretching languidly.

'You're only on hold, Michael,' she mumbled, 'and bring your dad as well, if you like.'

Chuckling softly, she crossed to the dressing-table and dared herself to look in the mirror.

'My God, girl,' she shrieked, 'you look awful without make-up.'

Holly looked anything but awful when she entered reception at Bridgetown police station, twenty minutes later. And Sergeant Ward, actively guarding a fresh mug of tea, marvelled at the sight of her as she approached the desk. She had on a two-piece black suit which hugged her figure, and her hair was fluffy and brushed back high on her head.

'Morning, Bert. Where's the guv'nor?'

'Morning, Holly,' Ward managed to say; indeed it was all he could do to stop himself drooling. 'He's in interview room one.'

Holly's huge eyes grew even larger as she surveyed the inviting mug of tea. 'I couldn't, could I, Bert? I didn't get time to make one.'

Before the sergeant could protest, she had taken the mug and was drinking from it.

'Jim's been waiting for some time,' he told her, hoping to salvage some of the tea.

'Oh, he'll keep,' Holly assured him between gulps.

Ward watched resignedly as she drained the mug.

'You've saved my life, Bert. I owe you one,' she said, backing away from the desk. 'Anything you want, just name it.'

'You wouldn't agree to it,' Ward chortled.

'Try me,' she teased, with a wide grin and a wave, as she disappeared along the corridor.

The buffet bar at Euston railway station was packed, and Lenny Spencer's tension eased slightly as he merged with the crowd.

After three cups of tea and an endless number of cigarettes, he realised it was time to make a move. But where should he go? Sure, he had contacts in London, but he was too frightened to approach them. If no one knew where he was, he might just pull this off. Pocketing his cigarettes, he reached for his cases.

An accommodation agency – that was his best bet.

Holly knocked on the door.

'Come in,' Ashworth barked.

31

Inside, Reginald Carter was sitting stiffly erect; he looked tired and edgy. The chief inspector was facing him, a frown marring his face.

'This is Detective Sergeant Bedford,' Ashworth stated briskly.

Holly gave a nod and, without wasting time, skirted round the uniformed officer at the door to announce the start of the interview into the tape recorder.

'Mr Carter,' Ashworth began, 'this is now a formal interview and a statement will be taken from the recording.'

'Am I suspected of anything?' Carter asked.

'Not at the moment, sir, you're merely helping us with our enquiries.' Ashworth leant forward. 'Now, you're aware from our earlier discussions that a body was discovered yesterday at your home, number twenty-five Lilac Avenue.'

Carter appeared tense. His 'Yes' was hardly audible.

'At first we assumed that it was you. Have you any idea who the dead male might be?'

'I've told you all this,' he said, exasperated.

'Tell me again,' Ashworth replied patiently, 'for the recording.'

Inhaling sharply, Carter said, 'I have a house guest, Terence Wells. We go back a long way. We were at school together. He lives in Rutley, and he's staying with me.'

'I see. And how long has Mr Wells been staying with you?'

'All last week. I was called away on Friday to Amsterdam. I'm an antiques dealer.'

'You have proof that you were out of the country?' Ashworth probed.

'Yes.' Carter sighed and reached into the inside pocket of his jacket. 'My airline ticket.'

Ashworth examined it and, for the sake of the tape recorder, said, 'Mr Carter has shown me his airline ticket, which does indeed confirm that he was in Amsterdam.' He handed the ticket back. 'Now, I have to inform you that we're treating this case as murder.'

He studied Carter's face for any sign of surprise, but the man's expression remained passive. 'Mr Carter, can you think of anyone who would want to harm Mr Wells? Does he have any enemies?'

'None that I can think of, but then I know very little about Terence's personal life.'

'Does Mr Wells drive a car?'

'Yes, a Mercedes.'

'What year?'

'It's an M reg.'

'Good, it's in your garage. And what do you drive, sir?'

'A Mercedes. Mine's an L reg.'

'Right, that's cleared that up. As it's Mr Wells's car in the garage, it looks increasingly likely that he's the victim.'

Ashworth shifted his position in the chair and was silent for some minutes; Reginald Carter continued to stare directly into his face.

'Now, sir,' Ashworth said eventually, his tone harsh, 'when you returned from Amsterdam you came straight to the police station. Why didn't you go home?'

Carter rolled his eyes towards the ceiling, and when he spoke his words were slow, intolerant. 'I did go home, and as I was opening the gates I could just make out a vehicle parked near the house. I got back into my car and put my headlights on full beam to get a better look. There was a man sitting in the car. It was three thirty in the morning.' He shrugged as if that explained everything. 'That's why I came to the police station.

'Thank you, sir,' Ashworth said. 'Now, I'm afraid I have to ask if you'd be willing to identify the body.'

'I suppose so.' He sounded almost bored. 'Can I go home now?'

'I'm afraid that won't be possible, sir. Your house is the scene of a murder. It'll be at least two more days before we're finished there.'

'This is ridiculous,' he protested.

Ashworth said firmly, 'Nevertheless, that's how it is. Have you anywhere else to stay?'

'No, I'll book into a hotel,' Carter said, getting to his feet.

'We'll have to know where you are, sir.'

'Chief inspector, I've been travelling all night, and my patience is wearing a little thin ...'

'So is mine, sir,' Ashworth snorted. 'I'll get the officer here to escort you to a telephone where you can make your reservation, and then he can take your particulars.'

Carter glared at the chief inspector for several seconds then abruptly broke eye contact. 'All right,' he said, striding to the door.

'Oh, Mr Carter,' Ashworth called after him.

'Yes?'

'Is there anything you want to ask me?'

'No, I don't think so.'

'Well, thank you for your help, sir.'

As soon as Carter and the uniformed officer had gone, Ashworth turned to Holly who was still dealing with the tape recorder.

'Well?' he asked.

She folded her arms and leant against the table. 'Cool, calm, very controlled. Definitely not frightened of the police, and not very upset by the death of his friend.'

'Quite,' Ashworth said, returning to his seat. 'We weren't at school together, were we, Holly?'

'No, guv,' she laughed. 'I would have remembered you. When I was eleven, you would've been thirty-seven.'

'But if I'd met an untimely death, even on our relatively short acquaintance, you'd want to know how I died. Wouldn't you?'

'Ah, I'm with you. Carter showed no interest, or even surprise, in the fact that his friend was dead. Do you think he was involved in the murder?'

'I'm ruling nothing out. His ticket shows he was out of the country...'

He rubbed his tired eyes and leant back in the chair. 'I don't know, Holly, we've got two and two here, and they're not adding up to four.'

She studied his preoccupied expression, and said, 'What's next, guv?'

'Get Josh.'

'I phoned him before I came in. He's on his way.'

'Good girl. We want anything on computer about Reginald Carter and Terence Wells. Oh, and go and make sure we know where Carter is. After he's identified the body, we'll have to take him to the house. We need to find out if anything's missing.'

Sergeant Ward had, yet again, returned to front reception with a mug of tea, and was happily contemplating the end of his shift in under an hour's time, when he caught sight of Josh running up the station's front steps.

'Oh, no,' he groaned, swiftly removing the mug to a shelf behind the desk. 'Morning, Josh,' he called cheerfully.

At first it appeared that Josh might ignore the greeting but then, seemingly preoccupied, he raised a hand in a perfunctory gesture and started for the stairs to CID. The sergeant shook his head in bewilderment, because Josh was well known for his good humour, and it was most unlike him to snub a colleague.

'Not too bad, Josh, thanks,' Ward mumbled cynically. 'Apart from your mob drinking my tea all night, I'm fine.'

It was then that two uniformed constables crossed reception, all the time staring enquiringly at the sergeant who continued to mutter to himself between sips from the mug.

Chapter 4

The young detective hardly had time to close the door before Ashworth started firing orders from his desk.

'Josh, get that computer on. We want everything there is on a Terence Wells, late of Rutley.'

Without a word, Josh removed his leather jacket and placed it on the back of his chair.

'You all right, lover?' Holly called from behind a pile of papers.

All she got back was a morose nod and a bleep from the computer as it was switched on. Josh sat down and stared at the empty screen.

'I've a feeling this is going to be an interesting day, albeit a long one,' Ashworth said. 'Firstly, we need to find out about Mr Wells, what he did for a living, that sort of thing. So, it doesn't look like I'll be going home for breakfast.'

He rubbed the stubble on his chin. 'Josh, you keep a shaver in your drawer, don't you? Can I borrow it?'

With a suddenness that startled them, Josh spun round. 'You wouldn't want to use my shaver, guv. You wouldn't want to touch anything of mine, believe me.' Then, with equal swiftness, he stormed out of the office, leaving the door open behind him.

'What the hell's wrong with him?' Ashworth huffed.

'I don't know,' Holly said worriedly.

'We've got a heavy workload today, Holly. This is no time for him to be throwing a tantrum.'

'Please, guv, no references to him being gay, all right? I think we could have a case of a lover spurned here.'

'We've all got our problems,' Ashworth said doggedly, 'but we mustn't let them interfere with work.'

'He's probably gone to the canteen. I'll go and have a

word with him. Can I order some breakfast for you while I'm there?'

The thought of breakfast without Sarah's muesli, bran, and other healthy ingredients made Ashworth's eyes sparkle.

'Yes, Holly – eggs, bacon, sausage and mushrooms,' he said. 'Double bacon. Tell them it's for me, and they'll know that means at least six rashers.'

'Right, guv.'

Holly left him contemplating a call to Sarah; she would have to be told he wouldn't be home until evening. He started to dial, then dropped the receiver back into its cradle and raced to the door.

'Holly, fried bread and coffee, as well,' he called, with keen relish.

She ordered the breakfast, and then joined Josh where he was sitting in an empty corner of the canteen. He was gazing gloomily into his coffee which he stirred carefully and continuously.

'Hi, Josh, sorry about last night,' she said, easing herself into a chair. 'I just didn't feel myself.'

'It's okay,' he answered, all the while stirring the drink.

She smiled. 'You'll wear a grove in the bottom of that cup.'

Without looking up, Josh withdrew the spoon and tossed it on to the table.

'Come on, lover,' she coaxed, 'tell me what's the matter.' 'Nothing,' he snapped. 'I just need some space.'

'You can't walk out on the guv'nor like that. He doesn't like it.'

'Okay then, I'll go back and find out about Wells.'

He started to leave, still averting his eyes, and Holly banged a fist on the table, causing coffee to spill out of the cup

'For God's sake, Josh, what's the matter?'

37

'Nothing's the matter,' he flared back. 'Why can't you just leave me alone? I don't want you in my life.'

Too shocked to speak, Holly watched as he picked a way between the tables and vanished into the corridor.

'Yes, yes, that's fine,' Reginald Carter said irritably, after the hotel porter had asked if he wanted the suitcases in his bedroom. He folded a ten-pound note and, when the man re-emerged, pressed it into his palm.

'Thank you, sir,' the porter said, surprised. 'Is there anything else I can do for you?'

'No, no,' Carter replied, ushering the man out of the room.

Once alone, he looked quickly around the suite, the best on offer in the Gainsborough Hotel. Then, taking a bottle of scotch from his suitcase, he poured a good measure and knocked it straight back.

Sitting on the bed, he reached for the telephone receiver, and stabbed out a number with obvious annoyance.

'Hello, it's Reggie,' he said sharply when the connection was made. 'I've just heard about Terry.'

Pouring another scotch, he listened. 'Yes, the police, of all people, told me. What's the news on the street?'

The computer noise was beginning to grind on Ashworth's nerves, even though he continued to breathe deeply in order to calm himself.

A while earlier he had despatched Holly to Carter's hotel. She was to accompany him to the mortuary, where he was to identify the body, and then on to his home to carry out a check of its contents. So now there was little else to do but watch Josh attempt to extract information from that infernal machine. And his mood was not helped by his stomach protesting violently after the fried breakfast.

Josh, still subdued, turned to face him. 'No joy, guv.'

Ashworth flexed his hands in frustration.

'Could try aliases,' Josh said helpfully, 'but it's a long shot.'

He nodded for Josh to try, then sat pondering. A body discovered at the home of a seemingly respectable businessman was unusual in itself. But the method used in the murder was beginning to disturb him. Reginald Carter was the only trail he had to follow. He would have to grill the man, find out all he could about Terence Wells, and backtrack from there …

'Guv, I've got something,' Josh said, pointing to the screen.

Ashworth hurried across and stared over his detective's shoulder.

'My God,' he exclaimed.

'Three hundred quid a week?' Lenny Spencer snorted, as he looked around the dingy room.

The landlord was a heavy man running to fat, with a shaven head and a brown sauce stain down the front of his dirty-grey vest.

'Take it or leave it.'

'I'll take it,' Lenny said, reaching for his wallet, and counting out the money. The landlord's piggy eyes gleamed as he viewed the wad of notes.

'Forget it,' Lenny warned, as he passed the money across. And to emphasise the point, he opened up his suitcase and retrieved the .38 pistol.

'Okay, okay, don't get heavy,' the landlord said.

Pointing the gun, Lenny hissed quietly, 'Just don't fuck with me – all right?'

'All right, all right,' the man replied, his arms held up in a position of surrender. 'You new to the Smoke?'

'Yeah.'

Still holding the gun, Lenny looked around the room; and although a luxurious home had never been one of his requirements, the bare floorboards, the dirty mattress thrown into a corner, made his nose wrinkle with displeasure. He pulled back a curtain which substituted for the kitchen door and peered at the chipped enamel sink, the wooden draining board, and the ancient gas cooker.

The landlord, who appeared to be happier now that he had edged closer to the door, said, 'You on the dodge?'

'What makes you ask that?'

The man shrugged. 'You didn't give no name, and you've got enough money to get somewhere decent.'

'You should be on *Mastermind*,' Lenny grinned.

He considered the man and decided to take a chance. 'Do you know where I can get some papers?'

The fat man's eyes rose into a question.

'A passport,' Lenny explained needlessly.

'Oh yeah, I know what you mean.' He stared at the pitted white walls and frowned, as if giving the question much thought. 'I can give you a name, but it'll cost you two hundred quid.'

'I thought it might. Can you arrange a meet?'

The landlord pursed his lips. 'That'll be three hundred.'

'Don't you do anything for free?'

'No,' he said with a humourless chuckle. 'I even charge my old lady for a seeing-to.'

'Is this guy any good?'

'Manny Fredricks is the best. His fivers have got the Royal Mint confused.'

'Fix it then.'

The man said nothing, simply stood there, rubbing together his greasy thumb and forefinger.

'No money yet,' Lenny told him. 'When the meet takes place.'

'Okay.' He opened the door, then turned back. 'Look, if you don't want to go out for any reason, I can get you anything you need. Booze, fags, food, a bird …'

'How much?'

'Hundred a week?'

'Your prices are coming down,' Lenny smiled, once again reaching for his wallet. 'Okay, get me some vodka – three bottles – and some bread, cheese and baked beans. And call me Lenny.'

'I'm Bruce.'

'Well, Brucey boy, when you come up those stairs, you knock on that door three times and you say: It's Bruce – nice and loud.' A smile stretched his mouth, but his eyes remained cold. 'The first time you don't do that, you're gonna have blood all over this luxury apartment of yours.'

With the door open and the corridor in view, the landlord's courage was strengthened. He grinned. 'Okay, hard case, I've seen it all before.'

'Fuck with me,' Lenny warned, grabbing his throat, 'and you won't see nothing again.'

Some of the colour had drained from the fat man's face as he closed the door, nodding profusely. Lenny straight away slid the bolts into place.

Crossing to the window, he looked down into the empty street. If he had to lose himself for a couple of weeks, he supposed the East End of London was as good a place as any.

Holly was not enthusiastic about viewing the body of Terence Wells for the second time in as many days; she felt sick when the sheet was pulled back and Reginald Carter, without a flicker of emotion, made the identification.

She drove him to his house and kept in close proximity while he checked whether anything was missing. He seemed preoccupied, and not in the least upset by the remaining evidence of the murder in his library. Eventually, he announced that everything was in order. Holly had reservations, however; to her mind, he had not been particularly thorough in his inspection. Nevertheless, she was glad that the morning was over, for although he had behaved with impeccable manners throughout, there was something about him which set warning bells ringing in her brain.

She dropped him off at the hotel and returned to the police station to find Ashworth waiting in reception, his expression forewarning her that the ball had started rolling. At the sight of her, he hurried forward.

'Well?' he asked.

'The dead man is Terence Wells, and there's nothing missing from Carter's house. I've got Wells's address in Rutley, so we can start looking there …'

Ashworth shook his head. 'No, we start looking closer to home. Mr Carter's got some explaining to do. Let's go and ask him some questions.'

'But when I left him, he was going to bed, guv.'

'Then he'll have to get up again,' Ashworth said sourly. He shepherded Holly towards the door, relating hastily the information Josh had discovered from the computer.

'Terence Wells?' she said. 'But it doesn't make sense.'

'Of course it doesn't,' he replied slowly, as if speaking to a child. 'It's our job to make sense of it.'

'Look, guv, can I just collect something from the office?'

'Yes,' was his peevish reply; he was in a hurry to get the case under way. 'I'll wait in the car.'

There was nothing to collect from the office. She wanted to see Josh. His outburst had hurt her, but overriding that hurt was a feeling that he was in serious trouble, and her first instinct was to offer help. Hoping for a good reception, she pushed open the door and went in. He looked up, and a slight flush coloured his cheeks as he turned away. Flattening herself against the wall, Holly worked her way around the perimeter of the room.

'Look, Josh, I'm giving you all the space I can,' she said, hugging the wall. 'I've just come in to collect something.'

For a few worrying moments, she thought he was going

to ignore her, but then he laughed. 'I'm sorry, Holly, I didn't mean any of it.'

Crouching beside his chair, she said, 'We're mates, aren't we? You don't have to be sorry. If something's gone wrong in your life and you want somebody to kick, I'm here. Just don't shut me out, okay?'

'Can I talk to you? After work?'

'Okay,' she said, standing up. 'I'll let you buy me a drink.'

She was hastening to the door when Josh called, 'I didn't mean any of it. I think you're great.'

'Don't be nice, Abraham, it doesn't become you.' But then she stopped, suddenly serious. 'We'll sort it, Josh.'

Ashworth was impatiently revving the Scorpio's engine as Holly dashed across the car-park. She scrambled in, and was still pulling at the seat belt when Ashworth steered out into the road.

He gave her a quick sideways glance. 'Have you found out what's wrong with him? I take it that's why you went up to the office.'

'Not yet, guv. We're having a drink after work.'

'Good.'

Holly settled back to consider his strong profile, and wondered how it was that nothing could get past this man.

Reginald Carter was not happy. That fact in no way displayed itself in his manner, which remained polite at all times, but it was all too evident in his body language. It was Holly's considered opinion that if this man was pushed, he could turn into an extremely unpleasant character.

Carter emerged from the hotel bedroom, fastening his navy blue silk dressing-gown. 'I protest, chief inspector,' he said mildly.

'Your protest has been registered, sir,' was Ashworth's cursory reply. 'But we have some more questions to ask.'

Carter settled into a chair and motioned for Ashworth

to do the same. Holly remained standing by the door.

'What questions?' he asked.

'It's come to our notice that you've been less than truthful with us.'

Carter frowned. 'You're accusing me of lying?'

'No, of withholding information.'

'Such as what?'

'You didn't tell us your friend, Terence Wells, had a long criminal record,' he said, watching the man closely.

'You didn't ask me,' Carter bristled. 'There might be some truths not told.' He gave the chief inspector a condescending smile. 'I don't suppose you know where that line comes from.'

Ashworth's irritation showed as he rose to his feet. 'I'm not here to play cultural guessing games, Mr Carter. Terence Wells had convictions for extortion, robbery, grievous bodily harm; and he was charged with murder, but acquitted at trial.'

Carter remained unperturbed.

'He also used a number of aliases –'

'Chief inspector,' Carter interrupted, a forceful note creeping into his tone. 'Terence had not been convicted of any crime in the last twenty years. As far as I know, he had become a respectable citizen – having paid his debt to society, as they say.'

'What did he do for a living?'

'He was a florist,' Carter said with a faint smile. 'He owned a shop in Rutley.'

'I'm going to dig into his life … and yours,' Ashworth warned quietly.

Carter's smile now became a laugh. 'I'm sure you will. Just make sure you can prove anything you may say about me.'

The reply took Ashworth off guard. 'And what do you mean by that?'

'Just what I say, chief inspector. Now, if that's all, I'd like you to leave.'

In the corridor, Holly fell in beside him. 'There might be some truths not told – what did he mean by that, guv?'

'It's Jane Austen. A quote from *Emma*,' he said absently. 'I distrust people who quote from the classics as a form of brinkmanship.'

'Is that the only reason you don't trust him?' she asked, as they descended the wide elegant staircase.

'No, there's something very strange about Reginald Carter. It's as if he knows we're going to dig something up about him, but he's not worried.'

'Might be something we couldn't do anything about,' Holly ventured. 'As in, non-criminal.'

'Could be, but it just might be that Mr Carter thinks he's above the law.'

'That could be his downfall, guv.'

'It definitely will be, with me as sheriff,' he assured her.

The request put through to Rutley police station to allow officers from Bridgetown to move into the area and investigate the murder of Terence Wells should have been a formality, but this was proving not to be the case. An impatient Ashworth waited for the telephone call which would give him clearance, and by late afternoon he was still waiting.

Finally, he rang Rutley station for the fifth time, and the way in which he slammed down the receiver told that he was about to erupt.

'What the hell's happening?' he growled. 'Every time I phone, no one I know is available. I just keep getting some young girl telling me my request is being processed. What in God's name does that mean?'

'Guv, you're losing your temper.'

'I want to know what's happening, Holly.'

As if in answer the telephone buzzed, and Ashworth

pounced on the receiver.

'Hello?' he said expectantly.

'Is that Chief Inspector Ashworth?'

'It is.'

'This is Inspector Derry, Rutley station.'

'Derry? I don't know you, do I?'

'No, I'm Special Unit.'

'Special Unit?' Ashworth echoed.

'Yes, I'd rather not go into that now. I understand Terry Wells turned up on your patch, very dead. Now, I'd like to send a couple of my people over to get the facts, and then we can take it from there.'

'Hold on, hold on, I've made a request to come on to your territory to investigate the murder –'

'And I'm saying I'd like to relieve you of that duty. We're well aware of Terry Wells's and Reggie Carter's activities, and hopefully, this murder's the lead we've been waiting for.'

Ashworth's livid expression made Holly cringe, and she glanced across at Josh who gave her a detached smile.

'I'm not understanding this,' Ashworth said, tilting his chair back to glower up at the ceiling. 'There's been a murder on my patch, and I'm going to investigate it –'

'We're Special Unit,' Derry interjected. 'We're better equipped –'

'I don't care if you're the Grenadier Guards,' Ashworth flared. 'You don't sideline me.'

'I've been through the Chief Constable with this,' Derry declared hotly.

'And what did Ken Savage say?'

'He said to talk to you first, and try to convince you that this is really our province.'

'Well, you haven't done that, son.'

'I could go back to Savage, ask him to make it an order that you turn the case over to us.'

Ashworth looked set to explode. 'All right, you do that,

but in the meantime, I'll see you in the morning. I'll be arriving at nine-thirty. Goodbye.'

He slammed down the receiver, and glared at Holly. 'I'm still in the police force, aren't I? We haven't been taken over by some special unit?'

'Yes, guv, you're still in the police force,' she said, smiling. 'Do you think we could call it a day now?'

Still scowling, Ashworth looked at his watch. 'I suppose so. It has been a long day. Bright and early in the morning, mind.'

Chairs scraped and shoes scuffed as the two detectives left the office. Linking her arm in his, Holly marched Josh along the corridor.

Chapter 5

Inspector Steve Derry pursed his lips and stood staring at the telephone receiver before dropping it back in its cradle.

'So that was Jim Ashworth,' he muttered.

Derry was Afro-Caribbean with strong, even features, and was casually dressed in jogging bottoms, trainers and a brown leather jacket. The loose-fitting garments concealed well the bulge of his automatic pistol in a holster beneath his armpit. A tall, athletic man, he moved lightly and gracefully.

He thought for a moment, and then went out into the corridor, a long subterranean passage in which endless lines of strip lighting gave off an artificial glow, for Inspector Derry's office was in the bowels of Rutley police station, and beyond the reach of any natural light.

Half-way along, he opened a door and strode into the room, narrowing his eyes against the thick haze of cigarette smoke. Nine detectives sat about on plain wooden benches behind formica desks, and all were dressed along the same lines as the inspector. On the wall ahead of them was a blackboard which held half a dozen photographs of various men, including Reginald Carter and Terence Wells.

Russell Pearson, Derry's detective sergeant, caught his superior's expression. 'Problems?' he asked.

'Nope,' Derry said as he made his way to the blackboard. 'Ashworth's proving difficult, but he can be sorted.'

'Their files have arrived from Bridgenorton. I think we can expect some resistance from Ashworth.'

'Tell me,' Derry said, still studying the photographs.

'Seems he's a good copper –'

'He might be good at catching kids nicking sweets from the corner shop, but this is big league.'

'He's an elderly guy,' Pearson went on. 'Known for his temper, can explode if pushed far enough. Very much a loner. Had some real bust-ups with the Chief Constable. He was asked to resign once because he was thought too old for the job.' Pearson suddenly laughed. 'According to this, he's offered to fight a few guys who've rubbed him up the wrong way.'

Steve Derry turned to his men. 'What do you know, guys,' he laughed. 'And we thought we invented that approach. Who's Ashworth's sidekick?'

'Holly Bedford seems like the favourite to be with him.'

'Holly?' Derry said, taking a matchstick from his pocket, and placing it in the corner of his mouth. 'You mean as in …?' He traced the outline of a female figure.

'The very same,' Pearson said, as he offered his inspector Holly's file.

Derry studied her photograph for a few seconds. 'Nice pair of tits,' he said dismissively, tossing the file on the desk. 'Right, guys, our country cousins will be arriving at nine thirty tomorrow morning …' He bit on the matchstick and grinned. 'And by ten o'clock, they'll be heading back with their tails stuck up their backsides.'

Someone shouted, 'Couldn't we keep the bird?'

'No,' he said with a laugh, 'we send her back to entertain the yokels.'

The bar in the Bull and Butcher was not the most exotic of places, but it was conveniently close to the police station, and always relatively empty early in the evening.

Josh chose the table farthest away from the counter, and sat facing Holly. She watched him running his finger around the rim of his glass, and noted that he hadn't yet taken a drink.

'If we're going to talk, we'd better say something, hadn't we?' she ventured.

He looked into her eyes, but remained silent.

'Is it Greg?' she coaxed.

Josh nodded.

'He's come back, and you don't know whether you can trust him – is that it?'

A harsh smile touched his lips. 'You don't understand, Holly.'

'I'm trying to,' she said, leaning forward, 'but you won't tell me anything.'

'I've …' He broke off, picked up his glass and took a long drink.

'This is something serious, isn't it? It's not just you and Greg, is it?'

He set the glass down and blurted, 'I could be HIV positive.'

Holly's mouth sagged open. 'You what? But how, Josh?'

'Greg,' he said simply.

'Have you two …?'

'No, no,' he replied, shaking his head morosely. 'I told you that when we were together, Greg messed around a lot – well, since then he's developed full-blown Aids. He's worried he picked the virus up when we were together and passed it on to me.'

'But isn't there a chance he got it after you two had split?'

'I suppose so,' he said wistfully. 'He was diagnosed twelve months ago, and from what I can gather, he was still very promiscuous.'

'Look, Josh, I know this thing with Greg still hurts, but we've got to make sure you're all right. Have you arranged to have the tests done?'

'No tests,' Josh said firmly.

'Don't be so bloody silly,' Holly flared. 'I'll ring tonight and make the appointment.'

'I don't want to take the tests.'

'Oh Christ, you're doing my bloody head in. Do you want to go through life frightened to death every time you get a cold? Is that what you want?'

'You don't understand,' he muttered, staring into his glass.

'Oh, I understand, Josh. You're behaving like a great big kid. You don't even know whether you're positive, and already you're swimming around in self-pity.'

He continued to study his drink, refusing to look at her. Finally, she stood up.

'I'm going.'

Immediately, Josh gripped her arm. I'm scared, Hol.'

'Of course you are,' she answered softly, holding on to his hand. 'But you can't run away from it.'

'I know.' He sighed and sank back in the chair. 'I'll take the tests. I know I've got to.'

Holly sat down and smiled encouragement. 'We'll get through it, Josh, you'll see.'

'I feel better already,' he said, smiling back. 'I thought if you or the guv'nor found out, you wouldn't want anything to do with me.'

'Thanks a lot,' she huffed. 'You thought I'd turn my back on you if you were in a mess?'

'People do, don't they? They're frightened to use a cup you've drunk from; frightened to use the loo after you; frightened you might touch them …'

'Josh –'

'I've seen it happen, Hol.'

'You might have done, Josh, but I'm not going to shun you, and neither will the guv'nor.'

'I'm not so sure. He doesn't understand gays, does he?'

'No, he doesn't, but bloody hell, Josh, he's not going to turn his back on you when you're in trouble. That's just not his way.'

'I hope you're right.'

'I'll phone tonight and make an appointment then.'

'Thanks for listening,' he said gratefully.

Holly drained her glass and winked. 'You're a pain in the neck, Abraham, but I still love you.'

Ashworth stretched and yawned. He was sitting at his desk, still pondering over the murder of Terence Wells. There was precious little he could do about it until the morning, but his obsessive mind had fastened on to the case like a limpet mine, and he found it impossible not to dwell on it.

The office door opened, and Superintendent Newton stood framed in the doorway. 'Still here, chief inspector?'

'Yes,' Ashworth said, glancing at the clock. 'I'm surprised you are, though.'

'Some paperwork to catch up on,' Newton said stiffly.

'I take it the problem with Rutley has been cleared up by the Chief Constable,' Ashworth said, in a victorious tone.

'Yes,' Newton replied, with clear disapproval. 'The official line is that for the moment the case is yours but, to be honest, we'd rather hand it over to the Special Unit.'

Getting to his feet, and pulling himself up to his full height, Ashworth said, 'Well, I wouldn't.'

Newton considered the towering figure. 'Yes, quite. I'll bid you goodnight then, chief inspector.'

'Goodnight, sir.'

As the superintendent closed the door, he thought how nice it would be to lose the taciturn Ashworth for a time.

Josh arrived home still shrouded in a cloud of worry. Just a few days ago, his world had seemed close to perfect. His home was small, tiny in fact, but the mortgage was well within his means. And living in isolation was not a problem for him, just the reverse: with only himself to worry about, he was beginning to develop as an individual.

For as long as he could remember, Josh had wanted to paint, but had been afraid that people would somehow link this to his sexuality. Now, however, away from prying eyes, he was able to purchase the necessary equipment, and take the first hesitant steps towards putting paint on canvas.

Josh had felt alone for most of his life. His father, a Yorkshire miner, refused to have anything to do with his son upon discovering his homosexuality; and his mother, a tiny mouse of a woman, was physically and mentally incapable of acting as mediator. Greg Albrine was his only lover, and when their relationship ended, Josh felt that something important inside himself – the ability to totally love another – had died.

And now Greg was back. When Josh answered the knock at the front door, and saw Greg standing there, that part of him stirred with life again. But then came the bombshell which brought the world tumbling down around him. Greg had Aids, was dying from it, and Josh could be carrying the virus.

As he pulled the car into the garage, a weariness swept over him and he knew Holly was right: he would have to take the tests. If he refused, he would fear the worst every time he felt tired or a little washed out.

Greg was waiting in the kitchen. 'I've made a pot of tea,' he said, placing cups and saucers on the small breakfast bar.

'Great.'

Josh went through to the hall to hang up his jacket, all the while wondering how he could have missed the signs. He might not have seen Greg for three years, but it was so obvious that he had lost weight. And that grating cough, which even now was drifting out from the kitchen – well, Josh had simply put that down to his chain-smoking habit.

In the kitchen, Greg asked, 'Rough day?'

'A bitch. That Carter guy's turned up, alive and well. It was his friend's body that we found at the house. So far we've been unable to find a motive for the murder, but it seems some sort of undercover team from Rutley's working on the case … Hey, Greg, you all right?'

He had slumped against the wall, his face a pasty grey. 'Yes, don't worry,' he said. 'I get days like this.'

Josh sighed. 'Sorry, I'm talking shop, aren't I? But I've got all the reports to type up tonight. It's one of the jobs I've landed myself with.'

'It's all right, Josh, it's just that you keep talking about murders, and when you're dying, it seems such a waste of life …'

'Point taken,' Josh said. 'I won't discuss the case any more.' He hesitated. 'There's a lot we do need to talk about, though.'

Greg wandered over to the window and gazed out at the garden. 'I know.'

'How far have you …?'

He gave a bitter laugh. 'What stage am I in – is that what you're asking?'

'Yes,' Josh admitted, turning away.

'About as far in as you can get and still be walking about.' He turned from the window, his eyes dark with anger. 'Josh, if I could find the bastard who did this to me, I'd kill him.'

Then, sinking back against the worktop, he let out a long breath, and said, 'I feel so bloody tired all the time, and the weight's falling off me.'

'I shouldn't have brought it up,' Josh said quickly. 'I'm sorry, Greg.'

'What the hell, you've got a right to know. At the moment, antibiotics are keeping me alive, but the next bout of pneumonia could be my last.'

Josh fixed his eyes on the floor tiles and stayed silent.

'I suppose you think it's a cheek dropping in just to die,' Greg said, going over to sit with Josh. 'I'm just trying to put things in order before I go, pay back some debts. I've sold my house up north, my car, everything. I'm leaving all the money to you.'

When Josh started to protest, Greg stopped him. 'You were something special to me, okay? I just realised too late.'

Another silence followed, during which an awkwardness crept between them, and in order to allay it, Greg picked up the files, and said, 'Look, I'll type the reports for you.'

Josh shook his head, too frightened to speak in case tears came with the words.

'Go on, it'll take my mind off things.' He was heading for the door, when he stopped. 'You know, if I haven't passed this on to you, I'll die happy.'

As he listened to Greg's step on the stairs, as he heard the ring of the typewriter, Josh let the tears fall.

Ashworth was not a city man. The roar of traffic, and the air pollution accompanying it, had an adverse effect on his mood.

Rutley, in common with many other cities, hid behind a façade of opulence; but away from the showpiece shopping centres, it was a mixture of tower blocks and decaying turn-of-the-century properties, with each small area being served by run-down shops, supermarkets and off-licences.

'Are we staying over, guv, if we have to?' Holly asked, as the Scorpio mounted a ramp leading to the first floor of the carpark.

'No,' he grunted. 'They couldn't pay me enough to stay here.'

They climbed from the car, and Ashworth looked across at the police station, another structure built almost entirely of glass which in the strong morning sunlight looked little more than a huge reflector.

'I wonder if anyone ever thought of building a police station in anything other than glass,' he growled. 'Like bricks, for instance.'

They emerged into the bright sunshine, and headed for the entrance to the police station.

'Guv, I think there're people here who're going to give us a hard time.'

'Oh no, Holly, there are people here who'll *try* to give

us a hard time. Whether we let them is up to us.' His tapped his forehead. 'Positive thinking.'

Lenny Spencer's first reaction was to reach for the revolver. His fingers curled around the butt and he withdrew it slowly from beneath the dirty pillow. In one movement he was on his feet.

'Lenny, it's Bruce.'

Relaxing, he threw the gun on to the mattress and got into his boxer shorts. 'Hold on,' he called.

At the door, he drew back the bolts and turned the Yale lock. Opening up just a fraction, he peered through the crack. 'What do you want? I was asleep, for fuck's sake.'

Bruce held up the watch on his thick wrist. 'But it's ten o'clock.'

Last night's vodka, almost a bottle of it, was slowing down Lenny's ability to formulate an answer, and before the string of expletives could reach his lips, Bruce said, 'I've just been talking to Manny Fredricks on the blower.'

Lenny's expression was blank.

'Manny Fredricks,' Bruce said slowly. 'The passport man.'

'Oh yeah, what about him?' Lenny snapped.

'He could come here tonight for a meet, but he just wants to make sure you've got the dosh.'

'How much?'

'It's gonna cost.'

'How much, Brucey?'

'I dunno. Manny'll tell you.'

'Okay.'

Lenny closed the door and stood with his back pressed against it. How much would the bastard try to con out of him? Five thousand? But whatever the amount, it had to be worth it to get out of the country. He thought of what lay before him if he stayed, and suddenly money seemed of little consequence.

Chapter 6

Holly was right in thinking there were hard times ahead. When Ashworth announced their arrival at reception in Rutley police station, the bored young constable, after telephoning Inspector Derry, told them that he was tied up, and would be with them as soon as possible. For fifteen minutes they stood kicking their heels. Holly viewed Ashworth's impassive expression with annoyance while she fumed at the inspector's ill manners.

Suddenly, Ashworth exhaled sharply. 'Come on,' he said, motioning for Holly to follow him to the desk.

Is Inspector Derry available yet?' he asked, his accent sounding slightly countrified in those strange surroundings.

'No,' the police constable said firmly. 'He'll be here as soon as he's free.'

'Could you check that he hasn't forgotten us?' Ashworth persisted. 'We have been waiting rather a long time.'

'Inspector Derry ordered that he wasn't to be disturbed.'

'Son,' Ashworth said slowly, placing his hands on the desk and leaning forward menacingly, 'unless Inspector Derry is either dead or has been taken hostage, would you please pick up that phone and tell him to get to reception immediately.'

The constable glanced with surprise into Ashworth's angry brown eyes, and said, 'Yes, sir,' as he reached for the receiver.

Within two minutes, the man was striding towards them.

'I'm sorry I kept you waiting,' he said.

'Inspector Derry, I presume?'

'Yes, that's me, look -'

'We've been treated with a distinct lack of courtesy,' Ashworth informed him tartly. 'Kept waiting for God knows how long.'

'This is a busy city station,' Derry said, taken aback. 'We haven't got time for the niceties you people indulge in.'

'May I remind you, I'm a senior officer, here on a case.'

'I was briefing my team,' Derry explained, defensively.

'Briefing them on the Terence Wells case?' Ashworth asked sharply.

'Yes.'

'So, while we've been waiting around here,' he said, with great restraint, 'you've been briefing your team about my case.'

Inspector Derry turned away, clearly irritated, then said, 'I think we'd better talk, don't you?'

'I think it's imperative,' Ashworth replied with candour.

As she followed the men to the rear of reception, Holly dwelt on the fact that she had been totally ignored by Inspector Derry. On arrival, he had swept his eyes over her body and glanced briefly at her face, but from then on it was as if she did not exist.

Their footsteps echoed on the stone stairway leading down to the basement where a musty smell of damp greeted them as they emerged into a long, depressing corridor.

'We're a special unit, set up about three months ago,' Derry said, 'so things are still a bit chaotic.'

'A special unit to deal with what?' Holly asked.

'I'll come to that later,' the inspector grunted, before turning back to Ashworth. 'But it's very important that we stay underground.'

'I see,' Ashworth murmured, taking in the dingy surroundings.

'Excuse me,' Derry said, as he stopped and opened a door. 'Okay, guys, move your butts,' he called into the room. Soon, a procession of detectives filed out, all of them casting inquisitive glances at the newcomers.

Through the open doorway, Ashworth caught sight of the blackboard holding the photographs. He was intrigued to see the face of Reginald Carter there, and strove to read the words written below it in white chalk. To the side of it was a head-and-shoulders shot of a black-haired man, with the name, Terry Wells, again written in white chalk.

Inspector Derry followed Ashworth's eye-line, and in order to prevent the chief inspector from seeing more, he quickly closed the door as the last of the detectives exited.

'My office is just along here.' He opened a teak door and unceremoniously pushed past to enter the room, leaving them to follow behind.

Ashworth cast his eyes around the confined space, with its bare brick walls and exposed water pipes, as Derry pulled two plastic chairs in front of his desk.

'Okay,' Derry said as he settled into his own chair. 'Let's talk.'

'Just show us the space that's been allocated to us, tell us what you know, then let us get on with it,' Ashworth said cheerfully.

The inspector began fiddling with a pen from his desk, and said, 'It's not that simple. Now, I've looked at your records. You're both good coppers –'

'We're not here for a job interview.'

'The fact is, I don't want you on the case.'

'Whether you like it or not, we're going to work together,' Ashworth insisted. 'I'd rather not have any bad feelings about it. Anyway, why don't you want us here?'

Derry considered him, as water gurgled along the pipes. 'You want me to be blunt?'

Ashworth nodded.

'Okay. A: you're too old. B: you're not trained to deal with this. And, C: I don't believe you're subtle enough for the job.'

'And me?' Holly asked, before Ashworth could argue.

'I'll be just as blunt,' Derry said, eyeing her with disdain. 'I like my officers to have balls.'

Holly's face flushed with anger, and Ashworth got to his feet. 'Right,' he said, 'I take it that was an Operations Room back along the corridor?'

Derry gave a resigned nod.

'Then take us to it, and explain what you've got.'

'Okay. Follow me.'

The Operations Room, which smelt strongly of cigarette smoke, was empty but for Detective Sergeant Pearson, who was lounging in a chair when they entered. He did not stand up.

'My DS, Russ Pearson,' Derry said, waving laconically in his direction. 'Russ, this is Chief Inspector Ashworth, and Detective Sergeant …' He snapped his fingers impatiently as he tried to remember the name.

'Detective Sergeant Bedford,' Holly said, glaring at him.

Pearson gave a tiny salute. 'Hi, people.'

Ashworth was ushered across to the blackboard, and Derry said, 'Right, Reggie Carter, you know, and Terry Wells, you've viewed the remains of.'

'What are their photographs doing here?'

'Carter is probably the biggest villain this country has ever produced,' Derry said lightly. 'And Wells has carved up more people than you've had hot dinners. It's reputed that he once ran with the Kray twins.'

Moving to the far side of the blackboard, he went on, 'Now, this gentleman is Bernie Williams. Looks like everybody's favourite uncle, doesn't he? Bernie's one boast is that he never deals in drugs – he thinks that makes him Jesus Christ. But he has no qualms about prostitution, extortion, robbery…' He spread his hands and shrugged. 'You name it, Bernie's into it.'

Ashworth flashed Holly a disbelieving look, and said, 'Are you saying Reginald Carter's a gangster?'

'You've got it,' Derry said, stabbing a finger at Ashworth's chest. 'That's what you've stumbled into. Now until recently, Bernie Williams had the east side of town, and Reggie Carter had the west. They controlled everything, and lived in relative peace …'

'I can't believe Carter's a gangster,' Ashworth said, still studying the photograph.

'And we can't prove that he is,' Derry said. 'Reggie's as clean as well-scrubbed dick. If you called him a villain, he could sue. Terry Wells was the front man, with a record as long as your arm – some of it earned carrying the porridge for Carter, or so it's been claimed.'

'And this photograph?' Ashworth said, pointing to a shot of a black man.

Derry pursed his lips. 'This is where the problems start. That's Hedley Ambrose. He's just moved in, but he has no intention of sharing the spoils. He wants the city for himself. He's already moved into most of the casinos, made inroads into the flesh trade and drugs markets. Bernie Williams and Reggie Carter are being squeezed.'

'Gang warfare,' Ashworth intoned.

'Right in one. My first guess is that Ambrose has started his push – he's blown Terry Wells away.'

'And what's your second guess?' Ashworth asked.

'That there's trouble in the two white gangs about how to deal with Ambrose, and they're falling out.'

Derry went and sat on a bench. 'One thing I do know for sure is, whoever wasted Terry Wells had better be protected by one of the gangs, or he's right up shit street.'

'Oh, we'll protect him,' Ashworth smiled. 'We'll give him thirty years inside.'

'This is an area I don't think you fully understand,' Derry said, taking a used match from his pocket and sticking it into the corner of his mouth.

'Pray, enlighten me,' Ashworth said with heavy sarcasm. He waved a hand in the direction of the blackboard, and

61

added, 'You've interviewed these people, surely?'

Derry exchanged an amused glance with Pearson. 'This is what you're not seeing,' he said. 'These men all hide behind respectable business fronts. If we went charging in, asking them about Wells, they'd deny even knowing him. Our brief is to watch, wait, and listen –'

'I wish I had your job,' Ashworth broke in.

'And if the balloon goes up, we're to try and limit the damage to gang members only.'

'What do you mean, make sure they only kill each other?'

'That's about it.'

'Well, that won't do for me,' Ashworth huffed. 'We're here to prevent crime, not to decide who can kill whom, while we look the other way.'

'Have you tried infiltrating the gangs?' Holly asked.

'You've been watching too much television,' Derry scoffed, without even glancing at her.

'And you watch too many American cop movies,' she threw back. 'Try answering the question.'

'Lady, you don't get anything past these people.'

'What about Hedley Ambrose?'

'He only uses black muscle.'

'What about his legit business?'

'He's a bookie,' the inspector said, finally giving Holly his full attention. 'On that front, he's an equal opportunity employer – pillar of the community.'

'So, if we could get me in there as a typist, say …' She looked hopefully across at Ashworth.

'No way,' Derry said, jumping to his feet. 'These boys play rough.'

'I can look after myself.'

'Not at this level, lady.'

Ashworth caught her arm and pulled her to one side. 'I don't know, Holly,' he whispered. 'It's going to put you at risk.'

'What's the alternative, guv? Just wait and clear the bodies away?'

Ashworth was still not convinced, and Holly said, 'Come on, guv, I am trained in martial arts.'

'Your DS's out of her tree,' Derry told him.

'And you're getting on my tits,' Holly hissed in a low voice.

'Hard shit,' Derry sneered.

Ashworth was preparing to intervene, when the inspector strode angrily towards her, saying, 'Look, lady, I need to prove this to you – these guys play rough and dirty – '

'Stop calling me lady,' Holly flared.

'Jesus Christ,' Derry muttered, edging back. 'Where are you people coming from?'

He crossed to a steel locker in a corner of the room and pulled open the door with such force, it clanged against the wall.

'You want to try a work-out in the gym – show me how tough you are? Is that what you want?'

'Yes, let's do it,' Holly hurled back.

'Okay.'

Derry retrieved two tracksuits from the locker and threw one at Holly. 'Like you said, let's do it … lady.'

Josh was finding the empty CID office depressing. On his own, with the other two in Rutley, he felt unable to resist wallowing in self-pity.

In the hope of clearing his mind, he set about scrutinising the reports of the Terence Wells case and was relieved to find them all in order. But even that task led his mind back to Greg, for it was he who had typed them the previous evening. All thoughts steered a course to Greg – that was Josh's problem.

As he sat there, Josh was horrified to find himself speculating as to how much money he was likely to inherit upon the death of his friend; but however hard he tried to dispel the thought, it refused to go away. Far better to think about that than the Aids test. Holly had arranged an appointment for five thirty that afternoon, and Josh was dreading it.

Could it be as much as fifty thousand pounds? Sixty thousand? What would he do with that amount of money? Pay off the mortgage?

Before Josh left the house that morning, Greg had had a very bad coughing bout. Could this be the beginning of the end? Would he soon have to nurse his sick friend, as life slipped away? The thought terrified him.

Perhaps focusing on his inheritance was a way in which to block more disturbing thoughts from his mind. Perhaps by concentrating on good things, he could nurture a more positive attitude to the future.

He *would* pay off the mortgage. And what then? A new car, the paintwork bright and shining?

But what if he were travelling the same road as Greg? What if all he had to look forward to was swollen glands, months of diarrhoea, devastating weight loss …

It would make a nice change to have a car in which the seats were not worn or scuffed.

… the crushing tiredness …

To have an odometer set at nil, a sleek, modern dashboard.

… the high temperature, the night sweats …

To feel the engine purring smoothly as it kicks into life at the first turn of the key.

… shivering, cramp-ridden night sweats that come as his body works overtime to produce antibodies…

A heartbreaking sob suddenly broke in Josh's throat, and he fell forward in the chair, cradling his head in his hands.

The gym stank of male odour. At the far end stood a boxing ring, and Holly walked purposefully towards it, her bare feet padding on the varnished floor. Steve Derry was already in the ring, kitted out in purple tracksuit bottoms and white trainers. Ashworth stood with Detective Sergeant Pearson outside the ropes.

'What size trainers do you wear?' Derry shouted.

'Fours,' Holly yelled back.

'Fours? You ain't gonna hurt anybody with those tiny feet. Russ, get the lady some trainers.'

Pearson hurried to a cupboard and riffled through a pile of shoes while Ashworth, with grave reservations, watched the inspector limbering up. Derry was a slim man, but his swarthy chest bulged, and muscles rippled on his torso. In comparison, Holly appeared slight at five feet eight of well-rounded female, slight and vulnerable.

She ducked between the ropes and shot a withering glance at the smiling inspector. Pearson passed her the trainers and she retired to a corner to put them on. While she was tying the laces, Derry appeared at her side, and before she had time to straighten up, he had kicked into her ribs, sending her sprawling, half outside the ropes.

'Hey,' an incensed Ashworth roared.

'First lesson, folks,' Derry said, from centre ring. 'These men are rough, and they play dirty. They don't wait until you're ready. You've gotta be able to look after yourself.'

'You'd better be able to, as well, son,' Ashworth said as, grimfaced, he started climbing through the ropes.

By this time Holly had regained her feet; white-faced, and clearly experiencing discomfort, she was struggling to drag air into her lungs.

Ashworth was half-way through the ropes when she called, 'Leave it, guv. Please.'

'But I can't let this go on, Holly.'

'Guv,' she said, feeling tentatively around her ribs, 'this is my pride on the line.'

Ashworth was about to speak but her eyes were pleading with him, so he bit back his words and climbed reluctantly out of the ring as Holly turned to face Inspector Derry.

'Come on, lady, show me what you've got,' he goaded, waving her to come forward. 'Show me.'

Holly circled around him, never looking away from his eyes. 'Yes,' she screamed, kicking out with first her right foot, and then her left. But Derry blocked both blows and counter-attacked by throwing a series of crushing chops with both hands.

Holly covered herself well, even though the vicious blows made her forearms tingle and lose sensation. Then an unexpected kick grazed the side of her head, causing stars to explode before her eyes.

'Show me what you got, lady. Come on, show me.'

He kicked again, but this time Holly saw it coming, saw the long, sweeping arch of his left leg which was meant to be the killer blow. Almost in slow motion, she watched it travelling towards her, and she saw the effort on Derry's face as every ounce of strength and balance went into the move. Holly made no attempt to block it, and as the foot hit her right cheekbone, she threw herself sideways, travelling with it, negating its force. Her shoulder jarred on the canvas, and Derry was above her, his face set in a winning smile, certain that it was over. But in one quick movement, Holly rolled between his legs and reached up for the bulge of his testicles, yanking them down hard, and screaming, 'You son-of-a-bitch.'

Derry howled with pain and sank to his knees, while Holly rolled clear and leapt to her feet. The gym was now strangely silent, and a look of total disbelief travelled across the inspector's face as Holly sank her foot into his chest. He fell forward, bemused, and failed to spot her knee until it collided with the side of his face. Finally defeated, he rolled over on the canvas, still clutching his groin.

Holly stood over him, fighting for breath. 'You'd better believe I've got more balls than anyone you've ever met,' she spat.

Derry attempted a smile and held out a hand, 'Draw?' he suggested.

'Not in my vocabulary,' Holly hissed back.

Pride alone brought Inspector Derry to his feet and allowed him to walk out of the gym, casting scathing glances at Ashworth and Pearson on the way. As the door swung shut, Pearson studied his shoes in an embarrassed silence and Ashworth chuckled quietly to himself.

Pearson gave an awkward cough. 'Chief inspector, can I take you two round the city, show you the sights? There's time, while a flat and a job with Ambrose are being arranged for DS Bedford.'

'All right,' Ashworth answered. 'And I'll need some office space.'

Pearson nodded eagerly. 'I'll sort it.'

'Let's go then,' he said, already heading for the door.

Holly called, 'Give me time to change, guv.'

'Surely,' he said, as the detective sergeant fell in beside him.

The rasp of her tracksuit zip sounded above their footsteps and at the door, Pearson turned back to find Holly down to her underwear. Totally transfixed, he took in her long, long legs and the ample cleavage which showed above her scanty bra. Pulling on her blouse, Holly glanced at him and, without embarrassment, her eyes held his until he looked away.

Chapter 7

Ashworth had never dealt with gangsters before, and so he had little fear of them. He could not understand the Special Unit's reluctance to step on their toes for he saw stepping, rather forcefully, on the toes of wrongdoers as an integral part of his job.

Sitting beside Russ Pearson in the passenger seat of the Ford Orion, he closed his mind to most of what the detective was saying, letting in only the relevant facts. Every so often, he would glance at Holly who had a bruise developing swiftly on her right cheekbone, but for most of the time he glared out at the city. The sickly-sweet stench from a chocolate factory mingled with the traffic fumes, and fuelled still further Ashworth's dislike for the place.

Their first call was to the florist's shop, owned by the late Terence Wells. Standing on the corner of a shopping parade, it was closed now, with multi-coloured shades drawn across its windows.

Pearson kept the engine running while he stopped on the busy main road. 'Terry Wells's shop,' he told Ashworth.

'Did Wells own it?'

Pearson shrugged. 'Anybody's guess. My bet is, it belongs to Reggie Carter.'

There was a persistent tap on the driver's window, and Pearson wound it down to stare up into the stern face of a uniformed policeman.

'Do you realise you're causing an obstruction on a major road, sir?'

The detective sergeant, digging around in his pockets for his warrant card, ignored the officer and turned to Ashworth.

'We'll have to wait and see if the shop opens again. If it doesn't, it means Carter's out of business.'

He found the card and flashed it at the policeman. 'Now, beat it,' he snarled. 'We don't need attention drawn to us.' The officer seemed tempted to make a retort but instead, he turned and sloped off back to his patrol car.

'The local fuzz are always trying to score points off us,' Pearson said.

'Nobody seems to love you,' Ashworth commented drily.

'That's true,' he laughed. 'And we can't claim to grow on people.'

'Is there much more to see?'

'There's Ambrose's place, and Bernie Williams's book-shop,' he said, slipping the car into first gear.

'A bookshop? Flowers, books, horse-racing …' Ashworth smiled. 'I really can't believe these men are as dangerous as you say.'

'Believe it. They've learnt a lot from the sixties. They know if they go around with shotguns, we can pull them in. So, they hide behind respectable fronts. Did you know, they even do a tax fiddle in reverse?'

He laughed at Ashworth's confused expression. 'Yeah, you see, the old-time hoods used to slip up because they had extravagant lifestyles with no visible means of support, Nowadays, they set themselves up in business and falsify the books to show a healthy profit. They pay tax on say, fifty grand – a drop in the ocean for them – and another avenue of investigation gets closed to us.'

'Clever.'

'You bet. They literally get away with murder.'

'Not on my patch, they don't,' Ashworth said, as he viewed with horror the congested road ahead. 'I've changed my mind, Russ, take us back to the station.'

'It would be useful to see where Ambrose and Williams conduct their business,' Pearson advised.

'I'll be going to see them tomorrow, and Reginald

Carter, as well,' Ashworth said firmly. 'It's about time some-body tried a little straight talking with these people.'

Holly was enjoying the city very much. When they arrived back at the station, where Ashworth got out of the car and stomped off up the front steps, she elected to go with Pearson to what he called 'the car pound', and was not overly surprised to find that it was simply a large car-park at the rear of the building.

The uniformed branch was about to change shifts, so the car-park was full, and Holly attracted many admiring glances.

'Your stock's risen considerably,' Pearson told her. 'News got round about what you did to my guv'nor.'

'Is that the only reason they're paying me this much attention?' she asked, as a wolf whistle rang out.

Pearson eyed her from head to foot. 'That, and the rest of the package.'

He lit a cigarette, and Holly was all too aware of her sexual frustration as she watched him draw on it and glance at her, the wind tousling his thick blond hair.

'Fancy a drink when we're finished?' he asked, expelling smoke from his mouth and nostrils.

His eyes caused excitement to ripple through her body, but Holly fought it off and shook her head.

'No, I don't think so,' she said stoutly. 'I'm off mixing work with pleasure.'

'Suit yourself,' he shrugged, 'but you might just have turned down the experience of a lifetime.'

Holly grinned. 'I'll risk it.'

'Come on,' he said, laughing mildly. 'Let's go inside.'

Bernie Williams was in good shape for a man close to sixty, with bulging muscles spoiling the fine cut of his corduroy jacket. He was small, around five feet eight, and his receding grey hair, together with the rimless spectacles perched on the end of his nose, lent him a scholarly bearing, not the least out of place in the office of a book-shop.

Holding the telephone receiver to his ear, he listened impatiently to the ringing tone, and was about to put it down, when a male voice growled, 'Hello.'

'Reggie,' he chuckled, 'by the sound of your tone, you need to watch your blood pressure.'

'Ah, Bernie,' Carter said, his voice returning to its cultured purr.

'I just rang to say how sorry I was to hear about Terry Wells.'

'Don't be a hypocrite, Bernie, you're glad he's dead.'

'I can place my hand on my heart, and say that's not true,' Williams said mildly.

'Since when did you have a heart?'

Bernie Williams smiled into the mouthpiece and Carter said, 'You could have blown Terry away. You had reason.'

'So did you Reggie. I'd heard that things were not all sweetness and light between the two of you. By the way, did you know the Bridgetown law were in the city?'

'Yes, but don't worry, it's just some thick copper named Ashworth. He'll soon get fed up and go away.'

'Reggie –'

'Listen, Bernie, when he's gone, I'm going to sort this out, and if I find you had anything to do with Terry's death –'

'Oh, don't threaten me, Reggie. It's so uncivilised.'

'Ambrose's people are denying any knowledge of the murder,' Carter said, abruptly changing the subject.

'Well, they would, wouldn't they?' Williams laughed. 'What's going to happen to the flower shop?'

'It's in Terry's name. He has no children, so we can't reopen it,' Carter spat, suddenly angry. 'As it's part of Terry's estate, it'll no doubt pass to his idiotic brothers.'

'You can stand the loss,' Williams said smoothly.

'Maybe,' Carter hissed between gritted teeth, 'but somebody's going to pay for this. And don't for one minute think that your boys can move in on my territory.'

'They remain as they were before, Reggie. You're getting paranoid.'

He replaced the receiver, and sat looking at it.

'And when you get paranoid, the blood's likely to start flowing.'

He leant back in his chair, hands behind his head, murmuring, James Ashworth, something tells me you're far from being a thick copper. You've already got your associate inside Ambrose's organisation. That means you're determined.' He laughed softly. 'But old Bernie Williams knows everything that happens in this city, and all of this could be to my advantage.'

Holly found Ashworth in Steve Derry's underground office. The two men were engaged in urgent discussion, and when she entered with Pearson, Derry looked up, and said, 'Leave us, would you, Russ?'

Taking in their stem faces, Pearson left without question. Derry leant against the desk and smiled.

'DS Bedford,' he said, 'the chief inspector and I are just ironing out some details.'

Holly raised her eyebrows but did not speak, and the inspector, angered by her sullen expression, said, 'Okay, this needs to be sorted. Look, lady, there's absolutely no animosity on my part for what happened this morning. I'll get some stick off my boys –'

'Why?' Holly interjected. 'Because I'm a mere woman, and you're a big, butch man?'

'I'm not doing this very well, am I?' he said, irritably. 'What I'm trying to say is, you can look after yourself. All right?'

When Holly simply gave a non-committal nod, Derry exhaled sharply and abandoned any attempt to pacify her.

Hitching himself up on the desk, he said, 'We've been working out how to avoid stepping on each other's toes. Wells's murder is connected to our work, but there's no reason why your investigation should get in our way. If you draw a blank, as I suspect you will …' He caught sight of Ashworth's offended expression, and laughed. 'Seems I'm making a habit of rubbing you people up the wrong way.'

That statement was not denied in the pause that followed, and he went on, 'I've arranged a flat for you.'

Leaning back on the desk, he took a ring holding two keys from one of the drawers, and passed it to Holly.

'We've pulled a few strings with a temp agency. They're taking one of their girls out of Ambrose's betting shop, and you'll be replacing her, as from tomorrow. Now, I'd like you to liaise directly with me, because anything you uncover about drugs, etc, will be vitally important to us.'

Jumping briskly to his feet, Derry added, 'Look, I don't think we've got off to a very good start, so can I offer to buy you a drink?'

The invitation was meant for them both, but the way in which his gaze held Holly's eyes left little doubt that it was primarily aimed at her.

'No, thank you,' Ashworth said. 'I've seen enough of the city for one day. I'm heading back to Bridgetown, but I'd like a word with Holly first.'

'Okay,' Derry said, heading for the door. 'Be my guest.'

As soon as the inspector had gone, Ashworth turned to her. 'I want you to be extremely careful.'

'Yes, guv.'

'You're going to be very much at risk. At the first hint of anything going wrong, just get out.'

'Yes, dad.'

Despite his misgivings, Ashworth grinned. 'And ring me every night.'

'Why don't you tell me about the birds and the bees while we're at it, guv?'

'You're incorrigible,' he moaned, shaking his head. 'No doubt, you'll make out.'

'Oh, I'll make out,' Holly assured him, as she settled into Inspector Derry's chair. 'You're not working down here, are you, guv?'

'No, they've given me an office upstairs. I've got an idea it's the stationery cupboard. Still, as long as I don't put on any weight, I should be all right.'

Holly was pensive for a while, and then she said, 'We may not see each other for weeks, guv, and I think there's something we should discuss.'

Ashworth turned enquiringly. 'Yes?'

'It's about Josh.'

'What about him?'

She paused, aware of his expectant expression, and then she launched into an explanation of Josh's problem. Ashworth listened, stony-faced, until she had finished.

'HIV? Aids in a police station? That's bad, Holly. If the news leaks out, a lot of officers could panic.'

'It's not confirmed, yet. He might have to wait up to twelve weeks before he knows.'

'But mud sticks. There are those at the station who'll believe the lad has Aids, even if he's in the clear.'

Holly was alarmed that Ashworth seemed more concerned about station morale than about Josh, and she said, rather angrily, 'Well, I think we should help him through it.'.

'I know what needs to be done,' he stated, in a tone which did not invite debate. 'Josh may not like it, though.'

Holly sat in Derry's office for a long time after Ashworth had gone. She could not believe the way in which he had reacted to Josh's predicament. Her volatile nature was such that her liking for someone could, within the space of a second, turn to hatred if she felt let down. Ashworth, she decided, was no better than all those who refused to sit in the same room as an Aids sufferer.

She was hitting out at the desk top with some force, when Steve Derry returned.

'Are you beating up the furniture now, just to keep your hand in?' Taking a spent match from his pocket, he placed it between his teeth. 'I'm trying to give up cigarettes,' he explained.

'Good for you,' Holly said, glaring at him.

'How about coming for that drink?'

'No, thanks.'

'Look, lady, have I just caught you on a bad day, or what? We're gonna be working together –'

'Yes, and that's all,' she flared. 'I feed you the information – end of story.'

'Is there something wrong with your hearing? I asked you out for a drink, for Christ's sake, I never mentioned dropping your knickers.'

He crossed to a filing cabinet, and was silent for a few moments while he searched among its papers. Presently, he turned to her.

'Is it because I'm black?'

'No.'

'Do you think we're all animals? Do you think we all lose control when we get close to a white woman?'

'I never said that. I didn't even imply it.'

'I know you didn't. I'm just trying to put you at a disadvantage.' He gave her a slow, lazy grin. 'I haven't had this much hostility from a female since I divorced my old lady. You know, if we carry on like this, we'll only be able to communicate through solicitors.'

Holly finally yielded and smiled at him.

'Sorry,' she said, 'it's just that somebody's let me down.'

'A guy?'

She sighed. 'Yes, but not in the way you think. I don't know, you think you understand somebody …'

'Is that a yes to having a drink?'

'It's a maybe. You can take me to see the flat, and then I'll need to collect my gear from Bridgetown.'

'I'll drive you there. We could have a drink on the way back.'

'Okay,' she said, getting to her feet.

'You'll get to like me, don't worry.'

Perhaps that's what I'm afraid of, she thought ruefully.

Chapter 8

The filthy room was beginning to disgust Lenny Spencer. He had spent most of the day squatting on the foul mattress, with the .38 revolver clutched in his hand, moving only when he needed to eat. His diet now consisted solely of baked beans and bread, with a shot of vodka straight from the bottle every so often to alleviate the monotony.

So finely tuned was his body's defence mechanism that he heard straight away the footfalls on the stairs; when the landing floorboards creaked, he gripped the gun with both hands and pointed it towards the door, his finger tightening on the trigger as a droplet of sweat trickled down his back.

The knock was tentative. 'Lenny, it's Bruce.'

Exhaling slowly, Lenny pushed the gun beneath his pillow.

'Manny Fredricks is here to see you.'

In two strides, Lenny was at the door, throwing back the bolts and lifting the lock. He opened the door a little way, and peered through the gap. Standing behind the sweating landlord was a slight, elderly man with a large, hooked nose and long, straggly grey hair. His overcoat collar was turned up, hiding his face, but in the half-light, Lenny could see his watery blue eyes darting from side to side. The old man stepped forward and smiled.

'Okay, Bruce,' he said, 'you can leave Lenny and me to have a chat, so make yourself scarce.'

The landlord, annoyed by the curt dismissal, muttered churlish oaths to himself as he lumbered off down the stairs.

'Well, Lenny, are you going to let me in? We cannot talk business out here.'

The door was pulled back, and Lenny slammed it shut

the moment Manny Fredricks had crossed the threshold.

'Nice,' Manny said, looking around the room. 'Very nice. Bruce could be named Landlord of the Year, don't you think?'

'You're not here to discuss my accommodation,' Lenny snarled.

'Easy, Lenny, easy.'

The old man wandered over to the window and stared out through the dirty panes. Then, turning sharply, he said, I understand you need a passport.'

'Yeah.'

'They cost fifteen thousand pounds.'

'Fifteen grand? You must be joking.'

'Money is the one thing I never joke about.'

'No way.'

The old man shrugged. 'You could always apply to Her Majesty's Government for a passport. I believe they are a lot cheaper than I am, but they have an irritating habit of asking so many questions.'

'How long does it take?' Lenny asked resignedly.

'Two weeks.'

'But I haven't got two weeks. I need it now.'

'These things take time. I have many customers who come before you. I cannot disappoint them.'

Lenny considered all of this, and grudgingly said, 'Okay.'

Manny beamed. 'Good, good. Now, half the money is up front.'

'Oh yeah, and if you do a runner with it?'

'That is a chance you must take.'

Much to Manny's amusement, Lenny rushed across to the mattress, and pulled the gun free of the pillow. Pointing it menacingly, he spat, 'You fuck with me, old man, and I'll blow you away.'

'Do not be so silly. I am here to help you.'

Lenny's nerves were taut, and it showed in his voice,

when he yelled, 'Everybody in this fucking place's taking my dosh off me.'

Manny stepped forward. 'Lenny, Lenny,' he cooed, 'my help costs money. I run risks. I have overheads.'

'Just get me the passport,' Lenny snarled.

'All right, all right. You are wise to trust no one. I will offer you no more advice that costs you money. Now, why do you think I want half the money up front?'

'I don't know.'

'Because I have to invest it in forging your papers and if, when I am finished, you are not here …' The old man shrugged.

'Why shouldn't I be here?' Lenny asked, wiping a hand at the perspiration on his forehead.

Manny reached forward, and pushed the gun aside, all the while staring into Lenny's eyes. 'Because the police might find you … or whoever else is looking for you.'

'Nobody knows I'm here,' Lenny insisted, fiddling nervously with the gun.

'So many people know you are here,' Manny said, his tone hypnotic. 'They do not know who you are, or what you have done, but they know you are afraid to go out, afraid to be seen. All the people in this house know you are on the run. If the police come asking questions …'

Lenny ran agitated fingers through his hair, and considered the old man's words.

'I could help you, Lenny. I may be the only friend you have in the world. Oh, but I forget, you do not want my advice. Give me half of the money, and I will go.'

'Okay, tell me what you've got.'

Manny hesitated. 'A safe house. No one, apart from me, will know you are there. A luxury flat,' he added, looking around at the squalor. 'I can arrange girls, boys, whatever is your preference. You pay only the going rate. For this, I take nothing.'

'How much?'

'Five thousand pounds. Look on it as an insurance policy,' Manny counselled, when Lenny looked set to argue. 'If you have paid me so much money, I have a vested interest in keeping you safe to flee the country. If I fail, I do not get the rest of my money.'

'Okay, okay.' Lenny said heatedly.

'Good.' Manny smiled. 'Money oils the wheels of the world, Lenny. Money buys anything.'

That evening, Inspector Steve Derry was a model of good behaviour and charm. He showed Holly the flat, which an estate agent would describe as 'compact', and afterwards took her to Bridgetown to collect her clothes.

Holly, assuming that the hundred-mile round trip would take up most of the evening was unable to quell a feeling of frustration at the thought that she was safe with this hunk of a man. But Derry drove his souped-up 1970s Ford Capri with the speedometer hovering at ninety, and the miles soon melted away.

'Aren't you frightened of being stopped by a patrol car?' Holly shouted above the wind rushing past the metallic-gold vehicle.

'No,' he scoffed. 'Being Special Unit has its advantages. I just flash my card, and tell them to go walkabout.'

Some miles outside Rutley, they stopped at a quaint country pub, and while Holly sat watching him order the drinks, she thought how unlike an undercover policeman he looked in his red jacket and well-cut beige slacks. She broached the subject when be sat down.

'I'm not undercover,' he laughed. 'They know I'm here. I'm watching them, remember, not the other way round.'

He took the head off his pint of ale, and watched as Holly poured tonic into her gin. She stared into the glass for a moment, and then gave him a challenging look.

'I've a feeling there's something you're not telling me.'

'My brief, you mean?' He chewed thoughtfully on the

habitual matchstick, and said, 'Watch and wait – that's about it.'

'But that's not telling me anything,' she persisted.

'Lady, you certainly push, don't you? Look, some of my information's classified. It goes right to the Home Office.'

'Okay, okay,' she huffed. 'Drink up, finish your match, and we'll be on our way.'

'You win,' he laughed, holding up a hand. 'Right, where to begin. We're supposed to stop prostitution for a start, but we never will. Women have been selling it ever since they found out men would pay.'

'And to think I've been giving it away,' Holly whispered to herself,

Derry cast a quizzical glance at her grinning face, and went on, 'The story with drugs is no different. However hard the Customs boys work, and however much of the stuff we seize, the traffic just keeps on hitting the streets.'

'So, you're saying it's a battle we can't win?'

'It's a battle we've already lost,' he said. 'The more junk we take off the streets, the higher the price rises, and the more crime the addict has to commit to finance his habit. The government's facing an ever-growing dilemma: should they persevere, or should they throw in the towel, and legalise drugs and the flesh trade?'

'I still don't see where you come into this.'

'I'm the little boy with his finger stuck in the hole in the dyke.'

'Am I supposed to be following this?' Holly asked, before finishing her drink.

Derry gave a rueful smile. 'While the government dithers, and it probably will for years, I have to try and keep the lid on things.'

Although they were the only patrons in the bar, Derry leant forward and lowered his voice.

'Look, Carter and Williams have never bothered the powers-that-be all that much; in fact, their reputations have kept the younger hoods out. But these two gents are coming to the end of their shelf life, so we get villains like Ambrose moving in.'

'Does that make any difference?'

'Of course it does,' he said, tossing the matchstick into the ashtray. 'Hedley Ambrose is your new-style villain. He uses more of this ...' Derry tapped his forehead. 'And he's after the whole of the territory.'

'Do you think Ambrose killed Terence Wells?'

'Hold on a minute, I'm coming to that. When Carter and Williams step down, and the young hotheads in their gangs take over, that's when we're likely to have a blood-bath, and that's what I'm here to contain. Now, did Ambrose kill Wells? I'll tell you one thing, Wells's death wasn't your normal gangland execution. If it had been, we'd probably never have found the body. It was a state-ment: You mess with me and, bang, bang, you're dead.'

Holly thought about this. 'So Ambrose has started a war?'

Derry shrugged. 'That's what my money's on, but it's still wide open. I do know that Terry Wells had a serious dispute with Bernie Williams recently, so your guess is as good as mine.'

He sank back in his seat and took a long drink. 'How good's your guv'nor?'

'He's good,' Holly said. 'In fact, he's very good.' She eyed him suspiciously. 'You don't think he's up to this, do you?'

'It's no reflection on his ability,' Derry stressed, digging into his pocket for another match. 'Ambrose is gonna meet him with righteous indignation; in fact, I wouldn't be surprised to see the writs start flying. Carter will admit nothing, and deny nothing; he'll just tell Ashworth to go and be silly somewhere else. And Bernie Williams, well, he'll milk the situation for his own advantage.

'I might come up with something,' Holly said brightly.

'Yes, you're a breakthrough – someone we can get on the inside. If you could come up with something on Ambrose, it'd make my life a whole lot easier.'

'Glad to be of service,' she said, inclining her head.

'Come on, lady, we'd better make tracks.'

Outside, where the night was cool, and a light breeze carried the scents of summer, Steve Derry gallantly opened the passenger door which squealed a protest on dry hinges. Holly grinned as she climbed in, and waited for him to join her.

'How old's this thing?'

'Watch it,' he warned. 'You're talking about the lady I love.'

'Your car's female?'

'Of course.' Then, with a straight face, he indicated the dashboard, and said, 'Delilah, meet Holly. Holly, meet Delilah.'

She laughed. 'You're crazy.'

'It's been said, lady.'

'Don't call me, lady,' she ordered, even though a smile still hovered around her lips.

'But it's a sign of affection.'

'Well, I don't want you addressing me with a sign of affection,' she told him, with as much firmness as she could muster. 'Our relationship is strictly professional.'

Derry moved closer, and whispered in her ear, 'Lady, it's gonna be a long time before I let you anywhere near my balls again.'

Holly giggled and, without thinking, leant forward until their foreheads were touching. 'You're bloody crazy.'

'I'll grow on you,' Derry told her softly.

His tempting lips were so close, and Holly knew that she should look away, but she couldn't.

'Hadn't we better be going?' she whispered.

'Put your seat belt on, then.'

She reached for the belt and the moment was gone,

and in order to cover her disappointment, she said, 'Shouldn't this thing be fitted with ejector seats?'

'Lay off Delilah,' he warned with a broad grin. 'She's the meanest thing on four wheels.'

The case was beginning to weigh heavily on Ashworth by the time he arrived at Bridgetown police station the next morning, and despite his outward display of confidence, he feared that a wall of silence would block his investigation, leaving him with only whatever information Holly might unearth.

Not relishing his meeting with Josh, he stomped up the station steps, gave a brief wave to Sergeant Dutton at reception, and took the stairs two at a time to CID.

Josh was lost in his thoughts, staring at the computer screen with unseeing eyes, when Ashworth entered the room.

'Good morning, Josh,' he said.

'Morning, guv.'

Ashworth settled at his desk, and studied the blotter for a few minutes.

'Holly's not in yet, guv.'

'Nor will she be,' he said, going on to explain her undercover mission.

Josh listened intently, and then let out a soft whistle. 'That's a bit risky.'

'Extremely. But you know Holly, once her mind's made up.'

There followed an awkward silence, in which Ashworth cleared his throat many times.

'Josh,' he said, eventually, 'Holly's been telling me about your problem ...' He waved his hand vaguely. 'About your friend staying with you.'

'The problem's called Aids, guv,' Josh said heavily, 'and I may have it.'

'Yes, well ...'

'I'll probably have to take two tests –'

'I know that. I had a chat with my GP on the phone last night. I didn't mention your name, of course.'

'Guv –'

'No, listen, Josh, I've got something to say,' Ashworth said firmly, as he approached the glass wall to look out over Bridgetown. 'You're not going to like this, but it's something that has to be done. I know you're a dedicated copper ...'

Josh closed his eyes and waited.

'... but for the foreseeable future you're going to be under a great deal of strain. Very likely, you'll make mistakes, possibly serious mistakes.'

'I can cope,' Josh insisted.

'I don't agree,' Ashworth replied sharply. 'And this case is fraught with enough difficulties as it is. Now, I've thought of sending you on sick leave, but that's going to start the others asking questions.'

Josh started to fear the worst. All right, if Ashworth was about to suspend him, he would not make a scene, he would simply walk out with dignity. Opening the drawer of his desk, Josh reached inside for his things, and sneered at the sound of his superior's voice.

'So, what I've decided is to check and double-check everything you do, every report, every enquiry.'

The sneer froze on Josh's face. 'Guv?'

'I'm sorry, Josh, I've got to be blunt, because that's the only way I can be. Basically, what it amounts to is this: when Holly gets back, we're going to have to carry you. I don't want anyone beyond these four walls knowing about this problem. There's a lot of ignorance and prejudice about these things. I know everything's going to work out, and I don't want to see your career ruined by something you have no control over.'

Josh continued to stare into the open drawer.

'I've talked this over with Sarah, and our door's always

open …' Ashworth gave Josh's shoulder a self-conscious pat, and said, 'You'll come through it, son.'

Then, imagining that he might be offended, Ashworth decided it would be best to leave Josh alone for a while, so he said briskly, 'Good man. Carry on, then,' and marched out of the room.

The office door closed softly, and Josh pushed the desk drawer firmly shut.

'Thanks, guv,' he murmured.

Holly was naked, and studying her reflection in the wardrobe's full-length mirror. After much scrutiny, it was decided that, rather than getting fat, she was merely becoming well proportioned.

With eyes still on her image, she stepped into a pair of scanty white briefs, noting with satisfaction that her stomach remained flat and taut as she leant forward. It was her first day at Hedley Ambrose's betting shop, and she had chosen to wear a white camisole top and tight jeans to high-light her curves.

'Okay, Mr Ambrose, you don't mind your workers dressing casually, so let's see what you make of me.'

Time was getting on, and Holly hurried into the kitchen to gulp down the lukewarm coffee she had made earlier then, collecting her shoulder bag from the tiny lounge, she prepared to meet the unknown.

After Ashworth left Josh, he went to call on Reginald Carter at the Gainsborough Hotel. Carter, in the middle of break-fast, was obviously not pleased by the interruption.

'Chief inspector,' he sighed, 'you'd better sit down.'

Ashworth lowered his bulk into a chair facing the break-fast table, and studied Carter as he cut into a slice of bacon.

'When can I move back into my house?' he demanded as he chewed.

'In a couple of days, I should think, sir.'

'Let's skip the "sir", and all the other niceties, shall we? I know you're a thorough man, so by now you'll have found out everything about me. In public, I'll deny it all … But in private, well, what's the point?'

'You admit you're a criminal?'

Carter cut into an egg, and laughed. 'Terry's death is none of your business, you know. I shall deal with the person or persons who did it.'

'I'm a police officer,' Ashworth retorted.

'Bollocks,' Carter threw back, his cultured tone lending a strange ring to the expletive. 'Ashworth, I've been a villain for forty years, and there is not one blemish on my record.'

'I could alter that,' he said, angered by the man's attitude.

'I've eaten better policemen than you for breakfast.' And, as if to emphasise the point, he scooped egg into his mouth. 'You're wasting your time.'

'I'll be the judge of that.'

Carter chewed slowly, as he took in Ashworth's resolute expression. 'Hedley Ambrose will tell you even less than I have. Bernie Williams will lead you along every false avenue he can – if you let him, that is. Where can you go?'

'A man has been murdered,' Ashworth said firmly, 'and I intend to find out who did it.'

'An admirable sentiment, chief inspector.'

With a casual ease, Carter put down his cutlery, and dabbed at his mouth with a serviette. Then he fixed Ashworth with a curious look.

'Tell me, what are you into – a middle-aged man like yourself? Girls? Young girls?'

Ashworth bristled at the question.

'No, I can see not. Scotch whisky, perhaps?' He chortled. 'Oh yes, I can see by your face that I've struck a chord.' He threw the serviette on to his plate, and settled back. 'I could have a case of the finest malt delivered to your home, four times a year. No one would know where it came from.'

'You're trying to bribe me,' Ashworth said, his eyes wide with incredulity.

'Merely offering you a gesture of goodwill.'

But then his manner changed abruptly, and when he spoke, Carter's tone was cold. 'You're a very determined man, Ashworth, and although this may sound crude, I would rather have you inside the tent, pissing out, than outside, pissing in, as they say.'

'Call me a detective if you must,' Ashworth mocked, 'but I just knew you'd possess a poetic turn of mind.'

Carter's face hardened. 'You're an irritant, Ashworth, nothing more, but one I could well do without.'

The chief inspector got to his feet. 'Sorry to disappoint,' he said, 'but I'll be urinating towards you.'

'You could regret that,' Carter warned.

Ashworth shook his head and tutted. 'First you try to bribe me, and now I get threats.'

'I don't threaten,' Carter declared, his lip curling with contempt.

'Which is just as well,' Ashworth said, placing his hands on the table, and straining forward. 'Because whoever you might think you are, with just the two of us in the room, that would be a big mistake. Am I making myself clear?'

Carter's face flushed. 'I could have you –'

'What? Beaten up? You may be able to arrange for it to be done but, believe me, you couldn't do it yourself.'

'Don't bother me again, Ashworth. I'm giving you fair warning.'

'Mr Carter,' Ashworth said, on his way to the door, 'I shall interview you as and when I see fit. Oh, and stick to an English breakfast. I'm a little more difficult to chew.'

Chapter 9

Many men turned to gaze appreciatively at Holly as she sauntered along the crowded road, smiling at those she passed, her hips swaying, her head held proud. She turned into Greenfield Terrace, a narrow alley bathed in sunlight, and her high heels sounded on the cobbles as she made her way up the steep incline.

A red, white and blue plastic streamer curtain marked the entrance to H. A. TURF ACCOUNTANTS, making it impossible to miss. Holly pushed through the strips, and went down two steps to find herself in a long narrow room which stank of stale cigarette smoke thinly veiled by air freshener.

At the far end of the room, behind heavy metal grilles at three windows, stood the cashiers' desks. The room was lit by rows of fluorescent lights which, for the moment, were turned off, leaving a single, shadeless bulb to glow dimly from the centre of the ceiling.

An elderly black man was leaning on a broom, the meagre light catching and accentuating the greyness of his curly hair.

'Well, glory be,' he called out. 'The power of prayer is a mighty force. I was askin' the good Lord for a beautiful woman, and you walks through the door.'

'I'm here to see Mr Ambrose,' she said, smiling. 'I'm Holly Bedford.'

'The new typist. Well, I'll be …'

Chuckling heartily, he limped between rows of easy chairs, all positioned towards a number of television sets high up on the wall, and reached for Holly's hand, shaking it enthusiastically.

'I'm Max, little missy. I sweep the floor, wash the tea things, keep the place tidy, and do whatever a poor man

89

has to do to keep bread on his table.'

Holly giggled as Max hobbled across to an open door on the right of the cashiers' desks, and pressed a bell at the foot of a steep flight of stairs.

'I'm ringin' to summon the master,' he said. 'And I just hope Mr Hedley's in a good mood, 'cause if he ain't, then old Max is in for the high jump.'

Is Mr Ambrose that bad?'

'Keep your voice down, missy,' Max cautioned. 'He's better than most … oh, yessir. He works old Max like a dog, but he gives him straw to sleep on at night.'

Holly was wondering what to make of this strange individual, when she heard footsteps thumping down the stairs.

'Don't say I talked to you, missy,' Max whispered urgently, before shuffling away.

Holly turned to see a powerfully built black man standing at the foot of the stairs, the strong light from the landing casting his long shadow across the room. He reached forward and flicked a switch, causing Holly to blink at the harsh light from the fluorescent strips. Hedley Ambrose stepped forward, his movements light for such a large man. He wore a white shirt, open at the neck, the knot of his striped tie pulled loose. His light grey slacks were well tailored, and his expensive leather-soled shoes made no sound as he strode towards her.

'Max,' he chided. 'Have you been doing your Roots act again?'

'I ain't done nothin', Mr Hedley. I ain't done nothin' at all,' the old man said, as he disappeared through a door at the back of the room, his infectious chuckle echoing in the corridor.

'Sorry about that,' Ambrose said, his hand outstretched. 'You must be Holly.'

'Yes, I am, Mr Ambrose.'

His handshake was firm, yet not heavy, and be surprised Holly, when he said, 'Max was an alcoholic, sleeping rough, when I took him in. He's straightened himself out now, I'm glad to say.'

He gazed down at her, his expression earnest. 'I believe one of the things missing from this great country of ours is the opportunity to give people a chance to help themselves.' Then, his smile disarming, he said, 'Sorry, that's a hobby-horse of mine. Max does have a strange sense of humour. I hope he didn't offend you?'

'No, I think he's great.'

She found herself warming to Hedley Ambrose too; and as she looked up into his handsome face, listened to the soft purr of his educated voice, she found it almost impossible to believe that he was a hardened criminal.

'Now, if I can just say a few things before we go upstairs,' Ambrose continued. 'I pay the wages, but apart from that we're all equal here. I want you to feel happy and relaxed while you're working for me. If anyone gives you any trouble, sexual harassment, or anything of that nature, just let me know.'

Holly would have welcomed a little sexual harassment, but she kept quiet and smiled.

'You'll be sharing an office with Janice, our telephonist. The poor girl's having boyfriend problems at the moment, but we're bearing with her, and I hope you can.'

'Right,' Holly said, nodding eagerly.

'If you'd like to come up, then.'

He strode to the door, and stood to one side for Holly to pass. 'Max!'

'Yes, Mr Hedley, sir?' he called from the rear.

'Could we have some coffee upstairs, please?'

'Right away, Mr Hedley, sir. I'll get it there as fast as these old legs will allow.'

Ambrose shook his head, and sighed. 'He swears he's dried out, but sometimes I wonder.'

'He's a real character.'

'He most definitely is, but the clients don't much like his

rendition of "Old Man River" in the middle of a big race.'

Holly laughed, and Ambrose said, 'Mind the stairs. They're rather narrow.'

Negotiating the sharp bend at the top, Holly found herself on a small landing, and surmised that Hedley Ambrose was not too worried about decor, for the walls were bare plaster, pot-holed and worn.

'Not luxurious, I know,' he said, as if reading her thoughts. 'But it's functional.'

He guided her along to a room at the front of the building, which Holly assumed was his office. An oak desk stood in the large bay window, facing towards the street, and a plush grey carpet and a long boardroom table added a touch of elegance.

'My office,' Ambrose announced. 'Now, if you'd like to come with me …'

She followed him on along the landing, and into what must originally have been the second bedroom. This room had an altogether different appearance. On a battered desk, which Holly took to be hers, there stood a tired, old electric typewriter. And in the opposite corner, the telephonist was positioned in front of an ancient switchboard. On the wall behind her was a Chippendale calendar.

'Janice, this is Holly,' Ambrose said warmly. 'Holly, meet Janice.'

The girl was around nineteen. She had long greasy blonde hair, and wore a baggy sweater over a short black skirt. She was considering Holly through red, puffy eyes.

'Hi,' Holly said, smiling broadly.

Janice sniffed. 'Hello.'

Ambrose, making a face, said, 'I take it you know how to use the old-fashioned typewriter?'

Holly assured him that she did.

'And the switchboard?'

She stood behind Janice, and studied the board. 'Yes, I think so. I flick those switches for incoming calls, put them through, then … yes, yes, no problem.'

'Good,' Ambrose beamed. 'Then I'll leave you two ladies to get acquainted.'

At the doorway, he said, 'Oh, and arrange lunch between yourselves. As long as the typing's done, and the switchboard's always covered, I'm not really bothered.'

Holly settled into her chair, dropped her bag on the floor, and flicked through the pile of letters to be typed. The top one was addressed to the local Conservative Head-quarters, others were for suppliers and various businesses.

'You all right, Janice?' she asked, more for something to say than anything else.

The girl, who seconds earlier had been busy filing her nails, suddenly pulled a handkerchief from the sleeve of her voluminous sweater, and put it swiftly to her screwed-up eyes.

'No,' she moaned.

Janice was obviously of the type who enjoyed being the centre of attention, pouring out her troubles to anyone willing to listen.

'What's the problem, then?' Holly asked, doing her best to sound chirpy.

'It's Tone, my boyfriend. He loves me, but says I've got to let him experience life before we settle down. He says if he doesn't get it out of his system now, when we're twenty-six, say, and married, it'll cause trouble 'cause he'll think he's missed out.'

'Chuck him,' Holly advised, as she fed paper into the typewriter. 'He's conning you.'

'But I love him,' Janice wailed, before picking up a glass of water and gulping down two aspirins.

This is going to be a bundle of laughs, was the thought behind Holly's sympathetic look.

Chief Inspector Ashworth found the drive to Rutley highly depressing. It was congested motorway for most of the journey, and as he sat in the Scorpio, hemmed in by petrol tankers and heavy goods vehicles, his mood was not helped by the thought that he would be making this trip every day for the foreseeable future.

Spotting a gap in the traffic, he pulled out into the middle lane, only to find his path blocked by a cattle transporter, and the fast lane crowded with vehicles crawling along at thirty-five miles an hour.

While cows bayed in front of him, and all around car horns blared, Ashworth abandoned his deep breathing exercises, and took to muttering darkly instead.

Max served the coffee, all the while teasing Janice. He could introduce her to the joys of sex with an older man, he said; and although the girl protested loudly, she did cheer up a little. Indeed, she seemed on the verge of smiling once or twice, but each time swiftly controlled the impulse.

The switchboard suddenly buzzed, and Janice flicked a switch.

'H. A. Turf Accountants,' she said, picking at a cuticle while she listened. 'Hold the line, please.'

Selecting another switch, she waited for Hedley Ambrose to answer his telephone.

'There's a Chief Inspector Ashworth, of Bridgetown CID, on the line. He's requesting an interview with you, this morning.'

The cuticle was once more under attack, and then she said, 'Okay,' and flicked Ashworth's switch. 'Chief inspector, are you still there?'

Holly swallowed a laugh as she visualised her guv'nor's craggy face set in a scowl at the sound of Janice's dithery voice.

'Mr Ambrose says he'll be happy to see you any time after eleven o'clock. Thank you.'

She looked across at Holly. 'That was a policeman.'

'Really?' Holly said absently.

She was looking at the Chippendale calendar, and wondering whether the poseur had something stuffed down his pants. No man was that big, surely?

Bernie Williams sat in his office above the bookshop. A life-long bachelor, he had developed a habit of muttering to himself.

'When will you get round to me, Mr Ashworth? Last, I shouldn't wonder. Will this turn out to be a meeting of great minds? We are, after all, in the same line of business: the government pays you to protect the public, and certain members of the public pay me to protect them. I wonder if you'll see it that way?'

He laughed softly, and a secretive look invaded his eyes. 'I am the only person, apart from the killer, who has the slightest inkling of why Terry Wells was killed. Should I pass this information on to you? Should I tell you that Reggie Carter has been a naughty boy? No, I don't think so. Maybe in the future, when many things have been turned to my advantage.'

Ashworth mounted the stairs to the office of Hedley Ambrose, and such was his size, he almost filled the narrow staircase. Max limped along the landing ahead of him, and knocked on Ambrose's door.

'Come in.'

Holly only caught a brief glimpse of Ashworth as he passed her office, but it was enough to confirm that he was not in his most benevolent mood.

Ambrose rose from his chair, and hurried to meet them. 'Chief inspector.'

'Mr Ambrose,' Ashworth replied flatly.

'Can I offer you tea, or coffee?'

'No, thank you,' he said, taking in the room,

Ambrose turned to the old man standing obediently in

the doorway. 'That'll be all, Max, and thank you.'

Ashworth waited until Max had shuffled from the room, and then turned sharply to Ambrose.

'Won't you sit down, chief inspector?'

They took their seats, as Ambrose remarked, 'I know your Chief Constable, Ken Savage. Well, to be more precise, I've met him once or twice at functions. I'm hoping to stand as a Conservative councillor. But that's by the by. How can I help you?'

'I believe you might be able to help us with our enquiries, sir.'

'I'm always happy to assist the police,' Ambrose said, smiling. 'Although I can't see how I possibly can.'

'Terence Wells,' Ashworth said, studying the man closely for a reaction.

Hedley Ambrose simply appeared blank. 'Terence Wells?' he repeated, shaking his head slowly. 'Oh, Wells, of course. The man found murdered in Bridgetown.'

'That's right, sir. Do you know him?'

'No. Should I?'

'Do you know a Reginald Carter?'

'No,' Ambrose said, puzzled.

'Bernie Williams?' Ashworth persisted.

'I don't know any of these men, chief inspector. Look, do you mind telling me what this is all about?'

'Terence Wells was a gangster, as are the other two.'

'Gangsters?' Ambrose said, his eyes widening in amazement. 'But I thought your lot had stamped out that sort of thing …' All at once he smiled, and leant forward. 'Oh, I know why you're here …'

Ashworth stared at him questioningly, and waited.

'You think those men are running a protection racket, and you want me to inform you the minute they approach me.'

It was Ashworth's turn to look amazed.

'Don't worry, you can rely on me. It's up to the ordinary

citizen to make a stand against this sort of thing, help to eradicate it from our society. Give me a number where I can get hold of you.'

Ashworth sat speechless as he listened to Ambrose fervently declaring that the public must help the police if crime was to be curtailed. If this was an act then Ashworth had to admit that the man was good.

Clearing his throat, he said, 'Mr Ambrose, it's been brought to my attention that you're engaged in illegal activities.'

Hedley Ambrose stopped in mid-flow, his mouth open with shock. 'Is this some sort of joke?'

'No, sir, it has been suggested by certain individuals that there's some sort of rivalry between you, Mr Carter, and Mr Williams.'

'Who on earth has suggested that?' he asked, bewildered.

Ashworth was beginning to feel slightly uncomfortable under the man's innocent gaze. 'I'm afraid I can't disclose that information.'

'I see,' Ambrose murmured.

He left his chair, seemingly disturbed, and crossed to his desk then, picking up the telephone receiver, he turned back to stare at the chief inspector.

'No,' he said, replacing it in its cradle. 'I was going to ring my solicitor, but I've decided against it. You've obviously been the victim of a cruel hoax, and I shall overlook it this time. But I must warn you that if these groundless accusations are repeated, I will feel compelled to take some action.'

Crossing to the door, be opened it wide with an air of finality, and said, 'I shall have a word with the Chief Constable, but ask that you be let off in this instance. Now, I must ask you to leave, chief inspector.'

A deflated Ashworth rose slowly, and made for the door.

'I wish you a good day,' Ambrose said curtly.

'Well, I'm not having one,' he muttered, as the door was shut firmly in his face.

Reginald Carter had the distinct feeling that he was being watched. There was nothing specific to suggest this but, even so, the uneasy sensation in his chest refused to go away.

Several times, on his way to the tobacconist's, Carter turned to search the crowded street with furtive eyes. He recognised no one, but that meant nothing, for the street was packed with shoppers, and anyone following could easily lose themselves in the crowd.

They wouldn't dare move against him. The thought was comforting, and yet the feeling persisted.

In the shop, Carter purchased five expensive Havana cigars, and then lingered at a display of birthday cards, all the while scanning the street through the large window.

Fifty yards away, a man had his eyes fixed on the entrance to the tobacconist's. Carter strained to pick out the man's features, but he was too far away. Something about his stance was familiar, though: the way in which he held his head to one side.

Carter left the shop, and stood on the pavement, surreptitiously watching as the man darted for cover in the milling crowd.

So, they were following him. He started to walk, and considered the implications.

'Most of the calls come between twelve thirty and two,' Janice said.

The switchboard had remained maddeningly silent since Ashworth's departure, and Holly was beginning to wonder whether anything would ever happen.

She was relieved when, at twelve twenty-five, the girl looked up, and said, 'Do you mind if I go now? Some weeks, Tone can only see me in his lunch-hour.'

'I suppose in the evenings, he's experiencing life,' Holly replied. 'Yes, off you go. And there's no need to hurry back, I'm on top of the typing.'

She wandered across to man the switchboard, and pointed to the calendar. 'That's what you need, Janice.'

'No,' she said dismissively. 'I saw them when they came to the Town Hall. Can't see the point of going twice.'

'I don't mean you need to see the Chippendales. I mean you need a hunky guy.' She peered closer to scrutinise the picture. 'But wouldn't it be disappointing if it was a sock, full of other socks.'

'If what was a sock?' Janice asked, touching up her make-up.

'Never mind.'

As the girl left the office, humming cheerfully, Holly settled in front of the switchboard and familiarised herself with the extension numbers.

The first call was outgoing, from the office of Hedley Ambrose. Holly held a hand over the mouthpiece as she listened in, identifying immediately the voice of Ken Savage, desperate to pacify his irate caller.

He was saying, 'Now, Hedley, you admit yourself that this must be some sort of sick joke. Let me have a word with the chief inspector, just to make sure it doesn't happen again.'

'It shouldn't have happened this time, Ken,' Ambrose insisted. 'I know we've only met a few times, but I felt you were the person to come to with this.'

'I'm glad you did, Hedley. I'll look into it, and make sure you receive a written apology.'

Ambrose made a number of other calls, all in the same vein: the local Conservative Club chairman was harangued about police harassment, and various business acquaintances were forced to listen patiently while he protested with an injured innocence.

Holly was baffled.

Chapter 10

Everyone was telling Ashworth he was out of his depth, and although he was not yet ready to admit it openly, deep inside he was beginning to believe that they were right. He had achieved nothing during his interviews with Reginald Carter and Hedley Ambrose, and he now approached the premises of Bernie Williams with fast-growing frustration.

The bookshop exuded about as much menace as the local branch of Mothercare, and Ashworth began to wonder whether the gangster theme running through this case was merely a figment of Inspector Derry's imagination.

An indifferent female assistant led Ashworth up a metal spiral staircase to Williams's office, where the musty smell of books mingled with that of fresh coffee. As he made his precarious ascent, Ashworth wondered why the girl had not asked for his name, or the reason for his visit.

Bernie Williams was perched on a ladder, selecting books from a shelf, and flicking through their pages. At the sound of their arrival, he turned, an amused smile settling on his lips. 'Mr Ashworth, I presume?'

The chief inspector's face creased into a puzzled frown. 'You're wondering how I know who you are. Your reputation precedes you, chief inspector.'

'Really?'

'You feel at a disadvantage – yes? I am on this ladder, so much higher than you. That makes you feel small, because you have to look up.'

Irritation showed on Ashworth's face, and Williams chortled. 'One of life's lessons, Mr Ashworth: always try to make the other person feel at a disadvantage. That way you increase your negotiating powers.'

'I'm not here to negotiate,' Ashworth snorted.

Williams descended the ladder with a nimble ease. 'I know why you're here,' he said. 'You will soon learn, my friend, that very little happens in this city without my hearing about it.'

'Then you're the person to answer my questions, Mr Williams.'

'Don't be so formal, or so stern. Take a seat. Enjoy some coffee.'

Ashworth settled in the chair, resigning himself to the fact that if Williams was going to tell him anything, it would be very much in the man's own time.

'You're learning already, Mr Ashworth. How many men could tell you to sit down at an interview, and have you obey? Already you know that your rank and position count for little here. Probably for the first time in your life, you realise you can't frighten those you're dealing with.'

Ashworth's sense of frustration soared as the small man placed the coffee in front of him.

'Fear is a very powerful weapon,' Williams went on. 'If others fear you, they will do your bidding without question.'

'I'm getting tired of being told I'm impotent.'

'I wouldn't suggest you're impotent, my friend. You're a very dangerous man … because you are naive.'

Once again, Ashworth's expression betrayed his annoyance, and Williams jumped in quickly. 'I have offended you, and that was not my intention. He who dares, wins, Mr Ashworth, and at this moment, you would dare.'

Williams settled into his chair, and sipped his coffee. Satisfied that it was to his liking, he scrutinised the chief inspector with mischievous eyes.

'You are naive in the sense that you have no comprehension of what you're dealing with. You simply cannot believe that many skeletons are out there, helping to support motorway bridges – the remains of those who gave offence.' His eyes narrowed. 'I have a feeling that when you do understand, you will still dare, but who knows? And now, I must ask you to leave. I have many things to do. But please, finish your coffee.'

The cup clattered as Ashworth set it down on the desk. 'I haven't asked you any questions yet.'

'Nor will you, my friend,' Williams said quietly. 'You must understand that I am as immune from the law as Carter and Ambrose. If I choose to help you, it'll be because I like you.'

'Maybe you'd enjoy having a policeman as a pet poodle,' Ashworth retorted. 'You could send it out on false scents. I'm sure that would feed your ego.'

Williams threw back his head, and laughed. 'You are as blunt as you are shrewd – these things, I like.' He became serious. 'If I tell you anything at all, it'll be after I've given due consideration to my own interests. Yes?'

'If you're leading me up the garden path, I'll come down on you like a ton of bricks,' Ashworth promised.

'Ah, but that you cannot do. So why waste time with empty rhetoric which does not impress me?'

The two men locked eyes, and for the first time, Ashworth felt the full strength of Williams's personality. Then, within seconds, it was gone and he was, once again, the benign scholar.

'Treat me as an equal, Mr Ashworth, not as someone you can interrogate, and we'll get along fine.'

Ashworth found the walk to the spiral staircase one of the longest he had ever taken, and after descending half a dozen steps, Williams's voice brought him to a halt.

'A word of warning…'

The chief inspector looked up to see the small man in his favourite position of advantage.

'Reggie Carter,' he said. 'Be extremely careful of him. He's a very vicious man, even by my standards. If he's hurt, he'll hurt back in any direction.'

'I'll keep it in mind.'

'Pray, do.'

He listened to Ashworth's departing steps, and when the shop door closed behind him, Williams let out a triumphant laugh.

'And there, my friend, is your first clue.'

Holly was also frustrated by a lack of progress, and she swore softly as her key refused to turn in the strange lock of her temporary home. Finally, she managed to get inside and, in a fit of temper, threw her shoulder bag on to the settee in the tiny lounge, forgetting that it was open. When most of its contents spilled out, she swore again, and stomped off to the kitchen.

Filling the electric kettle, she plugged it in and stood waiting for it to boil; when, after a couple of minutes, no sound came, and no steam, she felt the outside. It was stone cold.

'Balls,' she spat, storming off to the bedroom.

She quickly undressed, and climbed into the bath. At least the shower worked, and as the hot water started to soothe her body, the telephone rang. With no time to dry herself, Holly rushed back into the bedroom, dripping water, and snatched up the receiver.

'Hello!'

'Hello, Holly, it's Josh.' He sounded hesitant; no doubt startled by her harsh reaction.

'Sorry, Josh,' she said, sitting on the bed, and jumping up immediately to view the wet stain spreading on the sheet. 'I've had a sod of a day.'

Josh told her that he had been for the Aids test, and that the result would be ready in a few days. Holly was pleased that he had taken that first step, and then felt slightly guilty on hearing how Ashworth had dealt with what he delicately referred to as 'Josh's problem'.

'How is the guv'nor?' she asked.

'He came back this afternoon, breathing fire.'

'Then I'd better wait for him to run out of petrol,' she said, laughing. 'Jim Ashworth, in a bad mood, I can well do without at the moment.'

'I'll keep in touch, Hol.'

'Be sure you do, lover boy.'

As she let the receiver drop, Holly caught a glimpse of herself in the dressing-table mirror. Her hair was plastered to her scalp, and make-up ran down her cheeks. She was not a pretty sight, and she stuck out her tongue at her reflection.

Manny Fredricks's safe house turned out to be a flat on the top floor of a tower block. Compared to the lodging house it was luxurious, but hardly worth two thousand five hundred pounds a week.

The prostitute was not in the highest fee bracket, but having paid 'a hundred pounds for anything', Lenny expected class, and was subsequently disappointed. Nevertheless, so deprived was he that his demands soon outstripped the money he had already handed over, and the girl was insisting upon another twenty-five pounds to provide him with the 'head' he was requesting. Although reluctant, he counted out the money, keeping the roll of notes well away from her inquisitive gaze and, with the girl between his legs, he settled back on the bed to lose himself in fantasies involving long-legged, deeply tanned beauties from sultry, sun-kissed islands.

When it was over, Lenny went into the bathroom to use the lavatory, and while he was urinating, he heard the girl opening the drawers of his bedside cabinet.

'You fucking bitch,' he yelled, racing back to the bedroom.

The girl was searching the drawers for money, and when Lenny burst into the room, she blanched at the murderous expression on his face.

'Just looking for a tissue,' she stammered. 'Hey, what's

this?' From the drawer, she took out a small plastic skeleton, about two inches in length. 'What do you do with this? Hang it in your car?'

In two strides, Lenny was beside her. Snatching the skeleton from the girl's hand, he gave her a stinging blow to the side of the head.

'Leave that alone, you bitch.'

The girl cowered on the bed, screaming, 'Get off me. Get off.'

Lenny gripped her firmly by the hair and yanked her from the bed and on towards the door. She was still struggling and protesting when he threw her into the corridor. She stumbled and fell heavily, a hand between her legs, the other across her breasts. Lenny prowled around the room like a madman, scooping up her scanty clothes from where they had been thrown, and hurled them at the frightened girl.

'You come back here, bitch, you even set foot in this building, and I'll kneecap you. Now, fuck off.'

The girl opened her mouth to return the abuse, but before she could speak, Lenny slammed the door and kicked out at it until his anger was spent.

Back in the bedroom, he picked up the tiny skeleton, and sat staring at it.

'Bleedin' hell,' he said, 'I've got to get away from here.'

Holly had dried her hair, applied fresh make-up and was dressed in tight black leggings and a pink sweatshirt. In the flat, with its small windows and flattering light, her attractive face took on an almost angelic look.

She was waiting expectantly for the sound of the doorbell, and when it rang at eight fifteen, she deliberately took her time to answer it. Smiling to herself because Steve Derry was impatiently holding a finger to the bell, she opened the door which led directly out on to the street. He cast a cautious glance back over his shoulder and glided past her, their bodies almost touching in the tight confines of the hall.

'Hi,' he said.

'Hello. Come on through to the kitchen.'

'This place gets smaller,' he remarked, as they passed by the lounge.

Holly laughed. 'The two of us is as big as the party's going to get, unless it spills out on to the street. Coffee, or lager?'

'Lager, please.'

She could feel his eyes boring into her back as she fetched a can from the fridge. 'Glass?' she asked.

'No, as it comes,' he said, averting his eyes when she placed the can in front of him.

'Nothing to report, "M",' she said, flippantly. 'Are you sure about Ambrose? He's definitely not coming across as a gangster. At the moment, he's so squeaky clean, he's making the Pope look dodgy.'

'He's in there, don't worry.

'I'm not so sure.' She told him about Ashworth's visit, and the resulting telephone calls. 'Are you certain this isn't a wind-up?'

'I'm not following you.'

Holly filled a copper kettle and placed it on the stove. She lit the gas and blew out the match, saying, 'Well, where does your information come from?'

'The streets, the dealers.'

'You've nothing on Ambrose?'

'If I had, lady, he'd be in custody,' he said, reaching into his jacket pocket.

'Here, have one of mine,' she quipped, handing him the spent match.

She fully expected him to laugh, but he accepted the match with a poker face, and stuck it between his teeth.

'Cheers,' he said.

She was becoming a little concerned, for as far as

humour went, they were clearly not on the same wave-length.

'Is something worrying you?' she asked.

'No,' he said, chewing on the match.

When the kettle boiled, Holly turned it off and sat down with him at the table, the coffee forgotten.

'Look,' she said, 'we were getting along fine yesterday. Has something happened?'

'It's your guv'nor. He's making ripples.'

'He does tend to,' she said, smiling.

'It ain't the way, lady. He spent some time with Bernie Williams – now that guy's gonna feed him false information, because he'll profit by getting rid of the other two firms.'

'Ashworth's clever,' Holly insisted. 'No one's going to get anything past him.'

'Maybe, but while he's out there doing his raging bull act, the gangs might just put everything on hold.'

'I don't think "raging bull" is fair comment,' Holly flared.

'Listen, there's a rumour going round that Reggie Carter threatened your guv'nor, and he responded by promising to wrap Carter's feet around his neck. People don't talk to Carter like that.'

'Well, my guv'nor does,' Holly said, grinning widely at the thought.

Derry got to his feet and dropped the empty larger can and matchstick into the waste bin. Then, leaning against the wall, hands in pockets, he stared down at her.

'Can't you persuade him to lay off?'

'No way.' Holly was emphatic. 'This is just a ploy to get him off the case.'

'No, it's not,' Derry said, crouching by her side. 'Russ Pearson put this to me: while Ashworth's out there, the firms'll just shut everything down. They know he'll only be there for so long, and they can wait.'

Holly frowned thoughtfully, and Derry sensed he was getting through to her.

'You know he's not going to get anywhere,' he said persuasively. 'I know he's not. Maybe by now, he realises it. We're likely to miss a golden opportunity with you inside Ambrose's organisation. After all, some of his business must go through the office. What a waste if he just closes down until Ashworth's gone.'

'I don't know,' Holly said doubtfully. 'You said he's built up some sort of relationship with Bernie Williams. He's not going to leave that.'

'There's no need for him to. Bernie's gonna lead him round in circles and then back to the start, while whatever's happening between the gangs is going on behind the scenes. All I want is to put it about the streets that unofficially the Terry Wells murder's being dropped.'

'That might start them doing business again, but it won't find Wells's killer, and that's what my guv'nor's after.'

'We'll know who did it, don't you worry. There'll be recriminations, and whoever's responsible will end up dead.'

'I know you're right ... Okay, I'll do my best.'

Derry stood up, and planted a kiss on Holly's forehead. 'Lady, you're beautiful.'

'I'm not making any promises,' she said, pointing a finger sternly.

Derry looked at his watch. 'I'd better go, I've got a meeting with my team. The word is, there's a big consignment of drugs coming into the city.'

On the way to the hall, Holly gave voice to her biggest worry. She said, 'This Bernie Williams – he's not going to put my guv'nor in any danger, is he?'

'No,' Derry assured her, 'Williams is like a praying mantis. He'll just sit it out, and wait to see how many of his rivals are dead when the dust settles. In fact, it wouldn't surprise me if he'd had Wells killed just to start this whole thing off.'

Holly sighed, and said, 'I don't understand any of this, Steve.'

'Lady, that's the problem,' he said, smiling down at her. 'Just trust me with it, okay?'

She nodded.

'I'll call some time tomorrow,' he said, opening the front door.

They lingered awkwardly on the step for a moment, and Derry explained unnecessarily that he had left his car in the next road so as not to draw attention to it, and then he left. Holly watched him until he was out of sight, and then closed the door.

'I've put on too much weight,' she told herself. 'That's why he doesn't fancy me.'

Chapter 11

Every day now, Josh felt a depression envelop him the moment he entered the house. Apart from the worries about his own health, Greg's condition was giving rise for concern. He had developed a dry cough, and seemed permanently short of breath. Josh feared that he might be developing pneumonia, and if that was the case, the end could be very near.

He felt he should be angry with his friend for not only jeopardising his future, but also inflicting upon him this great burden of care, and yet Josh could only summon up feelings of sorrow and regret. They were in this together, and it seemed right that Josh should help him until the end.

Upstairs the typewriter was clattering away, and Josh's step was heavy as he made his way to Greg's bedroom. He stopped in the doorway to find his friend stooped over the typewriter, deeply absorbed in Ashworth's rough notes.

He was muttering, 'Can I get away with it?'

'Greg?'

'Josh,' he said, turning quickly in surprise.

'Can you get away with what?' Josh asked, with a smile.

'Oh, I was wondering whether I could type all the interviews on one report, rather than separating them.'

'Yes, 'course you can. They're only for our reference, not for the file.' He thought how tired Greg looked, and added, 'I can do that, if you like.'

'No, I want to do it. I know I said dead bodies weren't my subject, but reading these reports, well, I'm really getting into it.'

Josh sat on the bed and studied Greg's profile. 'What's brought this on?'

He shrugged. 'I don't know, maybe I should have been

a policeman.' Then, with a fierce intensity, he turned to Josh, and said, 'I read somewhere that we die when we run out of reasons for living. Josh, I'm going to fight this thing. I don't want to die.'

'And you think studying this case could help you?' Josh asked lightly.

'Working on it could.' He saw that Josh was startled, and laughed. 'I don't mean working on it like you do, but getting involved in it, helping you.'

'Well, from what I can gather, we're not making any headway on it, so any ideas you might have …'

'Don't laugh at me, Josh,' Greg pleaded.

'I'm not,' he said quickly. 'I'm just saying that so far we've come up with nothing, no lead's, no clues. Forensic –'

'You're looking in the wrong place,' Greg interrupted eagerly. 'Think about it. Who could have got close enough to this Wells guy without raising his suspicions? He was a vicious gangster, remember.'

Suddenly the answer presented itself, and Josh grinned. 'Reginald Carter. Of course.'

'Exactly,' Greg said, full of enthusiasm. 'Look at this, I've made a chart.'

He picked up a sheet of foolscap paper and fixed it to the wall with a drawing pin. On it, he had written Terence Wells's name near the top, with arrows pointing down to Reginald Carter, Bernie Williams, and Hedley Ambrose, and relevant points and theories were scribbled against each name.

'What I've worked out so far is that one of these three must be the murderer.'

'That's as far as we've got,' Josh told him. 'But Carter wouldn't murder his first lieutenant, and just leave the body in his own house for us to find.'

'Who says that's what he intended? If it hadn't been for his nosy neighbour, the police wouldn't have found the body. It would still have been there when Carter got back from his supposed trip abroad.'

'You've got a point there. But what would Carter's motive have been?'

Greg shrugged. 'Who knows? But, don't forget, when Carter did get back, he saw the police car in his drive and panicked. Anyway, he could have worked out for himself that the police would think it unlikely he'd kill somebody in his own place and just leave the body there.'

Josh laughed. 'You're really taking this seriously, aren't you?'

Greg's face took on a resolute look. 'I'm determined to beat this thing. Do you know what my life expectancy is? Anything from three months to three years. If I could just make it to four years, five years … By then there might be a breakthrough; a cure might be possible.'

Discussing the case had been enjoyable, had taken Josh's mind off things, but now reality was back. He pushed himself up from the bed.

'I'll fetch your antibiotics, and bring you a cup of coffee.'

'I was in the park today,' Greg said softly, 'and I felt such a strong surge of spirit. I don't want to die.'

At the doorway, Josh shuffled his feet, wishing he could offer some words of comfort. But what could he say? He could only do his best for Greg, make life as easy as possible.

'I'll fetch your antibiotics,' he repeated.

Holly decided not to telephone Ashworth before nine forty-five p.m. By that time, he would have at least one glass of malt under his belt, lightening his mood considerably.

When the receiver was lifted at his end, Holly could hear the dog barking.

'Hello.' Ashworth's tone was gruff.

'Hello … dad,' she said cheerfully.

He chuckled. 'You cheeky young madam. I hope you've got some good news for me.'

She set about telling him of the telephone calls Ambrose had made.

'And nothing else?'

'No, sorry.' She hesitated for a second, undecided, and then said, 'Listen, guv, I've been talking to Steve Derry, and he thinks it might be a good idea for you to keep a low profile. He's working on the assumption that nothing's going to break while you're probing about.'

Ashworth's laugh had a hollow ring to it. 'Oh, I see, this is Derry's way of getting me off the case, isn't it?'

'It's not, guv. I've been thinking about it, and –'

'All right, all right, I don't have much choice, really. I'm drawing blanks everywhere I go. No one will let me investigate. I'm still going to chase up Bernie Williams, though.'

'Steve said that's fine. He just wants to pass it around that the police have dropped the Wells investigation.'

'Well, thank him for letting me continue,' Ashworth muttered with a good deal of hostility.

'Guv –'

'Don't worry,' he chuckled. 'I'm beginning to realise that we've got to play it Derry's way. I just hope that you come up with something.'

Over the next two days, that hope grew increasingly forlorn. Nothing untoward was happening at the betting shop, and Holly was finding that typing letters for a living was the most mind-numbing of occupations.

Janice, however, was happily settled on Cloud Nine, ever since Tone had agreed to see her two evenings a week; and Holly was fast discovering that a happy, chattering Janice was far more daunting than the old suicidal one. Added to which, Max's impersonation of an American slave was beginning to irritate.

Hedley Ambrose had not put a foot wrong all the while

she was there, and Holly was wondering if it was time to pull the plug on the whole operation.

The dreary undercover job was not the only thing exasperating her: Steve Derry's attention was proving to be elusive, and she could not understand why. So far, all she had got from him was a light peck on the cheek as he left the flat one evening, and last night, an even lighter kiss on the lips.

When he had gone, Holly stormed around the flat, taking out her frustration on the furniture. Then she rang Josh, and was glad that she did, for he told her that he'd had a negative result from his Aids test and sounded delirious with relief. Of course, he was not in the clear yet – a second test would have to be done after another nine weeks – but the news did lighten her mood.

She rang Ashworth to report, yet again, that there was nothing to report, and his rather peevish chatter eventually guided her to the gin bottle which, in turn, led her to a drink-induced dream in which she satisfactorily seduced Steve Derry, only to find herself at the police station next morning, faced with a charge of 'date rape'.

Back in the office, her judgement was in danger of being clouded by a hangover and soaring sexual frustration. Janice was happy and smiling, while Holly, her brain jangling at the sound of the typewriter, was the one gulping down aspirin.

At eleven o'clock, Max served the coffee.

'Here you go, Miss Holly,' he said, limping across and placing the cup on her desk. 'Hope you'll forgive an old man for taking so long, but these ankle chains, they sure do slow me down.'

Piss off, Holly thought. Piss off, before I thump you. At twelve twenty-five on the dot, Janice jumped up. 'Do you mind if I go to lunch, Holly? Only I want to look round for an outfit. Tone's taking me out tonight.'

'Yes, go on,' Holly scowled.

'Tone's taking me for a pizza. Do you think a jacket, leggings, and a blouse'll be too formal?'

'No,' Holly said, closing her eyes, 'that sounds just about right to me.'

Janice sniggered. 'Tone's being ever so attentive … if you know what I mean. He says it keeps his skin clear, 'cause he's got a tendency towards spots.'

Holly began to count and, luckily, by the time she reached ten, Janice was already walking down the stairs.

The switchboard buzzed, and Holly rushed across to it. Flicking the switch, she said, 'H. A. Turf Accountants.'

'Hedley, please.'

'Who shall I say is calling?'

'Winston.'

'Hold the line, please. I'll see if Mr Ambrose is available.' Something about the man's voice alerted Holly, and after putting the call through, she listened in diligently, recording the conversation in hurried shorthand.

When Ambrose put down the receiver, she punched the air, and called out softly, 'Bingo.'

Ashworth had deliberately left Bernie Williams alone for a couple of days. He was not used to being brushed aside, and the feeling it instilled in him did not settle well. Indeed, his anger was building, and he was determined that today he would get the upper hand.

'Mr Ashworth,' Williams greeted him warmly from his desk. 'This is a pleasure.'

'No doubt,' Ashworth said, taking a seat without being asked. 'Bernie, I'm fed up with being messed about. I could take you in for questioning – you do realise that?'

'Don't be silly, Mr Ashworth. Of all the things I could take you for, a fool would be the last. At the moment you're frustrated, but you must learn to control your anger.' He paused. 'Have you heard of self-knowledge?'

'I'm studying it at the moment.'

'Then study harder.'

Ashworth's face flushed.

'I've decided to tell you many things,' Williams continued smoothly, 'because I like you. Things that you will not hear from any other source. Then, you must mull them over, and see what conclusion you reach.'

Although unused to playing a passive role, if there was information to be gleaned then Ashworth was prepared to listen. Settling back in the chair, he felt his body relax.

Williams took a pen from his desk-tidy, and fiddled with it, as he began, 'In the sixties, there were just two gangs operating in Rutley. Reggie Carter ran one, and I, the other. You must understand that we were young men then, suffering from more than our fair share of pride, ego, and all those other distasteful things that afflict the young. Reggie stayed in the background. I doubt if more than a handful of people knew that he was involved in illegal activities.'

'How many know now?' Ashworth asked.

'You could count them on your hands. Terry Wells knew, but he won't be telling anybody. Then there's me, and several others in my organisation.'

'Does Hedley Ambrose know?'

'I think I see what you're getting at, but let me finish, please, then you can ask questions.'

Deflated once more, Ashworth subsided.

'As time went by we learned to live beside each other. After all, there was more than enough for both of us, so we showed respect. Of course, there have always been black gangs, but we stayed away from their areas of the city. They were fragmented, anyway, badly organised. We held no fear for them, you understand, they were useful to us; because of their lack of finesse, they were often picked up by the police, so it appeared that the guardians of law and order were tackling crime.'

He paused to stare into the middle distance, a resigned

smile on his lips. 'Then, about eighteen months ago, Hedley Ambrose moved in, and things changed. He may be as remote as Reggie Carter, but he's an ambitious man. Hedley Ambrose wants the whole city all to himself.'

'Do you think he killed Wells to start a gang war?' Ashworth asked.

'Who knows? It's possible, I suppose, but let me finish. Ambrose's people made overtures to both Reggie – through Terry Wells – and myself. My answer was simple: I am not a young man, and I told him that if he could wait a few years until I retired, then he could have my part of the city. But Ambrose is a man in a hurry. We negotiated with his people – Terry and myself, that is – and an offer of one million pounds for each of us was put on the table. For that, we would be expected to disband our organisations and retire immediately.'

'One million pounds each! Where would that sort of money come from?'

'You know nothing about the drugs trade, my friend,' Williams said, laughing. 'I read in the newspapers of people winning twenty million pounds on the lottery. In this part of the world, the annual turnover from drugs would be the equivalent of winning such a jackpot five or six times over.'

'And what was your reaction to this offer?'

'I was tempted. So was Terry. We were neither of us young men. But when it was put to Reggie, he was against it, he wanted to retain his power. He and Terry had violent arguments about it. In the end, Terry had to go back and decline the offer. Ambrose's people were threatening bloodshed, or so I believe.'

'Did Ambrose know of Carter's existence?' Ashworth asked, totally absorbed.

'Ah, your bloodhound instinct is aroused,' Williams mocked. 'I see what you're getting at. If Ambrose didn't know about Reggie, he may well have thought that by killing Terry, he was having a rival gang leader executed.'

Ashworth waited. 'Well?'

'It's possible,' Williams said, after a long pause.

'Or Carter could have killed Wells during one of their violent arguments.'

'Again, possible. But if that is the case, then it's back-fired on Reggie. He and Terry went back a lone way. It's even been suggested that they shared the same father. Now, Terry's gone, and so few of Reggie's associates know him, so his empire is falling apart. His people are simply drifting away, and Reggie has no control.'

'So, Hedley Ambrose has got his way, up to a point.'

'Not quite. You see, Reggie's boys are drifting our way. We're moving into the territory. It's a natural progression: the boys controlling the area aren't going to side with Ambrose.'

'Now, Bernie, that means you could have killed Terence Wells to secure a two million pound jackpot,' Ashworth stated boldly. 'You must have known the way things would go after Wells's death.'

Williams's laugh was loud and startling. 'I promised you information, Mr Ashworth, not solutions.'

'And do you have any more information?'

'Yes, as a matter of fact, I do.'

He replaced his pen in the desk-tidy, and withdrew a small object which Ashworth could not see. Sitting back, he began shaking it in his hand like a dice.

'I had a dispute with Terry Wells just before his death,' he said. 'Some of his boys were pushing drugs on my patch, and I had to rap Terry on the knuckles about it.'

'You didn't rap him with a .38 automatic, by any chance?'

Williams shook his head slowly. 'No, I registered my displeasure, and Terry gave me his word that it would not happen again.'

Suddenly a slyness crept into his manner, and he asked,

'What are you finding out about Terry?'

'Very little,' Ashworth had to admit. 'He lived over his shop. We've searched the flat, but that's produced nothing, and we're having difficulty in locating his next of kin.'

'Terry had three brothers,' Williams told him. 'Two are working on building sites in Germany, and the other – Brian Wells – works for me.'

'Terence Wells's brother works for you?' Ashworth said, astonished.

'Yes, that's right.'

'And where is he now?'

'On holiday.'

'How convenient.'

'Yes. I'll be totally honest with you, I'm so concerned about this, I've put word around that I'm willing to pay twenty thousand pounds for information leading to the arrest of the killer.'

Ashworth was surprised. 'The arrest?'

'The arrest,' Williams confirmed. 'I don't want Brian Wells reaching any conclusions and deciding to seek revenge.'

'Because he could reach the wrong conclusion,' Ashworth said, 'and think that you killed his brother.'

He waited for a reaction to that statement, but Williams merely nodded towards the spiral staircase.

'I'll keep you informed of any progress, Mr Ashworth.'

When he was alone, Williams again shook the object in his hand, then tossed it on to the desk. The small plastic skeleton skidded across the blotter. It was two inches long, and its fleshless skull appeared to be smiling.

Chapter 12

That evening, Holly could hardly contain her excitement. As soon as she got back to the flat, she called Ashworth to tell him of the information she had derived by listening in on Hedley Ambrose's telephone conversation. He was immediately charged with enthusiasm, but offered a note of caution.

'Holly, if things are hotting up, you'd better be very careful.'

'I will, dad.'

'You can joke,' Ashworth said, 'but these men are dangerous. I just want you to be careful.'

'Will do, guv. I'll ring you tomorrow.'

After the call, she showered and fixed her make-up, and had just put on her bra and pants when the doorbell rang. Pulling on her blue bathrobe, she rushed to answer it.

Steve Derry looked her up and down, and smiled. 'Hi, lady.'

'We're off first base, Steve,' she told him, excitedly.

Pulling him through to the kitchen, she said, 'Ambrose had a telephone call today, from somebody called Winston.'

'And?' Derry asked, taking off his red jacket and draping it over the back of his chair.

She held up a sheet of paper. 'I've written it all down. Here, have a look.'

Holly perched on the table, while Derry settled in his chair, and read:

Winston: The sellers are getting nervous, man. They want to unload the junk.
Ambrose: Tell them they'll have to wait till we're ready.
Winston: But they're really pushing. They say they're not

prepared to wait.

Ambrose: Tell them to sell elsewhere, then.

Winston: The streets are quiet, man. Word is, the Special Unit goons have been pulled off Wells's murder.

Ambrose: We wait.

Winston: We dealt with Wells at the wrong time.

Ambrose: Wells was dealt with when it became necessary. There was nothing else we could do,

Winston: I still don't like it, man. These dudes are real uptight.

Ambrose: This has got nothing to do with Wells.

Winston: The sellers say they can't hold on to the stuff much longer. If the cops get word of it and raid them –

Ambrose: The more nervous they are, the better. There's no other firm that can pay out six million for smack. The longer we keep them waiting, the better price we'll get.

Winston: Okay, man, you're the boss, but I'm still worried about Wells. If the cops uncover anything –

Ambrose: They won't. Ring back in a couple of days, and we'll start to finalise plans.

Derry looked up into Holly's smiling face. 'Brilliant,' he grinned. 'Brilliant.'

Holly, realising that most of her shapely legs were on display, shifted her position, and said, 'This is as close as we can get to an admission that Ambrose had Wells killed.'

'Yes,' he said, 'and to take six million in drugs would make a hole that the gangs might never repair.'

'Want a beer?' Holly asked, pushing herself off the table.

'Yeah.'

'Or you could have a big boy's drink. I've got some scotch.'

'I'm driving.'

'Just one?' she coaxed.

'Okay.'

Holly could feel Derry watching her while she moved around the kitchen, and a warm glow enveloped her as she poured a scotch for him and a gin and tonic for herself. They drank sitting at the kitchen table.

In many ways, Steve Derry was one of the strangest men Holly had ever met. He was given to long, brooding silences which would suddenly be broken as he strove to articulate an important point or idea, his deep brown eyes animated. He was sipping his drink, and studying the sheet of paper.

'Have you told Ashworth about this?'

'Yes, of course. Why?'

He looked pensive for a while, and then said, 'If you uncover too much about Wells's murder, your guv'nor's gonna want to go bulldozing in there, and he could blow the drugs thing.'

'He wouldn't do that.'

'He would, and you know it. You couldn't play down any information you get about Wells, could you?'

'No, I couldn't do that, Steve. He's my guv'nor. I owe him my loyalty.'

'Just hold it back, then. Please? I'd rather get Ambrose and his friends for six million quid's worth of drugs, than for topping Wells.'

'I'll hold it back,' she said grudgingly, 'but before anything happens – and I mean, anything – he's got to know.' She started to feel guilty before the words had even left her mouth.

'Deal,' he said. Then, glancing at his watch, he picked up his glass and knocked back the scotch. 'I'd better be moving.'

Holly could barely hide her disappointment as he followed her towards the hall. At the front door, he leant forward and his lips brushed hers. She instantly responded, throwing her arms around his neck, and pulling him close. Derry's movements were urgent and hurried as his hands slid around her waist, his fingers digging into her flesh. But then he pulled back, suddenly rigid, his eyes closed as he rested against the wall, his breathing shallow. And there was an almost indefinable sadness in his eyes when he opened them.

'I'd better go,' he said.

But Holly placed her hand on the wall to bar his exit, and asked angrily, 'What gives with you?'

'Nothing,' he muttered. 'There's just somewhere I need to go.'

'Have you got a wife tucked away, with two little Steves? Is that it?'

Derry shook his head, and Holly considered his impassive attitude.

'Don't you fancy me? Just say it, if that's what's bothering you. I won't mind.'

He looked down at her body then, and a slow, sexy grin brightened his features. Holly followed his gaze, and saw that her bathrobe had come loose and was gaping open, revealing her underwear.

'It's not that,' he said, turning away.

She put a hand to his cheek and pulled his head round, forcing him to look at her. 'Then, what is it?'

He sighed. 'I've just come through a lousy divorce. I don't want to get involved with anybody.'

'I don't remember getting the white dress out, or talking about booking the church.'

'It's a chance I'm not prepared to take. Okay?'

'Steve,' she said softly, 'I'm not going to give you my life story but, believe me, I'm not looking to get into anything I can't get out of without scars.'

He searched Holly's face, and then, pulling apart the bathrobe, his hands returned to her waist, sending a shiver coursing through her body. Their lips met, their bodies touching, and no sooner were they apart than they fused together again, with Holly pushing hard against him, thrilling at the feel of his growing erection.

'I want it,' she murmured in his ear.

Derry gasped, the breath catching in his throat, as Holly ran her fingers along his groin.

'I want it, Steve.'

The next two days passed slowly at H. A. Turf Accountants, but Steve Derry had at least taken the edge off Holly's dislike for the job. He had proved to be an enthusiastic and skilful lover, solving most of her emotional problems, and she was back to her normal happy self. Indeed, her strong yearning ache had been so expertly satisfied that there were times when she almost forgot why she was working for Hedley Ambrose.

On the third day, the first thing of any real significance occurred. At four o'clock that afternoon, Ambrose looked into the office.

He said, 'Holly, I wonder if you could do me a favour? I've got to go out on some business, and I'd like you to lock up when you all leave at five thirty.' He leant across her desk, and lowered his voice. 'I'd rather leave the keys with someone I can trust,' he told her confidentially, indicating Janice who was applying varnish to her fingernails.

'Yes, I'll do that,' she said, smiling, and trying to look honoured at being entrusted with the task.

'You can leave the alarm system,' he said, handing over the keys. 'I'll be back at six thirty, so I can see to it.'

That night, Steve Derry arranged for duplicate keys to be cut.

The neon lights of the Nite On The Town flashed on and off, green and red, the name of the club alternating with a line of chorus girls.

Bernie Williams emerged from his car, flanked by two of his henchmen who, despite their advancing years, looked solid and fit. Williams viewed the flashing lights with distaste, and then shouldered his way through the swing doors, bringing an immediate hush to the foyer.

Two bouncers, immaculate in evening dress, were manning the doors, and their build, their malicious demeanour, suggested that they would be good at the job. The larger of the two swaggered over to Williams and his party.

'What do you want?' he scowled.

Williams bristled at the insolent welcome, but said softly, 'I want to see Mr Morgan, the manager.'

'He's on his way, then you're outta here,' the bouncer said, flexing his huge forearms.

Williams smiled. 'We shall see, my friend.'

Through the open inner door to the club could be heard soft smoochy music, laughter and conversation, the clink of glasses. Morgan, with the other bouncer following at his heel, was picking a way between tables towards the foyer, now and then stopping to acknowledge his guests, always the genial host. But in the foyer, with the door firmly closed, his manner changed.

'You shouldn't be here, Bernie,' he stormed. 'Terry wouldn't like this.'

'Terry's dead, my friend.'

'His boys still look after us. My people are on the phone to them now.'

Williams smiled, and wagged a finger, saying, 'No, my friend, Terry's boys work for me now. You're protected by my firm.'

A look of total alarm flitted across Morgan's face, and his eyes went to the bouncers who were backing away.

'Your staff have been most discourteous,' he continued. 'They are extremely lucky not to have received a slapping –'

'Mr Williams,' Morgan stammered.

'You must not interrupt me, my friend. That is most unwise.'

He withdrew a slim gold case from his inside pocket, extracted a cigarette and lit it, his mocking gaze never leaving Morgan's fear-filled eyes.

'And now, you will have a cigarette,' he said.

'I don't smoke. Look Mr Williams, I'm sorry –'

'If I say you smoke, you smoke.'

He looked towards his henchmen who immediately positioned themselves either side of Morgan, and gripped his arms. Williams came forward cigarette slowly, and placed the cork tip of the cigarette between the man's lips.

'Draw on it deeply, my friend. Good, good. Now inhale and blow it out.'

Morgan spluttered as smoke streamed from his mouth, and he tried desperately to turn away, but one of the henchmen grabbed his neck in a grip of steel and forced him to face his tormentor.

'You learn quickly, my friend,' Williams encouraged. 'Again.'

By the time he had smoked half of the cigarette, Morgan was clearly unwell and was coughing profusely. Bernie Williams chuckled as he dropped the cigarette on to the white carpet and ground it out.

'Now, I have some questions to ask you, Mr Morgan. I believe a man named Leonard Spencer works for you.'

Morgan nodded fearfully.

Williams beamed. 'Good. Now, I am interested in the whereabouts of Mr Spencer.'

'I don't know where he is,' Morgan stuttered. 'He hasn't been in for a few weeks.'

'Is that so?' Williams tut-tutted, and took out the cigarette case again. 'Don't worry, my friend,' he said, as Morgan eyed the case with rising nausea. 'I'm not going to damage your chest further.'

He selected another cigarette, and took his time in lighting it, then drew on it again and again until the tip was red hot.

'This time,' he said, his smile gleeful, 'I will put in the lighted end first and stub it out on your tonsils. That often jogs the memory. Open his mouth.'

'No, no, for God's sake, no.'

Morgan tried to break free, but his struggles were soon contained, and his mouth was forced open. The cigarette burned his lips as it brushed past, and when its heat could be felt on the back of his throat, he began to gag.

'He's pissed himself,' one of the henchmen chortled.

Williams looked down and watched with satisfaction as the urine trickled over Morgan's expensive Italian shoes.

'I'll talk, I'll talk,' Morgan said, the words muffled.

'Good,' Williams purred, withdrawing the cigarette. 'Now, Spencer, where is he?'

'I don't know, I swear to God,' he babbled. 'He left suddenly. His bird thinks he might have gone to London. That's all I know. You've got to believe me. I'd tell you if there was anything else.'

'All right, let him go.'

The cigarette was dropped and as it burnt a hole in the carpet, Williams approached the trembling man and slapped his cheeks lightly with both hands.

'In future, my friend, you will show respect. Yes?'

'Yes, yes.'

'Yes, what?'

'Yes, Mr Williams.'

'Good. Now, enjoy the rest of your evening.'

Outside, a smiling henchman opened the car door for Williams, and said, 'Just like the old days, eh, boss?'

'Yes, Don,' he replied wistfully. 'I miss them, you know.'

'What do you want done about Lenny Spencer?'

'Put word out in London that I want to know where he is. No one is to touch him, Don, I just want him located.'

Reginald Carter's empire was crumbling fast, and it seemed there was nothing he could do to stop it. This was something he had not predicted, but with hindsight he could see that it was inevitable. Once again installed in his house, Carter took to wandering into the library and studying the spot where Terry Wells was killed.

What would happen next? He knew someone was out there watching him. More than once he had looked through the front windows to see the same car parked on the road outside his gates. It was all so unnerving; so much so that on one occasion he had flung open the front door and charged along the drive towards the road, but the car pulled away before Carter could distinguish the driver's features.

Now, alone in the house, he spent more and more time dwelling upon recent events. With Terry gone, there was no one he could turn to, and for the third time in as many hours, Carter moved around the house, checking the locks on the windows and doors.

Chapter 13

Chief Inspector Ashworth had never been made redundant, but given the way in which this case was shaping up, he felt he had an insight into how it must feel. Seeing little point in travelling to Rutley, he stayed in the CID office at Bridgetown, spending most of the day watching the back of Josh's head as he worked on the VDU. As a matter of fact, Josh was adding to his irritation, for he had loaned Greg his car, wanting to make it easier for him to get around, and this meant that Ashworth had to ferry Josh about.

He wished he could turn his mind away from the case, but it was impossible; police work was more than just a job to him, it was an essential part of his life. For him, it was a fundamental principle to ensure that justice was seen to be done.

Ashworth's earlier euphoria, inspired by Holly's information regarding the Ambrose/Winston telephone call, was beginning to fade as the problems this created became apparent. It was without doubt a vital development but, on its own, was of little value. What if Holly was not on the switchboard when the second call came through? Say no more information was forthcoming, and the second call was merely to arrange a meeting? These scenarios would be typical of a case in which so many hard facts were common knowledge, and only proof was thin on the ground,

In an effort to quash his feelings of impotence, Ashworth flicked through the reports Josh had brought in that morning. They were very much for CID's own use, merely an accurate record of what had taken place, and held no official value. Turning over a page, he came across a folded sheet of notepaper, and opened it up to read the handwritten words.

'Josh,' he said, 'what's this?'

'Sorry, guv, it must belong to Greg. He typed the reports for me. It helps to keep his mind off everything.'

'I see.'

'He's getting interested in the case,' Josh explained, hugely embarrassed. 'He's almost obsessed. He thinks that if he's got a reason -'

'And he's forming opinions, I see. The way he's got it, all roads lead to Carter.'

'I'm really sorry, guv, I know I shouldn't be discussing it with him.'

'Nonsense, none of the suspects will talk to us, so we might as well discuss it amongst ourselves.' He laughed. 'This is quite good, you know. Greg's building a satisfactory case against Carter. But how does he explain what Holly heard on the telephone?'

He riffled quickly through the remaining reports, as Josh said, 'He's got an answer for that. If you look at the transcript, neither Ambrose nor Winston actually say they killed Wells, just that they dealt with him. They could have been doing a drugs deal with him, and we've just put the wrong interpretation on it.'

'That's a good point. Greg seems to be a very bright young man.'

'I suppose he is.'

'Which brings me to something else. I was talking to Sarah last night, and we wondered if the two of you would like to come to dinner.'

'But we're a couple of poofs,' Josh said, his mouth gaping open.

'Josh, I don't understand homosexuality, I admit that, but I'm not a bigot.'

'But Greg's got Aids, and I'm suspect.'

'Listen, if I called you a poof, you'd be offended,' Ashworth said stiffly, 'and rightly so. You're feeling sorry for yourself. You're expecting everybody to shun you, and when they don't, you go into this "I'm a poof" routine.'

'I don't need a bollocking, guv.'

'Yes, you do, you've got to face this thing. Now, I'd like to meet your friend, so are you going to accept our dinner invitation?'

'I'll have to check with Greg,' Josh replied, far from easy about it.

'Do that, and I'll tell you something else, young man, your language is getting worse. That's what comes from mixing with Holly.'

'I miss her.'

'So do I. She's like a breath of fresh air. I wonder what she's doing now?'

'I'm coming, I'm coming,' Holly cried out, her fingers sliding into the tight curls at the nape of Derry's neck.

Derry groaned, and thrust into her with increased vigour, moaning loudly as he ejaculated. Breathless, he slumped on top of her and was still.

'I love it, Steve,' she whispered in his ear.

Lifting his weight, Derry looked down into her eyes, and quipped, 'How was that for you, lady?'

'Awful,' she said. 'All the way through I kept thinking: I hope he leaves me alone once he's had his wicked way.'

He rolled off, laughing, and lay beside her on the single bed. 'You're one sexy lady, did you know that?'

'Yes.'

She turned on to her side and stared at him. 'Was it all right, Steve?'

'Fair,' he said.

Holly laughed, and hit out at him with the pillow. 'You bastard,' she said, as he got to his feet.

'Shit,' she muttered, scrambling from the bed. 'I forgot, I left the bath running. It went out of my head when you seduced me.'

'I seduced you? If you remember, lady, you came into the room with nothing on and said: Do you think you

131

can handle this?'

Holly popped her head back round the door, and said, with a wink, 'And I do believe you can.'

Derry sat on the bed and fingered the livid weals on his shoulders, left there by Holly's fingernails.

She was back again. 'You coming for a bath?'

'Yeah, why not?'

'I've poured drinks for us,' she said. 'Have you given up the matches?'

'Trying to,' he laughed. 'I thought. Who wants to be seen with a guy who's always chewing on dead matches? – so I bought some cigarettes.'

They were in the bath, sipping their drinks, when Derry said, 'Why the long face, lady?'

'It's not right, Steve, I should have told him. This could cost me my job.'

'I just asked you to hold it back for a couple of days, that's all.'

'But it's vital information in a murder enquiry. I should have told Jim Ashworth.'

'Ashworth,' Derry scoffed, as he lay back and positioned his head between the taps. 'That man's getting to me.'

'I don't care about that. Just think how it would look on my record. Today, I'm listening to Ambrose and Winston on the telephone. Winston warns Ambrose to get rid of the .38 revolver – I repeat, the .38 revolver – and Ambrose says it's better where it is, in his office safe, because the police haven't got the powers to look there.'

'Lady –'

'Steve, it's a .38 gun we're looking for in connection with Terry Wells's murder. I've lied to Ashworth. That's a pick-up-your-cards-and-walk offence. Right?'

'And what else did Ambrose say? Go on, what else?'

Holly looked away.

'He called a meeting for the day after tomorrow, in his office, to discuss the date of the drug deal. And that's the one I'm after.'

'But Ashworth would wait.'

'He might not. It's a chance I can't afford to take. Look, I thought we'd settled this earlier.'

'I just hate lying to Jim Ashworth, that's all.'

'Ashworth, Ashworth. Why the fuck do I keep hearing that name? Have you got a thing about the guy, is that it?'

'Don't be so bloody stupid,' Holly yelled. But then she checked her temper, and lowered her eyes.

'The gun's still gonna be in Ambrose's safe,' he said, reaching over the side of the bath for his glass.

Derry stared at Holly's sullen face as he sipped his drink. Then, spilling bath water on to the floor, he moved his leg between hers and wriggled his toe in her crotch.

'Stop it,' she said, barely concealing a smile.

'Why?'

'Because I like it, now pack it in.'

She plunged her hand in the water and grabbed his leg, but instead of pushing it away, she held it firmly where it was.

'You're wasted in Bridgetown, you know. Special Unit could use you.'

'What is this? Screw yourself into a job?'

'I'm serious. You're good, you've got class and brains. You're wasted in that hick town.'

'Bridgetown is not a hick town,' she declared forcefully.

'You're wasted there. What's in the future? When the time comes for Ashworth to step down, they might make you up to inspector, or they might just sideline you. There ain't many women holding high office in the force, but that's about to change. If you were in the city, you'd be getting noticed.' Holly reached for her drink, and sat staring into it.

'You ambitious? Because if you ain't looking to be some-body's wife …'

'Yes, I'm ambitious,' she said slowly, before finishing her gin. 'It just takes something to activate it, that's all.'

'Like the rest of you,' he grinned.

Her empty glass landed with a dull thud on the floor as she smiled at him. 'The rest of me is already activated, lover boy.'

The bathroom carpet got another soaking when Holly straddled him. 'Right, are you going to screw me again?'

'And what if I don't?' he asked, a look of mock horror on his face, as Holly's hands disappeared under the water.

'I'll turn the cold tap on all over your head.'

By the following morning, Ashworth had begun to realise the futility in sitting around waiting for something to happen, so he busied himself with a spate of break-ins that had occurred on one of the local estates. He was sitting at his desk when the telephone rang. Josh took the call.

'It's Reginald Carter for you, guv.'

Ashworth pulled a face, and picked up the telephone on his desk. 'Chief Inspector Ashworth,' he barked.

'This is Reginald Carter.'

'Yes?'

'Well, I … I really don't know how to say this …' He sounded nervous. 'I think someone's watching me.'

'Someone's watching you? Why should anyone do that, Mr Carter?'

'I don't know, but I want you to do something about it.'

'What can I do, sir?' Ashworth asked, smiling at Josh with a great deal of satisfaction. 'Just a few days ago, you were telling me you were above the law.'

'Ashworth, I'm reporting this to you because I want something done about it.'

'Right, what form does this watching take?'

'Whenever I go out on foot, I feel there's someone following me.'

'You feel? You don't know, you just feel?'

'I've seen someone, and I know he's watching me,' Carter said, decidedly ruffled. 'And there's a car, small, metallic-silver, parked outside my gates sometimes, and the driver just sits there, staring towards the house.'

Ashworth was clearly enjoying himself, 'I see. Not much to go on, really, is it? All this could be put down to an over-active imagination.'

'But I'm not imagining it,' Carter insisted, 'and I want something done about it.'

'We are here to serve, sir,' Ashworth said, with heavy sarcasm. 'Right, let's get something down on paper, shall we? Do you have any enemies that you know of? Anyone who might wish you harm?'

'No,' Carter snapped.

'You haven't upset or … murdered anyone recently, sir?'

Carter gave an exasperated sigh, and said, 'Ashworth, you're beginning to annoy me.'

'That's intentional, sir, I'm gloating a little, you see. A few days ago, you were ordering me out of your life, and now you're asking for my help. And I must add, in none too polite a fashion.'

'Ashworth –'

'Mr Carter, unless you can give me something more specific such as, oh, I don't know, a villain you've upset in some way, or a murdered man's brother who's after you, then all I can do is ask for a patrol car to keep an eye on your property whenever it's in your area. So, if you remember anything, or you get even more frightened than you are now, give me a ring, furnish me with some infor-mation, and I'll act upon it.' He slammed down the receiver before the man could respond.

'Say it, guv,' Josh laughed.

'Not I,' Ashworth said, gleefully rubbing his hands together. 'Such words shall never pass my lips.' He went on to tell Josh what Carter had said.

'It fits in with Greg's theory that Carter killed Wells, guv.'

'It could do. Make sure a patrol car does check Carter's house every so often. If someone is watching it from a car, it could be useful to get the number.'

'Right, guv.'

'Oh by the way, Sarah wondered if Sunday night would be all right for you and Greg?'

'Yes, thanks.'

'Greg doesn't eat faddy food, does he? Vegetarian stuff, or anything like that?'

'No, guv,' Josh replied, smiling. 'He's just a normal straightforward poof.'

Chapter 14

Holly was experiencing a little discomfort after her sexual demands had been so expertly satisfied by Steve Derry, and she squirmed in the chair as she glanced across at Janice who seemed rather pensive.

'You all right, Janice?'

The girl looked up from the switchboard, and asked plaintively, 'Do you know anything about sex?'

'A bit, yes.'

'Should anything happen … you know … for a girl?'

'I'm not following you, Janice.'

'Well, what I mean is, when a girl's done it, should she know she's done it?'

Holly gave her a puzzled frown. 'She should know something's happened, definitely.'

'Because I'm worried, see.'

'What about, Janice?'

'Well …' Although no one else was in the room, Janice started to whisper. 'Me and Tone did it last night, in our house. My mum was out.'

'Thank God for that,' Holly said. 'On both counts.'

'We went into my mum's bedroom, 'cause of the double bed, right, and while Tone was doing it, I was counting the flowers on the wallpaper …'

The poor girl looked so miserable as she recounted her story but, even so, Holly had a job to keep from smiling.

She cleared her throat. 'How many flowers did you count, Janice?'

'About six.'

Holly closed her eyes, and bit down hard on her lower lip.

'This is really screwing me up, you know.'

'I bet it is,' Holly said fervently.

'I was awake all night, wondering what was the matter with me.'

'Janice –'

' 'Cause it has to be me. Tone's good at it, he said so.'

'Janice, listen to me for a minute. Do you think Tone's right for you?'

'How do you mean?'

'Well, it doesn't sound to me as if you two have much in common.'

'That's what I've been thinking,' Janice said dismally. 'But I'm confused, see, 'cause mum said she never got anything out of sex, and I wondered if that's how it was for women.'

Just then, footsteps sounded along the landing, and for a moment a tall, well-built black man stood framed in the doorway. He smiled at them and winked, and then went along to Ambrose's office.

'Hedley, my man, how goes it?' they heard him say.

And Ambrose laughed, and said, 'Winston.'

But then the door was closed, cutting off further conversation.

'Do you know who that was?' Holly asked.

'No, never seen him before,' Janice said, shaking her head. 'So what do you think my problem is?'

More footsteps could be heard, and Holly turned in time to see two smartly dressed Afro-Caribbeans making their way to the office.

'Get yourself a good seeing-to,' she advised absently.

Janice giggled, and said, 'Oh, you are crude.'

'It's a crude subject,' Holly told her, as she glanced at her watch. 'Look, would you like to take an early lunch?'

'But it's only twelve,' Janice protested. 'If I go now, it'll make the afternoon long.'

Holly's mind was racing. She needed to get rid of the girl so that she could find out what was happening in Ambrose's office. She could just make out the rumble of voices, and was desperate to know what was being discussed.

Crossing to the switchboard, she said, 'I'll skip lunch, so you needn't come back till two, and then we can really talk things over. Yes?'

'Do you mean it … about talking things over?'

'Yes, of course,' an agitated Holly promised. 'Just as soon as you get back.'

'Good,' Janice said, picking up her handbag. 'That's what I need, see. There's things you can't ask your mum, isn't there? Like, you know, how big should a man's thing be?' She giggled. ''Cause I've only seen Tone's, and I always thought they were bigger than that.'

Holly wanted to scream as she hurried the girl towards the door. 'We'll sort it all out when you get back.'

Interested as she was in the size of Tone's thing, there were other matters far more pressing, and as Janice disappeared down the stairs, Holly sat studying the switchboard and wondering how the hell she could tune into what was being said in the office.

Totally engrossed in this problem, she jolted with surprise when Ambrose came in, and said, 'Holly, could you do me a favour?'

She turned with a smile. 'Of course, if I can.'

He coughed, and moaned about cigarette smoke, then said, 'I'm having a business meeting, and I don't want to be interrupted.'

'I'll hold any calls for you, then. I'll get them to ring back at whatever time you say.'

'I'd rather you closed the switchboard down. This is a very important meeting.'

'Okay,' she said brightly.

'And, I wonder if I could ask you to go to lunch?'

'What? Now?'

'Yes,' he said, his eyes furtive. 'I'd rather not have anyone on this floor while the meeting's going on. It's very delicate.'

'Okay, I'll wash my hands, and then I'll go,' she said.

'Good.'

Holly watched him stride back to his office, and muttered, 'Balls, how am I going to find out anything now?'

By the time she had tidied herself up in the tiny wash-room, she had decided upon a course of action. Closing her mind to the dangers involved, and to the fact that her cover would be blown if she was caught, Holly knocked on Ambrose's door.

'Come in,' he called.

The room was enveloped in a haze of cigarette smoke, and there was a half-empty bottle of scotch on the desk.

'Just off, Mr Ambrose.'

'Thank you, Holly.'

The other men studied her with interest, and ordinarily she would have been flattered, but in the circumstances, their attentions were an irritant.

'All right, let's get started,' Ambrose said.

She pulled the door but did not close it properly, leaving a gap no wider than a strand of cotton, and although none of the room was visible, the sound of voices filtered through.

Holly noisily walked along the landing, and waited just around the bend of the stairs. A moment later the door came open, and a voice said, 'It's clear, man, the dame's gone. You're getting paranoid, Hedley – you know that?'

The man went back inside, and Holly swore beneath her breath. Her ploy with the door had not worked. Slip-ping off her high-heeled shoes, she cautiously made her way back along the landing and, nearing the door, she noticed that it was slightly ajar, in fact, the crack was wide enough for her to see into the room. Ambrose was standing up, leaning forward with his hands resting on the desk. He seemed to be studying a large map.

'What have you got for us, Winston?' he asked.

'It's a good deal, I'd say.'

Winston came into Holly's line of vision, and stood beside Ambrose.

'In fact,' he said, 'it's the best deal we've ever done. Crack, cocaine and heroin, man, with a street value of six big ones. I've negotiated with the sellers, and we get it for a million.' Ambrose whistled softly. 'That's good, Winston. Now, when and where's the drop to be?'

'Four days' time, at nine p.m. Right there,' he said, leaning across and placing a mark on the map with a felt-tipped pen. 'The stuff's in that area already. The sellers are keeping it in a warehouse until we've seen it, and as soon as we come up with the cash, we can arrange transport.'

'That's a lot of stuff to have on the road,' Ambrose cautioned. 'I don't think much of the police, but if one of their routine patrols stops the convoy –'

'It's all taken care of,' Winston said, laughing. 'Sinclair's got the plan. Come on, show him, man.'

'Yeah,' Sinclair said, as he moved towards the map. 'I've organised a little diversion of the race riot kind that'll keep the police pretty busy.'

'I don't want any violence,' Ambrose jumped in.

'There won't be any,' Sinclair assured him. 'My boys'll be controlling what's happening. It'll be just enough to keep the police thinking about riot gear, here …' He pointed to a position on the map. '… rather than what's on the road, here.'

'Good,' Ambrose said. 'Now, has anybody got anything they want to say?'

'Yes,' Winston replied. 'Me and the rest of the boys ain't too happy about the gun that wasted Wells being in your safe.'

'I don't want to hear another word about that,' Ambrose said curtly. 'Look, we decided we wouldn't top anybody unless we had to, but Terry Wells was in the way. Now that gun stays where it is, because if it goes back on the street, the police could pick it up.'

He moved out of Holly's eyeline then, and she changed position slightly in order to see if he was going to open the safe. As she did so the shoes slid from under her arm. She managed to catch one, but the other slipped through her fingers and landed with a soft thud on the worn carpet.

'What the hell was that?' she heard Ambrose shout as she scooped it up.

'What was what?' Winston asked.

As she scuttled along the landing, Holly could hear movement from within the office, and she made it to the small recess which housed the washroom just as the office door was thrown open.

'Look around,' Ambrose ordered shrilly. 'Make absolutely sure there's no one here.'

Holly darted into the washroom, and pressed an ear against the door. Determined footsteps were heading her way, so she rushed into the lavatory cubicle. But what could she do now? If she locked the door, they would know someone was in there. The footsteps were getting perilously close. Holly had to think quickly, and was almost on the edge of panic when she noticed an eighteen-inch gap between the open lavatory door and the wall; that was more than enough space in which she could hide, and if the searcher looked into the cubicle, he would think it was empty.

The washroom door was flung open, and Holly held her breath as leather-soled shoes sounded on the stone floor. The man was so close that Holly could hear his breathing.

'Hedley, you're paranoid,' he muttered, opening the door to exit.

Holly exhaled thankfully and sank back against the wall. But then the footsteps returned, and as the lavatory door was pushed open still further, she held in her stomach, and willed herself to melt into the wall.

The man was inside the cubicle, opening his trousers

and humming quietly to himself as his urine splashed into the lavatory bowl. Holly could hear her heartbeat, could feel her stomach rolling. He was so close. She could see the pores, glistening with sweat, at the back of his neck. If he turned to his right, he would be looking directly at her.

The cascade became a trickle, and when it stopped the man shook his penis and stuffed it back inside his trousers. Then he made a half-turn to his right, and Holly needed all of her willpower to keep from vomiting. But he turned back, flushed the lavatory, and moving to his left, he walked out. Holly was swallowing bile when the door slammed behind him.

Trembling violently, she sat on the lavatory seat, her head between her knees, and muttered, 'Jesus Christ, Jesus Christ,' over and over again.

Bobby Adams turned the patrol car into Lilac Avenue and could see, far down on the right-hand side, a silver-grey vehicle parked roughly where Carter's house was. He pressed down on the accelerator and, seconds before the number plate came into focus, he was spotted by the driver and the car sped off.

Bobby thought of giving chase, but then he realised how foolish he would look if he pursued the car only to find that the driver had a legitimate reason for being in Lilac Avenue. Instead, he parked outside Carter's house, and sauntered along the drive. Reginald Carter opened the front door the moment the bell was pressed.

'Good afternoon, sir,' Bobby said. 'I'm from Bridgetown police station.'

'Did you see the silver car?' Carter asked, highly agitated.

'I did, indeed, sir. It drove off just before I got to it.'

'It's been there all afternoon. I've been out to it twice, but I get half-way along the drive, and it pulls off. Then I go back indoors and ten minutes later it's back.'

'Leave it with me, sir,' Bobby said with an air of confidence. 'I'll be passing by on a regular basis from now on. I'll make sure you're not bothered.'

'Can you wait outside now?' Carter almost pleaded. 'It should be back inside ten minutes.'

Bobby tipped the peak of his cap, and said, 'Leave it with me, sir.'

He sat outside Carter's house for almost an hour, but there was no sign of the car. And when the radio crackled with a request for assistance in a domestic dispute, Bobby reached for the handset, and said, 'On my way, sarge,' in the deep voice he had adopted of late.

No sooner had Bobby reached the junction and turned left, than the silver-grey car began to cruise along the road from the opposite direction, coming to a halt at the top of Carter's drive.

Manny Fredricks's nerves were jangling as be put the finishing touches to Lenny's forged papers. The passport held no problems; he simply had to get hold of one pertaining to a deceased male in Lenny's age group and doctor the details accordingly. But work permits and other such documents had to be falsified with enormous care. It was the permit he was working on now, and he scrutinised his handiwork through a powerful magnifying glass.

'Who would know the difference?' he chuckled.

Manny had heard talk around the billiard halls and bars that someone was looking for Lenny Spencer. There was not a contract out on him; whoever it was simply wanted to be told of his whereabouts. Manny was experienced enough to know that those who were looking for Lenny wanted the information to give to the police, and that meant the offer of a reward.

Manny sighed as he glanced around the converted loft of his house. All of his equipment would have to be moved out. Such a big job, such a lot of effort, but it would have to be done if he was about to invite a visit from Johnny Law.

Chapter 15

Janice accepted the proof of Tone's inadequacy with fairly good grace, and after checking several times that they were talking about inches and not centimetres, she announced that Holly had confirmed what she already suspected: Tone's thing was undersized.

Holly's eyes kept straying to the wall clock. She could hardly wait for five thirty, when she could report to Steve Derry the events which had taken place during the lunch-hour. At last she grabbed her bag and made for the door.

'Night, Janice,' she called over her shoulder.

On the pavement, she opened out her umbrella against the light drizzle, and set off in the direction of the police station.

Josh collected fish and chips on the way home.

Greg was in the kitchen, pouring boiling water into the teapot, when he walked in, and Josh thought how much better he looked; those antibiotics which he consumed like sweets seemed to be winning their battle with his latest chest infection.

'Hi,' Greg said. 'I've made the tea.'

'Great.' Josh pulled out a stool at the breakfast bar. 'I've bought fish and chips.'

Greg poured the tea, and placed a mug beside Josh who was eagerly unwrapping the food.

'Anything exciting happen today?' he asked, as he sat down.

Josh shook his head, and crammed chips into his mouth. 'Not really. Carter thinks somebody's watching him. He's reported a car parked at the end of his drive.'

Merely picking at his food, Greg said, 'Have you got the make or registration?'

'No. The guv'nor's not taking it seriously. In fact, I think he's pleased that Carter's frightened.'

'So he's not taking any action?'

Josh took a sip of tea, and grimaced when it burned his lips. 'Oh, yes, he has to. A patrol car's keeping an eye on Carter's place every time it's in the area.'

'And there's been nothing reported?'

'Bobby Adams is on the beat at the moment. He reported a car there this afternoon, but he didn't think the driver was watching the house. Anyway, Bobby'll do a thorough job, and if anybody is watching Carter, he'll pull him in.'

Greg suddenly pushed away the remains of his meal, and sat staring at the opposite wall.

Josh, rather alarmed, said, 'You all right?'

'Yes, of course I am,' he threw back irritably. 'I'm not just going to keel over and die, you know. Christ, you're always on edge.'

'Sorry. What with you being ill, every time you go quiet, I wonder if you're okay.'

'It fits in with my theory, this does, Josh. Terry Wells's brother could be watching Carter.'

'We don't know that anybody is yet, and the way Carter tells it, this guy's just trying to unnerve him.'

'Make him suffer, you mean? Give him time to reflect on what he's done?'

Josh laughed. 'You're getting worse, you know. Anyway, you'll get a chance to discuss it with Jim Ashworth. He's invited us to dinner on Sunday night.'

'Has he? That's great.'

'Thank God you're pleased. I accepted for us, but I didn't think you'd be too keen to go.'

'What do you mean? I can't wait to meet the great man. What's his wife like?'

'Sarah? She's really nice.'

'And will it be just the four of us?'

'Yes, the guv'nor invited Holly, but she can't make it.'

'Good.'

'Oh, come on, Greg, Holly's all right.'

'But she doesn't like me, and I can't say I'm that keen on her.'

'You caught her in a bad mood, that's all. How she feels depends on whether she's getting it or not.'

Holly felt good in Steve Derry's underground office, as she passed on the information she had uncovered. He listened attentively, and let out a loud triumphant whoop when she had finished.

'Nearly got you, you son-of-a-bitch,' he laughed. 'Come on, we'd better talk this over with the team.'

Derry was almost at the door before he realised that Holly was reluctant to follow.

'What's wrong?' he asked, frowning.

'Jim Ashworth,' she said simply.

'Bear with me, please,' he implored. 'Look, if I can get this drugs raid set up, Ashworth can get a warrant to search Ambrose's premises at the same time.'

When she still looked doubtful, he went on, 'You told me yourself Ashworth's got tunnel vision, so if you pass this on now, he's gonna want to storm Ambrose's office, like, this minute.'

'But that decision's not entirely up to him, is it?' Holly countered. 'And it's far from certain that the drugs bust is going to come off.'

'That's my whole point. If the powers-that-be look at this now, what are they gonna see? An easy end to a murder enquiry. We could just walk in there and book Ambrose and his boys for the murder of Terry Wells. But the drugs thing needs a hell of a lot of work on it, so it might happen or it might not. They're gonna take the soft option, and get Ambrose off the streets any way they can, and fuck the drugs.'

Holly was still wavering, and Derry struck the desk top in a fit of frustration, and paced about the office.

'For God's sake, lady,' he said, stopping abruptly in front of her, 'I need this for my record, and for myself. If I can dent the gangs, I earn myself some street cred.'

'Listen, Steve,' Holly snapped, 'you're putting me in a really bad situation here.'

He gave a resigned sigh, and said, 'Look, I tell you what, if by Saturday it looks like we're gonna pull the drugs raid off, you can tell Ashworth. Then, whatever he might want, he'll be forced to wait until Monday.'

The whole business settled uneasily on Holly, but after a moment's thought, she reluctantly said, 'All right.'

Straight away, Derry pulled her to him, and kissed her lightly on the lips. 'Have I ever told you how good you make me feel?'

'Yes,' she said, nudging him playfully, 'and your language was filthy, but tell me again.'

'Come on,' he grinned, 'we've got work to do.'

They hurried along the corridor where stale sweat mingled with the smell of damp, and where gurgling water continued its unceasing journey around the pipes. Derry was chewing on a match, and did not speak until they were in the Operations Room, where half a dozen detectives lounged about.

Derry positioned himself in front of the blackboard, and said, 'Okay, guys, now you all know Holly ...'

'Yeah,' an athletic officer called out. 'She's the bird who threw you all over the gym.'

Derry, acknowledging their laughter with a wide grin, threw back, 'Just remember, she did what none of you jerks could.'

That sparked off a succession of catcalls and cheers, and Derry called, above the clamour, 'Okay, okay, that's enough. Holly's got something to pass on.'

A hush descended, and she joined the inspector by the

blackboard. Then, spotting Russ Pearson's friendly face, she shot him a grin and proceeded to relate that day's events, all the while enjoying the murmurs of approval emanating from within the group.

'What happened to the map with the marks on?' Pearson asked.

'I don't know, I was in the loo with this guy when it vanished,' she joked.

There was a ripple of laughter, and Holly said, 'No, seriously, it was still on Ambrose's desk after lunch. It went into the top left-hand drawer as you're facing the desk.'

Derry hitched himself up on to one of the tables, and asked, 'What are the chances of you getting a look at it?'

'Remote, I should think. Since I've been there, Ambrose has only been out of the office once; that was the day he left early, and we got the duplicate keys. So, the chances of that happening again between now and Sunday have to be nil.'

Derry patted the table, and Holly went and sat beside him.

'So, we have to go in,' he reflected. 'George, what have you got for us?'

George proved to be a portly man in his forties, with receding brown hair, twinkling blue eyes, and an easy smile. The double cheeseburger, never far from his mouth, was feeding his already ample waistline.

'George is our alarms expert, among other things,' Derry explained to Holly.

Stuffing the remains of the burger into his mouth, the man got to his feet, and dug a handkerchief from the pocket of his faded grey trousers.

He wiped his greasy fingers thoughtfully, and then turned to Holly. 'Do you know what kind of alarm system it is? What make?'

'No idea,' she replied.

'Okay then, what's the set-up? Is it a box on the outside

wall, with a point just inside the door where you turn it off with the key?'

'Yes, that's it,' she said.

'Do you know where the control box is? It'll be metal, about a foot square, usually tucked away somewhere.'

'There's a box like that in the stationery cupboard by my desk.'

'Sounds about right,' George said. 'Now, give me the layout from the front door to that cupboard.'

'Right, you go in the front door, across the betting shop to another door leading to the stairs, fourteen in all –'

'You count stairs as well, eh?' George interjected.

Holly smiled, and went on, 'You turn right at the top, go along the landing, and left into the office.'

'That sounds quite a distance,' George said.

'A fair distance, yes.'

'What are our chances, George?' Derry asked.

'Depends. I'll need some shots of the alarm, and the inside of the control box. If I can find out what the make is, I'll know how long we've got to get from the door to the box.'

'Hold on, is there something I'm not getting here?' Holly asked, bewildered. 'If the alarm goes off for a minute, say, what difference will it make? No patrol car's going to get there that quickly.'

George's eyes twinkled as he grinned, and said, 'Holly, you've led a sheltered life.'

'Hey, don't give the lady a hard time,' Derry said, smiling. He leant towards her, and explained, 'The alarm's not there to alert the police to a break-in. It'll be wired to a building nearby, with half a dozen of Ambrose's heavies in it.'

'Oh,' Holly said, feeling decidedly foolish.

'Stand up,' George said.

Puzzled, Holly obeyed.

'Now, just take a normal stride.'

She did as he asked, and her eyebrows rose questioningly when he knelt beside her and took a tape measure from his pocket.

He looked up at her, and laughed. 'It's all right,' he said, 'I'm not going to feel your legs.'

'Damn, and I thought my luck had changed.'

George measured her stride. 'Okay, now what I want you to do, is pace the distance from the front door to the stairs, then from the top of the stairs to the control box.'

Holly pictured the route in her mind, and covered the distance as accurately as she could.

Derry said, 'What do you think, George?'

'It's not looking good,' he said, scratching his head, 'unless we've got somebody who's won an Olympic Gold for the hundred yards sprint.'

'And there's nothing we can do to shorten the odds?'

George shook his head. 'Not really. The alarms are fitted so that nobody can get to the control box before the bell goes off.'

'So, it's just down to speed.'

'That's about it,' George said, with a shrug. 'Whoever does it, has got to move like their arse is on fire, and they're running for the water-butt.'

The next day, feeling like a Bond girl, Holly took the photographs with what George described as an espionage camera, an ingenious pen-shaped device.

During her lunch-hour, she dropped them off at the police station, and the rest of the day passed slowly.

Ashworth managed to clear up the break-ins. Six local youths were arrested, and a lock-up garage, packed to the ceiling with televisions, video recorders and microwave ovens, was discovered.

But still his mood was not good. He was frustrated by the lack of progress on the Terence Wells murder case. And he was concerned too about the change he had noticed in Holly during their evening telephone calls. Ashworth was astute enough to realise that she was holding something back, but that was not all: it was almost as if she were slipping away from him. Even her mode of speech was becoming that of the Special Unit, and he feared that before very much longer, he would be looking for a new detective sergeant.

Throughout the day, Reginald Carter was vigilant, scouring the road for the silver car, but it did not return, and his confidence began a tentative emergence at the sight of the panda car cruising past at regular intervals. And now, again positioned at the front windows of his house, he managed to relax for the first time in weeks.

It was early evening when he wandered into the library to stand at the spot where Terence Wells had met his death and, not for the first time, he searched his memory in an attempt to identify the face he had spied fleetingly behind the side window of the small car when he had rushed along the drive the previous day. It was not a fleshy face, in fact it had appeared almost skull-like.

Skull-like ...

Reginald Carter stopped in mid-thought and broke out into a cold sweat as an image flashed into his mind of a small plastic skeleton, about two inches in length.

Ashworth's assumption was correct: Holly was indeed slipping away from the relatively quiet life of Bridgetown, and was very much enjoying her attachment to the Special Unit. The excitement suited her temperament, as did the Unit's unorthodox manner of working.

A cocky swagger crept into her walk as she made her way to the Operations Room, where George and Steve Derry were at a table, studying closely a number of photographs while the other detectives sat around.

'Hi, guys,' she called.

'These are good photos, Holly,' George said, with an appreciative smile. 'They've told me exactly what I wanted to know.'

'Okay,' Derry said, clapping his hands, 'now Holly's here, let's make a start.'

Feeling honoured that they had waited for her, Holly took a seat next to Russ Pearson.

Derry handed the floor to George who stood in front of the blackboard.

He said, 'The only good news we've got is that the bad news can't get any worse. The alarm's made by T.C.Y. Systems, a local firm. Now, it goes off thirty seconds after the door's opened, unless the key's used to turn it off, of course. Going on the measurements Holly provided, it's thirty yards from the front door to the control box, and in that we've got two doors to deal with: the door at the bottom of the stairs, and the one on the control box.'

'Is it possible?' Derry wanted to know.

'Fifty/fifty chance, I'd say. It's as close as that.'

Turning to the assembled detectives, Derry said, 'Who fancies trying it?'

No one spoke, and after a few seconds Holly stuck her hand in the air.

'No way,' George said. 'We can't send a woman on this.'

'Oh, bullshit, George,' Holly retorted. 'I'm the lightest one in the room, and the fittest.'

'Lady, I'm with George in this,' Derry said firmly. 'I should do it. If anything goes wrong, these boys play rough.'

'And I don't?' she challenged.

The reference to his somewhat humiliating experience at Holly's hand caused the inspector to turn away, and one of his detectives shouted, 'Don't blush, Steve.'

'Can it,' he warned, with good humour. Then, to Holly,

'If one of us goes in there, we can carry a shooter. You can't.'

'Oh, yes, that would look great, wouldn't it?' Holly said, striding to the front of the room. 'Why don't you all go blasting in there?'

Inspector Derry idly took the match from his mouth, broke it in two, and flicked it across the room. 'You got a better idea?'

'Yes. I work there, so if I get caught I can say I was out jogging, heard the alarm, and went to see what was happening.'

Derry pulled a face.

'Okay, I know it's flimsy, but it's something. It could be enough to make Ambrose's goons stop and think. But if they catch a cop on the premises, there's nothing for them to think about.'

'It's risky,' Derry said stubbornly.

'Christ, where are you coming from? Of course it's risky, and it hasn't escaped my notice that we should be getting a search warrant for this.'

'We wouldn't get one. That's why I wanted to do it myself. If there's a can to be carried, I should be the one doing it.'

'That's insane, Steve, and you know it. I'm used to the place, I walk it every day. I bet I could find that control box blindfolded.'

'George,' Derry snapped. 'What do you think?'

The detective studied Holly's slim figure and gave a resigned shrug. 'Sorry, Steve, but this girl's built for speed, and she does know the territory.'

'Okay, I'm out-voted,' Derry said. 'Now, if I know you, George, you've already worked out somewhere we can practise.'

George laughed. 'Yes. I can't reproduce the actual scene, but I've worked out the distance, and got as close to the real thing as I can.'

Chapter 16

The simulation was, as George had said, pretty close. Fourteen stone steps led up to a corridor linking the underground headquarters with the main police station, and George had arranged for an alarm control box to be screwed to the wall at the prescribed distance.

'Right, Holly,' he said. 'Now, there's no bend at the top of the stairs, and there's no door at the bottom, so we need to fake that. We'll knock two seconds off to allow for it.'

Standing at the top of the steps, Holly gazed along the corridor at the control box, and then back down towards the start line. 'So, I've only got twenty-eight seconds,' she murmured.

'Yes, it's quite a way, isn't it?' George said, reading her thoughts. 'Let's do it.'

He started along the corridor, eyes glued to his stopwatch, saying, 'I'll wait by the control box. When I shout "Go," start running.'

Holly descended the steps, aware that the whole of Special Unit was paying considerable attention to her body, which was understandable because her outfit left little to the imagination. She had changed into skin-tight emerald cycling shorts which highlighted her pubis, and a matching short-sleeved top, beneath which her nipples thrust enticingly.

Inspector Derry was positioned by the chalked starting line. He gave her a wink and, when her toe rested on the line, he shouted, 'Ready to go, George.'

'Hit it,' he called back.

Holly began to run, surprised by her self-consciousness which made her clumsy, and her every bone seemed to jar with each stride she took. Reaching the stairs, she stumbled, but nimbly regained her footing and scrambled to the top. George seemed so far away, but she pounded on towards him and overshot, skidding to a halt. Going down on her knees, she swiftly wrenched open the door of the box, and then, fighting for breath, she looked up at him expectantly.

George shook his head. 'Forty-five seconds.'

'Christ,' Holly exclaimed.

'Relax, loosen up. You shouldn't be breathing heavy. Take your time, and use speed only when you need it. As you approach the box, slow down and go into it in one smooth movement.'

She acknowledged the advice with a nod, and made her way back to the start.

By nine thirty p.m. Holly had made the run thirty times. Her clothing was soaked in perspiration, and her hair was flattened and dripping wet. She slumped, with her back to the wall, beside the control box and took in a deep breath.

'Thirty-five seconds,' George told her, as the rest of the team gathered around.

'I'm not going to make it,' she stated despondently.

'Sure you will.'

A fizzing can of lager was thrust at her, and Holly received it gratefully, gulping down its ice-cold contents. She was still against the wall, her legs wide apart, and she ran the cold can over her face, around her neck, and deep into her cleavage.

Turning to George, she said, 'There's still seven seconds to knock off. I'll never do it.'

'You're just tired.'

'I'm not, you know, I'm bloody knackered.'

'Exactly. You're improving with every run. You're moving good, smooth, with no waste in your actions. Tomorrow, when you're fresh, you'll knock some more time off. Okay?'

She smiled. 'Okay.'

'Right, champ,' he said, patting her shoulder. 'Go and shower.' They watched her walk away, with George adding softly, 'I wish I was going in there with you, girl. Will you take a look at that body?'

'Forget it,' Derry advised. 'She'd kill you.'

'Probably, but that's got to be the only way to go.'

'Cut the shit,' Derry ordered, above the laughter. 'What are the chances?'

'Still fifty/fifty. Sorry, Steve, but the odds won't get any shorter than that.'

Holly opened the door to the stationery cupboard and slipped the catch of the alarm control box so that the front would swing open when she tugged at it.

Behind her, Janice was relating in boring detail how she had thrown Tone over the night before, after meeting Sean at a disco. Sean, she had soon discovered during a session of heavy petting, was far better endowed than Tone; but rather than pleasing her, this discovery worried Janice, who was now concerned that sex might move from merely uninteresting to downright painful. It seemed that she had targeted Sunday evening – while her mother was at the bingo - for the moment of truth.

But the pleasures of the flesh were far from Holly's mind, for she was all too aware that she would be facing her own moment of truth on Sunday evening as she moved like a bat out of hell through the confines within which she now paced with a restless boredom.

As she glanced around, Holly realised that there were many obstacles for which they did not allow during training. For a start, she would have to turn left into the office, and manoeuvre around the desk – movements that could eat up precious seconds.

'It's twelve o'clock, Holly,' Janice said, bringing her back to the present.

'Thanks.' She grabbed her shoulder bag. 'See you Monday, then.'

'Yeah, all right.'

Holly had almost made it out of the office, when Janice brought her to an impatient halt, with, 'How will I know?'

'How will you know what?'

'If I come?'

'Oh, you'll know,' Holly said, searching for words to explain. 'It, well, it just sort of hits you.'

'Oh,' Janice said, staring into space. 'You mean a bit like burning your mouth on a hot chip?'

'Almost, yes. Anyway, I'll see you on Monday. Good luck.'

The betting shop was packed with punters, and the cloying smoke from their cigarettes met her as she pulled open the door and shouldered her way towards the alley.

Then a familiar face made her stop in her tracks: blond hair, blue eyes, a mouth that turned down slightly. But as soon as she spotted the man, he vanished, lost in a sea of moving bodies.

'I'm sure that was Russ Pearson,' she said to herself, as she stood on tiptoe to scan the room. 'But it couldn't be. What would he be doing here?'

Outside, she dismissed the incident from her mind, convinced that her keyed-up state was causing her to see things that were not there.

Sarah Ashworth was noting her husband's detachment. In the supermarket, he pushed their trolley around the aisles with the air of a man whose mind was on a grassy river bank somewhere, or lost in the clubhouse at the local golf club. But Sarah knew where Ashworth's thoughts were focused – on the Terence Wells murder case.

'Chicken for tomorrow's dinner party?' she asked, stopping by the fresh meat refrigerator.

'Yes, why not?' he grunted.

She looked up into his handsome face, and longed to tell him to forget it, but knew the outcome of that would be the same as waving a red rag at a bull in the hope of pacifying it. Sensing her concern, he slipped his hand in hers, their fingers entwining.

'Fruit and veg?' he asked.

Sarah nodded. 'It will come right, dear,' she encouraged, as she walked beside the trolley.

'Not unless something breaks soon, it won't.'

Holly's first run had been timed at thirty seconds. Six more followed, but that first time could not be bettered, and yet by the same token there was no deterioration.

George then sent her home with the order to return later for one last attempt to get below that stubborn thirty-second mark, and after spending an energetic hour in bed with Steve Derry, she dropped off to sleep.

Reginald Carter's feelings were mixed. Since the regular police patrol in Lilac Avenue, the silver car had not put in an appearance, and his tensions were eased considerably.

But as quickly as that worry receded, another surfaced to take its place, and just when he was planning to leave Bridgetown and start a new life in another part of the country, this old problem – one which had been with him for years – suddenly burst back into the centre of his mind. For such a long time now, he had convinced himself that his anxiety was unjustified, he was one of the lucky ones, he had escaped that which he feared most.

But now the worry was back, and becoming more real as the hours went by.

Holly pressed the button that would kill the alarm, and looked expectantly at George who was staring at the dial of his stop-watch.

'Right, downstairs,' he said.

She followed him to where the rest of the team were waiting at the foot of the steps.

'Well?' Derry asked.

George looked at Holly, and beamed. 'Twenty-nine seconds.'

She eased herself down on to the bottom step, and said, 'However many times I do it, I'm not going to better that.'

'I agree,' George said. 'You've peaked. Any more tries at it now would only be counter-productive.'

Derry asked, 'What are the chances?'

'When Holly opens the front door, she'll get a shot of adrenaline –'

'Cut the crap, George. Is she gonna make it, or do we need to abort?'

'Wait a minute.' George said, holding up a hand. 'Like I said, Holly's going to get a shot of adrenaline. Now that could work against her, make her clumsy, or it could give her speed.'

'And?' Derry pressed.

'If it gives her speed, she might just make it, but then again, she might not.'

Derry considered Holly. 'Lady, it's up to you in the end.'

Looking around the circle of faces, Holly said quietly, 'Let's do it.'

George knelt by her side and grasped her shoulders. 'Good girl. Now, remember, until that front door's open, take your time – okay? But once it's open, just go, don't count the seconds, don't even think about it, just go for that box, because your life probably depends on you getting to it before that alarm goes off.'

'Okay, everybody,' Derry said, smartly, 'we go at twenty hundred hours, tomorrow.'

It was Sunday, early evening, and Ashworth was returning home with the dog. He had deliberately extended her walk across the fields in the futile hope of tiring her out but, true to form, her energy was hardly dented as she bounded along the drive towards the house.

Inside, his appetite, enhanced by the fresh air, was plagued still further by the tempting aromas wafting out from the kitchen. Hanging up his waxed cotton jacket to the sounds of the dog slurping up water from her bowl, Ashworth considered again his reasons for suggesting this dinner party. Had he invited Josh and Greg to demonstrate how broad-minded and caring he was? The only true answer was, yes. Sarah, of course, was a carer at the best of times, and had readily gone along with him, for she needed only a hint that someone was in trouble and would offer her help gladly.

He wandered into the lounge, still analysing his motives. Greg, it seemed, regarded him as some sort of master detective, capable of solving any crime, and he was flattered. Could that too have influenced his decision? Probably.

He looked at the clock. It was seven p.m. Their guests were not due to arrive until eight, so he could have half an hour with the newspaper. Picking up the *Sunday Telegraph*, Ashworth sat in his favourite armchair, and turned to the editorial.

The hand gripping Holly's shoulder crept slowly towards her throat, and she opened her eyes with a start to find Steve Derry standing over her, his fingers caressing lightly.

'Time to go, lady,' he whispered.

She touched his hand, squeezed it gently, and then pulled back the duvet.

'How're you feeling?'

Sitting naked on the side of the bed, she said, 'Do you watch the fights – boxing, I mean?'

'Some of them.'

'I always wondered how those guys must feel when they're sitting in their dressing-rooms before a big fight, knowing that the next hour or so will affect the rest of their lives. Well, now I know.'

'Yes?' he said, sitting beside her.

'Yes. I feel sick, Steve.'

'Are you sure I look all right?' Greg asked.

He was staring into the mirror, straightening his tie for the fifth time.

Josh, struggling with his cufflinks, glanced up. 'You look great. He's not going to inspect us, you know.'

'But he's the great detective. I feel really nervous about meeting him now.'

'Relax,' Josh said, reaching into the wardrobe for his sports jacket. 'He's a chief inspector in the police force, not Sherlock Holmes.'

Turning away from the mirror, Greg asked, 'Do you think I look any better lately?'

Josh took in the trendy suit which hung on his friend's frame, and sighed. 'You've lost a lot of weight, but you do look better than you have for some time.'

'I am going to beat this,' Greg stated, almost to himself. 'I'm determined to outlive the bastard that gave it to me.'

'Oh, come on, Greg, don't get bitter.'

'Don't get bitter? What do you expect?'

'We've discussed this so many times,' Josh said heatedly. 'You've probably already outlived him.'

'You don't understand, Josh –'

'I've got an inkling,' he retorted sharply. 'You could have given it to me – or had you forgotten?'

'Oh, God, I'm sorry. I'm so caught up with my own problems.'

'Yes, well, let's try and forget it for once and enjoy ourselves.'

'All right,' Greg said, trying a smile.

There was a hush of expectancy in the Operations Room.

'Okay now, listen,' Derry said, standing in front of the blackboard. 'In thirty minutes, we go. Now, Holly comes in my car, and I'll drop her off as near to the betting shop as I can. I want you guys to park in a circle around the immediate area.'

'Do we go in if Holly meets any trouble?' Pearson asked.

'No, leave me,' Holly said, swivelling round in her chair. 'Give me a chance to talk myself out of it.'

'Okay,' Derry said, 'but if they do catch you, and then try to take you out of the area, we'll be there.'

Holly's pent-up nerves were becoming hard for her to bear, and she glanced anxiously at her watch. 'Why do we have to wait for eight o'clock? Why can't we go now?'

'Because there's a police patrol goes past Ambrose's at a quarter to,' Derry explained, drumming his fingers on the desk.

He was as anxious as any of them to get the operation under way, and after a few more minutes in which tensions built further, he banged on the desk, and said, 'Come on, let's go.'

Holly looked again at her watch, and listened to her quickening heartbeat as she followed him out.

The dinner was proving to be less daunting than Greg had expected. Sarah was, as ever, the perfect hostess, and the meal was delicious. Throughout the starter and main course, their conversation remained on very general lines, and flowed effortlessly.

'Would you mind very much if I didn't have the sweet, Mrs Ashworth?' Greg asked, as Sarah placed a huge strawberry flan at centre table.

'Of course not, Greg,' she said with a smile. 'In fact, I'm rather full myself.'

'Me too,' Josh confessed.

Ashworth eyed the dish. 'Well, I'd rather like some,' he said firmly.

'Yes, dear, I thought you might,' Sarah remarked, as she cast a surreptitious wink at her guests.

While Ashworth consumed his large portion, they engaged in lively small talk, and eventually Sarah began to clear the table. Straight away, Josh leapt to his feet, and started to help.

'Can I give you a hand with the washing-up, Mrs Ashworth?'

'No, I wouldn't dream of it, Josh. Sit yourself down, and I'll serve the coffee.'

Taking her to one side, he said, 'Look, I hope I'm not being rude, but I think Greg would like to be left alone with the guv'nor.'

'Josh …' Greg protested.

'It's quite all right,' Sarah jumped in. 'Of course you can help with the washing-up, Josh.'

Chapter 17

Derry's car, Delilah, came to a halt about two hundred yards away from the betting shop.

'This is as close as we go, lady,' he said, reaching for the radio handset.

Holly, breathing deeply to calm herself, listened while he checked that all cars were in position.

'Okay, go,' he said softly.

She climbed from the car and immediately took up a slow jog towards Ambrose's premises. Her tracksuit was loose-fitting, and all that she carried were the keys to the shop and George's espionage camera.

No one paid her the slightest attention as she trotted along at little more than walking pace, and soon she was turning into Greenfield Terrace to be met by a large golden labrador loping towards her and barking furiously.

'Shift,' she snarled, and continued on.

The dog scuttled out of the way and viewed her with large, doleful eyes before padding off to inspect a torn rubbish sack further along the alley.

Holly stopped outside the door of the betting shop, and searched her pocket for the keys. And as her fingers curled around the metal, a male voice shouted, 'Hey!'

She had to stifle a cry of fear as she turned to see a large black man running towards her with a lumbering gait. For a few tense seconds she remained undecided: which would be her best course of action – fight or flight? She spread her feet and prepared to defend herself.

The man stopped in front of her, a metal chain swinging viciously from his hand.

'You seen a labrador?' he panted, holding up the chain. 'He's come off the lead.'

'Yes, he went down there,' Holly said, pointing to the end of the alley.

'Thanks.' The man trotted off, calling, 'Sam. Sam!'

'I hope you're enjoying yourself more than I am, Janice,' Holly muttered.

'Whisky and soda, Greg?' Ashworth asked.

'Thank you.'

'I've seen some of your work on the case,' Ashworth said, as he poured the drinks. 'It's very good. You seem to be taking a great interest.'

'It fascinates me. What do you think of my theory that Carter killed Wells?'

'As good as any at the moment. But tell me what makes you so sure?'

'The method used for the killing,' Greg said, leaning forward eagerly. 'It was a pro job, right? Carried out by somebody used to handling a gun.'

'Yes,' Ashworth said, sipping his drink.

'So that would mean it was a gangland killing, wouldn't it? But why didn't they get rid of the body so that the police couldn't discover it?'

Ashworth shook his head, and smiled. 'I don't know, but I think you're going to tell me.'

'Because without a body, there wouldn't be a war, and that's what Carter wanted.'

'So that his rivals could eliminate each other, you mean? Leaving him to take over the city?'

'Seems logical to me,' Greg said, nodding enthusiastically.

'Well, it's backfired on him, then. His empire's crumbled, and it seems he's lost everything.'

'Perhaps that's because it's common knowledge that he did the killing.'

'If that is the case, no one's telling me.'

As he spoke, Ashworth's thoughts returned to the

mysterious car parked outside Carter's home, and the man's vehement statement that he was being watched; and Greg's next remark only served to sow the seed of doubt more deeply in his mind.

'With respect, Mr Ashworth, you only know what this Bernie Williams character's telling you …'

Sounds of dishes being stacked and Sarah's laughter filtered through from the kitchen, while Ashworth contemplated his young guest's logical arguments.

'Anything could be happening out there,' Greg said, pushing home his point. 'Maybe Carter's gang's disintegrated because they know he killed Wells, and they want to remove themselves from the firing line.'

'If you're right, it's very likely that Carter's life could be at risk some time in the future.'

'That's the conclusion I've reached,' Greg said, with a smug grin. 'And surely that would be case proven and closed.'

'Not necessarily, you're missing a couple of important points,' Ashworth said, before pausing to drain his glass. 'If Carter did turn up dead, then we'd be looking for his killer, and we'd still need proof that he murdered Wells.'

'And you'd just run into another wall of silence.'

'Are you implying that the police are powerless in this case?' Ashworth asked, as he reached for Greg's glass.

'Can you deny it?'

Ashworth laughed. 'You're a clever young man.'

'So the case would be closed?'

'We never close an unsolved case.'

Whisky gurgled into the glasses, as Ashworth went on, 'I suppose that after we'd gone through the motions and come up with nothing, the powers-that-be would undoubtedly deem that any more spent from our hard-won budget would be a waste of money.'

'And that would be the same as case closed, wouldn't it?'

'As good as,' Ashworth had to admit.

'Have you looked into Carter's professional and private life?'

'Extensively. I am very thorough, you know.'

'Oh, I didn't mean to say you weren't,' Greg put in quickly.

'I know, I know,' Ashworth chuckled. 'Carter's private life is as big a puzzle as everything else about him.'

'How do you mean?'

'Well …' Ashworth took a sip of the scotch. 'To begin with …'

The key failed to turn.

Holly swore softly, strove to compose herself, then cursed the newly cut key and tried again, attempting to turn it until her thumb hurt from the pressure.

'Balls,' she mouthed, her eyes darting nervously along the silent stretch of alley.

She let go of the key and inhaled slowly and deeply, making a conscious effort to loosen the tension in the back of her neck, then, offering up a silent prayer, she persevered. This time, the key turned slightly, but then refused to budge.

'Turn, you bastard, turn.'

And as if obeying the instruction, the key turned and the lock clicked, allowing the door to swing open, but precious seconds ticked away before the message reached her brain and galvanised her into action.

Holly raced across the floor of the betting shop, and pushed open the door to take the stairs in one swift motion.

'Move, you bitch, move, move, move,' she chanted as her feet pounded the steps.

The bend at the top of the stairs loomed, and she negotiated it badly, slamming into the landing wall, and yet she kept on running.

'Slow. Slow for the doorway.'

Timing it perfectly, Holly skidded into the office and around the desk to fling open the door of the stationery cupboard. Her heart was pounding, and her breathing was erratic. Any second now, she expected to hear the siren sound of the alarm.

She fumbled frantically with the casing of the control box, and eventually managed to wrench it open with such force that the metal clanged loudly against the wall.

And then a bell sounded.

'Dong …'

'I checked out his professional life first,' Ashworth said, settling back into his chair. 'By all accounts, he's a first-class antiques dealer. He doesn't trade much, but then with the income he gets from his criminal activities, he doesn't need to.'

'What about his private life?'

'That's so private, I haven't been able to find out anything.'

'Any girlfriends?'

Ashworth shook his head. 'Friends of either sex seem non-existent. He was friendly with Terence Wells, that much we're aware of, but no one seems to know anything more about him.'

'And he just has the one address?'

The question caused Ashworth to frown. 'As far as I know. When he couldn't move back to his house after the murder, he stayed at a hotel. Why do you ask?'

'The double life thing.' Greg finished his whisky. 'Is it possible for someone to go through life without making any friends?'

'We haven't established that he has. Remember, Reginald Carter trusts no one. I suspect his right hand is suspicious of his left.'

Greg laughed, and Ashworth said, 'What I do know is

that a lot of his deals take place in the so-called sex capitals of the world.'

'And do you think that's relevant?'

'It could be, but until I find out more – who knows?'

'You're good,' Greg said, suddenly. 'You're really good.'

'Well, I like to think so,' Ashworth smiled.

'You've really tried to build up a complete picture of Carter, and with so little to go on.'

'I suppose I have. But just remember, I haven't come up with anything yet.'

'Dong …'

The bell sounded again, and a bead of sweat worked its way down her back, snaking over her skin, leaving goose-pimples in its wake, as Holly flicked the off switch inside the control box.

'Dong …'

The third chime marking the quarter-hour rang out, and at last the distant church clock fell silent. Holly sank back against the wall, breathing heavily.

'Front door. Must close the front door,' she mumbled, after a time.

Pushing herself up, she teetered for a second on legs that seemed unable to support her. Her head felt strangely light, and now that the initial danger had passed, she felt an uncontrollable urge to giggle.

'This is as much fun as dropping my knickers,' she grinned.

'Well, almost as much.'

Ashworth was placing cups and saucers haphazardly inside the kitchen cabinet, while his head spun pleasantly from the whisky.

'Josh is a lovely young man,' Sarah said. 'It's such a shame, what they're both going through.'

'Yes,' Ashworth agreed. 'When I was sitting in the

lounge, talking to Greg, I almost forgot that he was dying. It's such a waste. Sorry I left you with Josh.'

'Oh, I think that's how they planned it. Apparently, Greg was eager to talk to you.'

'He's an intelligent young man. I could see him in the law. He's got that sort of mind. He immediately grasps every aspect of an idea.'

Sarah pulled out a chair, and sat at the kitchen table.

'Josh still thinks the world of him, you can see that. He believes that if Greg involves himself in the case, it could prolong his life. Do you think that's possible?'

'I suppose so. Do you know, Sarah, when I was talking to him, I felt comfortable, totally at ease.'

Sarah eyed his tumbler of whisky, and asked suspiciously, 'How many drinks did you two have while you were talking?'

'Only one,' he lied.

'So you feel you've met your intellectual equal then?'

'Oh, I wouldn't say that, Sarah,' he said, immodestly, 'but the lad is clever.'

The champagne cork hit the ceiling as a laughing Holly sprayed the members of Special Unit with the sparkling wine.

'Hold it,' George shouted, 'that's booze you're wasting.'

A line of plastic cups was thrust in front of her, and she filled them all, whooping whenever the liquid escaped over the rims. When everyone had a drink, Holly picked up her own, and offered a toast.

'These are great photos,' Derry said. 'We've got all we need now to apply for a warrant.'

Champagne bubbles tickled her nose, and Holly giggled, and pulled the inspector to one side.

'Can't we go?' she whispered.

'This could go on for some time,' he said. 'These guys have a lot of tension to release.'

'And I don't?'

'Let's stay awhile. We'll slip out in about an hour.'

'But I feel horny, Steve. It's all the excitement.'

Derry smiled down at her. 'I told you this was the job for you. The offer's still open.'

'Why don't you take me somewhere, and persuade me?'

'Where?'

'What about your office?'

'My office?' He looked surprised, but definitely interested.

'Oh, come on,' she coaxed, grabbing his hand. 'I've never done it on police property before.'

It was a grim-faced Chief Inspector Ashworth who sat in his small office at Rutley police station, the next morning.

Holly gave a sheepish knock, and entered.

'Guv …'

'Hello, Holly,' he said sharply, indicating the chair in front of his desk.

'Can I explain?'

'There's little need for that. It's quite plain that information came to light about a .38 revolver in Ambrose's safe, and for some reason you decided not to tell me until this morning.'

'Because I was undercover, guv. I was waiting to find out where a very large drug deal was about to take place.'

'You were put in there as part of a murder investigation,' Ashworth stated hotly. 'That should have been foremost in your mind, not some drugs deal. And why did you hold back? Was Inspector Derry frightened I'd bluster in and spoil everything for him?'

'I'm not saying that, guv, it's just that Steve didn't want to move until we had all the information.'

'Which meant lying to me.'

'I didn't lie,' she said, averting her eyes.

'But you didn't tell me the whole truth, and that

172

amounts to the same thing.'

'Yes, okay, I realise this is a disciplinary matter, but I honestly thought I was doing the right thing.'

'Disciplinary matter? What are you talking about? This is our working relationship I'm discussing. I should be able to trust you in all situations.'

'Steve said –'

'Steve said. I couldn't care less what Steve said ...'

He stopped suddenly, his frustration fuelling his anger, and regarded her with an adverse expression. 'I take it you and he –'

'That's my personal business,' she flared.

'Not if it interferes with your work.'

'Oh, I've had enough of this. Guv, if I'd told you there was a .38 revolver in that safe, you would've gone barging in there.'

'No, no, I would have discussed it first.'

'Oh yes, you'd have discussed it first, and then you'd have gone barging in.'

'I don't know ... you're probably right.'

'You don't own me body and soul, guv.'

Just then there was a knock on the door, and Inspector Derry threw it open, but catching Ashworth's imperious glare, he wavered on the threshold. 'Have I chosen a bad moment?'

'An extremely bad one,' Ashworth growled.

Derry held up his hands and backed away, winking at Holly. 'Excuse me, then,' he said, closing the door.

Ashworth caught the look of admiration in Holly's eyes as she watched the inspector exit, and remembered when that look would have been directed at himself.

He said, 'Something tells me you're growing out of Bridgetown.'

'Steve has offered me a job,' she replied, unable to look directly at him.

'I see. Well, if you've decided to take it, I wish you

the best of luck.'

'Thank you.'

'I've seen the report, and it seems you did some excellent work, in very dangerous conditions.' She made no comment, so he added, 'I suppose after all that, Bridgetown and old Jim Ashworth seem a bit dull.'

She started to interject, but Ashworth continued, 'If the warrant comes through to search Ambrose's property, and I've no doubt it will, I shall be taking Josh. I feel it would be inappropriate for you to attend. It's far better that Ambrose doesn't know you were an undercover officer.'

'Thanks, guv.'

Holly got to her feet in the heavy silence that followed, and at the door, she said, 'Special Unit have requested that I attend the drugs raid. Do you have any objections to that?'

'None,' Ashworth told her sharply.

It was four p.m. before the magistrates issued warrants for the searches to the office of Hedley Ambrose and the warehouse allegedly containing the drugs shipment.

Ashworth made full use of the intervening hours by returning to Bridgetown for Josh – who seemed even more out of his depth in the big city than his chief inspector – and by arranging for the required number of uniformed officers to be present on the scene.

Chapter 18

Reginald Carter was in the lounge when the doorbell rang. He tensed automatically and sidled across to the window to glance out along the drive. On the road, directly opposite his gates, stood a small van with WHOPPLES – THE FLORIST stencilled on its side, and a man wearing blue jeans and a brown smock could be seen waiting at the front door. In his arms was an enormous bouquet of flowers.

Carter hastened into the hall, and shouted through the closed door, 'What do you want?'

'Whopples, the florists, with a delivery, sir.'

Flustered, and highly suspicious, Carter said, 'Just leave it on the step.'

'I can't do that, sir, I need a signature.'

Although reluctant, Carter lifted the latch, and drew open the door. The man grinned, and when he reached into his pocket, Carter ducked back, flattening himself against the wall, and kicked the door shut, expecting bullets to start flying at any moment. 'Hello, hello,' the man called, hammering on the knocker.

Keeping to the side panel, Carter peered through the pebbled glass and, seeing that the man held nothing more dangerous than a biro, he once again opened the door.

'Are you all right, sir?' the man asked, with a puzzled frown.

'Yes, yes,' Carter snapped, taking the proffered pen and clipboard.

'Sign on number thirty, please, sir.'

He scrawled his signature and snatched the bouquet, then slammed the door with some force.

The delicate fragrance of freshly cut roses and carnations was lost to him as he focused on a small envelope stapled to the cellophane wrapping. Tearing it open, he withdrew a card, and read the simple inscription: 'See you soon.'

A low mist swirled up from the river, and hung in the still, warm air. Steve Derry, with Holly in the passenger seat, slowly circled the industrial estate. All around was an eerie silence, stretching their taut nerves still tighter, and Holly jumped when the radio crackled into life.

Derry grabbed the handset. 'Yes?'

'We're in place, Steve.'

'Roger.' He turned to Holly. 'Better kill the lights. We're almost there.'

Without the comforting arc of the dipped headlights, the mist seemed to close in and envelop the car, cutting them off from reality, but then the long, aggressive blare of a heavy goods vehicle sounded reassuringly in the distance.

Ashworth's preparation for his part of the raid was far more sedate. The alley containing Ambrose's betting shop had been effectively sealed off, and uniformed officers placed at the front and rear doors of the property to ensure that no one entered. Satisfied that all was ready, he telephoned Hedley Ambrose at his home number, drumming his fingers while he waited for an answer.

Almost immediately, the man's pleasant voice drifted into his ear. 'Hedley Ambrose.'

Keeping his tone cordial, Ashworth said, 'Hello, Mr Ambrose. This is Chief Inspector Ashworth. I don't know whether you remember me.'

'Oh yes, I remember, but it's a little late for you to ring with an apology, and in any case, I told Ken Savage that one wouldn't be necessary.'

'I'm not ringing with an apology, sir, far from it. I believe you could assist me with my enquiries.'

'We've been through all this, chief inspector,' Ambrose said stridently.

'That we have, sir, but I was far from happy with the result.'

'I warn you, I shall ring the Chief Constable.'

Ashworth ignored him, and said, 'I now have a warrant to search your premises in Greenfield Terrace, and I would like to request that you attend.'

There was a stunned silence on the line, and Ashworth grinned widely. 'Are you still there, Mr Ambrose?'

'Yes.' The hectoring tone was now gone, replaced by a hint of anxiety. 'I'm going to ring my solicitor.'

'That's fine, sir. Now, if you would both like to meet me at Greenfield Terrace in fifteen minutes, I'm sure we can clear this matter up quite quickly.'

Derry pulled up in the car-park of a large DIY warehouse, where the vehicles of other members of the team were formed into a tight circle. A gentle breeze fashioned the mist into unearthly moving shapes, and Holly's rubber-soled shoes made weird slapping sounds on the concrete as she followed Derry through the semi-darkness.

'How goes it, Russ?' he asked, as they joined the large knot of detectives.

'About six guys have gone in. Looks like it's all in place.'

'Are Mike and George at the back?'

'Ready and waiting.'

Derry spat the ever-present match from his mouth. 'Right, let's do it,' he said.

Back at his car, Derry took an axe from the boot while Pearson whispered into the radio, 'Mike, we're going in. Wait for the signal.'

They moved silently and swiftly across the car-park, and scrambled through a low gorse hedge to the forecourt of the adjacent premises on which stood a large brick-built structure, windowless, with a plain wooden door. Excitement coursed through Holly's body as the six of them skidded to a halt, and Derry passed the axe to the largest of his detectives.

'Do we give them a warning?' Pearson asked.

'Of course,' Derry grinned. 'That's how the big book says it should be done.'

He leant against the wall, and whispered, 'Open up. Police.'

Then, pointing to the door, he yelled, 'Take the fucking thing – go,' while Russ Pearson screamed instructions into the radio.

'I think you'll find that the warrant's in order, sir,' Ashworth said serenely, handing the document to Ambrose's lawyer, James Davis.

The man studied the warrant while his client paced the floor of the betting shop.

'Well?' Ambrose asked, impatiently.

Davis's forehead creased into a frown, and he turned to Ambrose, shrugging resignedly. 'It's all in order, Hedley.'

'But there must be something we can do about this, James. It's outrageous.'

'Nothing we can do, I'm afraid.'

There was just a tinge of gloating in Ashworth's tone, when he said, 'Yes, there is, sir, you can let us search the property.'

'You're enjoying this, Ashworth, aren't you?' Ambrose sneered.

'I'm just doing my job,' he said, smiling, 'which I've always enjoyed.'

'Calm down, Hedley,' Davis advised. 'We've got to go along with the man.'

'Then what do I pay you for?' Ambrose barked, turning on the lawyer.

Davis shot him a cautionary glance, and turned to Ashworth. 'Where do you want to look?'

'Mr Ambrose's office, in the first instance.'

Davis said, 'I'd like to make it plain that my client objects to you being here.'

'I had an idea he wasn't happy,' Ashworth replied. 'Now, can we look at the office?'

Ambrose continued to protest all the way to the first floor. Inside the office, Ashworth directed Josh to remain by the door, and then he said to Ambrose, 'Right, sir, I'd like to look inside the safe, if I may.'

'Not the safe. I don't want them looking in the safe, James.'

The man was distraught, and fast losing control of himself, and when he started towards Ashworth, his fist raised, James Davis grabbed his arm and roughly pulled him back.

'Hedley, you must co-operate. You must.'

After glowering at the chief inspector, Ambrose went to the safe and began fiddling with the combination lock. Several clicks later, he turned the key, and the door gaped open. Then, while he moved moodily to the opposite wall, Ashworth crouched down and, under the watchful eye of the lawyer, began to remove papers from the safe, stacking them neatly on the floor.

The door splintered with the second blow from the axe, and the third wrenched it from the top hinge. Derry called a halt, smashing into the wood with his shoulder, and when it creaked and groaned and gave way, crashing to the floor, he ran across it, reaching for his gun, and shouting, 'Go, go, go.'

At the very centre of the enormous floor-space, under the insufficient glow from a single strip light, three men wearing startled expressions were leaning over a trestle table.

The detectives raced towards them, but half-way there, Holly's victorious grin changed to a look of puzzlement when the whole interior of the warehouse was suddenly lit up with a blinding light, followed by a strobe flashing orange, green, and red across hundreds of people moving slowly out from the perimeter walls, and dancing to the rap music which seemingly came from nowhere. All at once, the detectives were surrounded by grinning faces, edging ever closer. And then, as one, the crowd began to scream.

Ashworth pulled out the remaining drawer. It was empty.

And as he squatted amid piles of papers, the interior of the safe yawned mockingly back at him.

There was no .38 revolver.

Unable to comprehend, Ashworth glanced towards the two men, and found that both were grinning broadly.

'But it wasn't a wedding reception,' Derry insisted. 'Those bastards were waiting for us to bust in. We were fitted up.'

'The papers say it was,' Ashworth countered, throwing a tabloid newspaper on to the desk in his temporary office at Rutley police station.

'And that's not all,' he added, hotly. 'I've raided the office of a perfectly respectable black businessman. And at the same time, officers on the west side of the city tried to arrest a black youth and were on riot alert for the rest of the night –'

'That was the decoy,' Derry interjected. 'To keep our guys busy.'

'I don't care what it was,' Ashworth yelled. 'Can't you see what all of this looks like – especially when it's given a lot of help by the fine gentlemen of the press? It looks like we're setting out to harass and victimise the black community.'

'That's what the bastards want it to look like,' Derry said. 'Listen, that may have been a legit wedding reception, but those people were waiting for us. The whole thing was orchestrated.'

Ashworth, infuriated by the inspector's calm manner,

moved towards him, and said, 'I know that, son, I'm not senile.'

Over by the filing cabinet, Holly stood cringing at the loudness of Ashworth's voice and, hoping to turn the conversation to calmer waters, she asked, 'What's the Chief Constable saying, guv?'

He turned to glare at her, and then appeared to make a conscious effort to cool down. 'Ken Savage is staying with us for the moment, thank goodness. He knows Ambrose is a villain, and that this is something to do with the Wells murder, so he's going to make the right noises in the right quarters, and hope this dies down.'

Ashworth sat at his desk, and focused his attention once more on Steve Derry.

'Right, let's get on with the post-mortem. What the hell went wrong?'

'Ambrose knew what we were doing, and was one jump ahead the whole time. Everything Holly overheard was carefully rehearsed. They left the door keys with her overnight because they wanted us to get duplicates cut.' Derry shrugged. 'There never was a drugs deal, or a .38 revolver. We were set up.'

'For what reason?'

'To make us look like a crowd of dim arseholes, I suppose.'

'Very elaborate just to make us look silly, don't you think?'

'Perhaps the man's got a sick sense of humour.'

Ashworth frowned. 'But how did he know? For Ambrose to feed Holly all that false information, he had to know she was undercover right from the start. Who could have told him?'

'Dunno,' Derry said.

'Well, somebody must have told him,' Ashworth flared.

'Maybe he saw Holly with me. Or maybe he saw her coming to the station.'

'No,' Ashworth said doggedly, 'someone here told him. Someone inside this station is passing on information to Hedley Ambrose.'

Holly took a sharp intake of breath, for she suddenly remembered that day in the betting shop, the Saturday before the raid. *Could* it have been Russ Pearson she saw there?

'You'd better not be accusing any of my people, Ashworth,' Derry said, pointing a finger. 'I vet them all thoroughly. They've all got first-class records.'

'Don't point your finger at me, son,' Ashworth said, glaring at the inspector until he lowered his hand. 'Thank you. So, who else could it be?'

'Perhaps the CID here, or uniform ... who knows?'

'Well, that narrows it down nicely,' Ashworth spat.

'Look, I don't need this, man. My people are traumatised right now, and I need to spend some time with them.'

He strode to the door, and turned aggressively. 'If you need to look at my people, you're welcome to, but the leak didn't come from my unit.' The door was slammed shut.

'Traumatised,' Ashworth mocked. 'A raid that went wrong and everybody goes on sick leave. I don't know what the force is coming to.'

'It was fairly horrific, guv,' Holly said, sitting on the edge of his desk. 'That crowd was waiting for us. They walked into the middle of the room, laughing, and then they just started screaming, and they carried on until the press got there.'

'And didn't they get some fine pictures,' Ashworth remarked, as he glanced at the newspaper. 'And that smug look on Ambrose's face when I didn't find the gun in his safe ... I could have killed him there and then.'

'We've all been made to look first-class idiots,' she said. 'When I think what I went through at the betting shop on Sunday night, and the alarm probably wasn't even on.'

'You did some fine work, and it hasn't gone unnoticed.

I've had a word with CID here.'

'Are you pulling strings for me, guv?'

'Yes,' he admitted frankly. 'If you're thinking of moving on, you'd be far better joining a large CID, than running around with that load of extras from a Mel Gibson film.'

Holly giggled. 'I wouldn't have thought you'd watch Mel Gibson movies.'

'I have to,' he told her, smiling. 'Sarah likes him. Anyway, Holly, I want you to know that you're a valued member of my team, and I'll be very sorry to lose you, but if you want to move to where the promotion prospects are better, then I'll do all I can to help.'

'Thanks, guv.'

The telephone rang, and Ashworth beat her to the receiver. 'Yes?' he said.

'Mr Ashworth, I see you got your picture in the papers. It's a good likeness, but what a pity about the publicity.'

The mocking tone in Bernie Williams's voice brought a rush of colour to Ashworth's cheeks, and irritation showed in his tone when he said, 'If you've got anything sensible to say, then say it, if not, go and be silly somewhere else.'

'Oh, Mr Ashworth, you seem to have misplaced your sense of humour. Now, I have a name for you. Connected with the matter we were discussing the last time you were here.'

'Then give it to me,' Ashworth said, picking up a pen.

'Not over the telephone.'

'Bernie, I'm getting pretty near the end of my tether with you lot. If you have a name, then give it to me.'

'Now it is you who are being silly, Mr Ashworth. The events of the last few days should really have brought it home that you are not in the driving seat as far as this matter is concerned. I shall expect you at my shop at four p.m.'

The line went dead, and Ashworth threw down the receiver. 'I've been in the police force for thirty-five years, and never before have I run into people who seem to think they exist outside the rules of society. If this continues,' he added, snapping the pen into two pieces, 'I'm going to lose my temper.'

'You already have, guv,' Holly said, pointing to the pen.

He tossed the pieces into the waste bin and, with a sigh of despair, said, 'Do you know, Holly, I'm beginning to think there's only one thing these men understand, and that's violence.'

'I agree with you there. So, what was the call about?'

'Bernie Williams, telling me he has the name of the person who killed Terence Wells.'

Her eyebrows rose. 'Well? Who is it?'

'He wouldn't tell me. He's summoned me to his shop at four o'clock so that he can make the disclosure there.'

'That's something, I suppose.'

'After what's happened, can we believe anything this lot tell us?'

He reached for the newspaper. 'Many more fiascos like this, and we're going to lose what little credibility we have left.'

'Can I come with you, guv?'

'Of course, then we can both be made to look silly.'

Chapter 19

The spiral staircase in Bernie Williams's shop suggested a quaintness found lacking in its owner. His two heavies were lounging about in the back of the shop, drinking coffee. They paid little attention to Ashworth, but Holly caught and held their interest until her long, shapely legs disappeared from view up the stairs.

Williams looked up from his desk. 'Ah, Mr Ashworth,' he beamed. 'And unless I'm mistaken, this beautiful young lady is Detective Sergeant Holly Bedford.'

She cast Williams a suspicious look. 'How do you know my name?'

'I know everything that happens in this city, Miss Bedford.'

Ashworth stayed near the staircase, while Holly wandered over and browsed through the bookshelves. With her back to Williams, she said, 'So, presumably, you knew what Ambrose was planning, to make us look like fools.'

'I had an idea, yes.'

'So why didn't you tell us?' she asked, rounding on him angrily.

He gave a shrug. 'I'm not the police force's keeper.'

'Ambrose went to a lot of trouble to make us look silly,' Ashworth said.

Williams laughed. 'Mr Ashworth, you are so naïve – sometimes it is so funny. Yes, it's true that Hedley Ambrose is taking a great delight in your discomfort, but that's not the sole reason he went to so much trouble.'

'Well, enlighten little old naive me,' a terse Ashworth said.

'Think about it,' Williams suggested. 'Could the police ever get another warrant for anything connected with him?'

Realisation dawned on Ashworth's face. 'Of course, putting him even further above the law than he was before.'

'Exactly. Well done. But, believe me, he's not finished with you yet. He's going to push the point home, demand a disciplinary hearing, and certain officers …' He glanced at Holly. '… will have to explain why they apparently suffered from flights of fancy.'

Ashworth digested this, and said, 'So what's he after?'

'Getting the Special Unit disbanded. He knows they're watching him, so he wants them removed.'

Opening a drawer in his desk, Williams took out a plain white envelope, and offered it to the chief inspector. 'Here is the name of the person you're looking for. I don't know exactly where he is, but there's information in there that will help you to find him.'

'Bernie, if this is false information …' Ashworth warned, as he took the envelope.

'I don't have to help you make fools of yourselves,' he said, watching Ashworth tear it open. 'You're doing a good enough job on your own.'

Ashworth pulled out a thin slip of paper, bearing a name which meant nothing to him. Returning it to the envelope, he wandered back to the staircase, as Holly said to Williams, 'Are you saying that Ambrose is going to push to have me demoted?'

'That's my guess, yes. You must understand, my dear, that in this cat and mouse game, you are the mouse.'

Holly bristled and Ashworth, knowing the sign too well, said forcefully, 'I think we'd better be going, Holly.'

'Hold on, guv,' she said, 'I've been made to look a first-class prick …'

'I see you don't share Mr Ashworth's eloquent turn of phrase,' Williams commented drily.

'No, I don't,' she said. 'Okay, so you're telling me that shit is pushing to have me disciplined.'

'Correct, and believe me, my dear, he will be successful.'

'Then I think it's about time I started asking a few questions,' she said, crossing to the desk, and leaning over the man. 'How did Ambrose know I was working undercover?'

'He was told.'

'Who told him?'

'There's a member of the Special Unit who's been in Ambrose's back pocket for some time.'

'And do you know who he is?'

Williams, clearly enjoying himself, nodded enthusiastically, but kept silence.

'Then tell us.'

'Oh, no,' he said, shaking his head. 'Because it is also in my interest to have the Special Unit disbanded.'

'I want the name,' Holly demanded.

Ashworth judged that she was getting out of her depth and, fearing that she would go too far, he said again, 'I think we'd better go, Holly.'

'Take your superior's advice,' Williams said

'I could take you in for withholding information,' she yelled, banging the desk top.

Williams simply laughed loudly. 'Don't be a silly girl.'

Holly broke away and lurched towards the bookcases lining the wall. 'I'm getting nowhere, am I?'

'No, and you're not likely to,' Williams said. 'Now, please leave.'

Reaching for one of the bookcases, Holly wrenched it away from the wall, and sent it tumbling to the floor. It crashed on to the carpet, sending books flying across the room.

'Oh dear, look at that, the bookcase has fallen over,' she said, smiling innocently. 'That must have happened when you were resisting arrest. And, look, this is where the struggle took place.'

Williams's mouth hung open, and a horrified Ashworth looked on while Holly stamped wildly on the books, tearing the pages, and kicking them around as they became loose.

Managing to regain his composure, Williams pressed a button on the underside of his desk, and said, 'Mr Ashworth, this is so embarrassing.'

Footsteps immediately sounded on the steel rungs of the staircase, and the two henchmen came running into the room.

'Don, escort the young lady from the premises,' Williams snapped. 'Don't hurt her. I just want her removed.' Holly smiled sweetly as they came towards her.

'Come with me, love,' Don said, grabbing her arm, his fingers digging into her flesh.

The sound of the hard toe of her shoe coming into contact with his shin reverberated around the room. The force of the kick made him cry out in pain, and as he doubled over, Holly head-butted him. With a howl of agony, he went spinning back, hitting the wall beside Ashworth, and holding his nose in an attempt to stem the flow of blood that was pouring on to the front of his shirt.

Before anyone had a chance to recover, Holly aimed a kick in the direction of the second man's testicles. She missed, but caught him on the thigh, and when his head came forward, she knitted her fists together and with a loud grunt of exertion, smashed them into his face, pitching him across the room. He collided heavily with the chair in front of Williams's desk, and fell to the floor, the chair on top of him. He did make a few desperate attempts to get to his feet, but eventually sank back, barely conscious.

Striding across to the desk, Holly grabbed a stunned Williams by the front of his shirt, and hauled him to his feet.

'Give,' she snarled. 'Because you'd better believe I'm up to here with people taking the piss out of me.'

A greyness stole across Williams's face, and he shot a

pleading glance at Ashworth, who was making a great show of studying his fingernails, and resisting the urge to laugh.

Manny Fredricks was expecting a visit from the police. Such was the underworld's grapevine, that none of the Metropolitan Police business escaped detection, and it was now common knowledge that Lenny Spencer was wanted in connection with their enquiries into the murder of Terence Wells; and Manny, after several brushes with the law, was always near the top of the list of interviewees when a wanted man was likely to flee the country.

His house had been cleared of all equipment pertaining to his livelihood as a forger, and he rather regarded this cessation of employment as a holiday.

Lenny Spencer's papers had been safely delivered, and Manny realised he would not be sorry to get the man out of the country and out of his life, for the psychopathic behaviour which had led to Lenny's days on the run had been very much in evidence recently, as he became more and more edgy.

Manny was preparing a cup of hot milk when there was a loud knock on the front door. He sighed heavily.

'Only Johnny Law knocks in such a way, when there is a perfectly good doorbell,' he muttered, making his way along the passage to let them in.

Holly's shoes sounded angrily on the spiral staircase, and Ashworth made no attempt to suppress his laughter as he observed the chaos left in her wake. The two heavies were now on their feet, but still trying to stop the blood flowing from their various injuries. Bernie Williams's face was the colour of chalk, and he was clearly distressed by the sight of the torn books and displaced bookcase.

'I'm going to lodge a complaint about that girl,' he warned Ashworth.

'You're above the law, Bernie,' the chief inspector

reminded him, with a mocking smile. 'You can't just opt back in every time you bite off more than you can chew.'

'I'll mark that girl,' he threatened.

Ashworth, shaking his head as he glanced around the room, said easily, 'I can't really regard that as a serious possibility.' He made his way, still chuckling, to the staircase and, looking back for one last glimpse of the shambles, he descended the stairs, calling, 'I'll be in touch, no doubt.'

He had enjoyed Holly's impulsive, if unlawful, display of anger, but foremost in his mind was grave concern regarding the name of the informant she had so masterfully dragged from Williams.

Police swarming all over the building was not an unusual occurrence, for the tower block where Lenny Spencer had been hiding out boasted more than its fair share of petty criminals, pimps and their prostitutes, and people who would not welcome the close attentions of the DSS fraud officers.

But armed police was another matter.

Although any visit from the law sent shock waves through the building, most of the residents quite rightly knew that their trifling crimes would not bring the armed police down on their heads, and so they became curious. Uniformed officers had to hold them back at the end of the corridor as their armed colleagues, together with two burly detectives, made their way to the flat.

The police marksmen took no chances; in an atmosphere charged with tension, they broke down the door and made a thorough search of the accommodation before the detectives were allowed in. When the exploration was completed, their nervousness was pushed aside by good-humoured banter. One of the marksmen peered out into the corridor, and said, 'Okay, girls, you can go in now, it's safe.'

'Ha, ha,' said Detective Sergeant Rob Willis of the

Metropolitan Police. 'When you grow up, they'll give you bullets for that thing.'

Detective Constable Pete Collins followed him into the flat, saying, 'He's gone then, sarge.'

'Spoken with your usual gift for stating the obvious,' Willis replied. 'Take a look in the bedroom.'

While Collins carried out the order, Willis fished around in the sparse cupboards of the kitchen.

'Sarge,' Collins called.

Willis rushed to the bedroom door, and saw his detective constable bending over an open drawer in the bedside cabinet.

'There's a .38 revolver in here, sarge, and a small plastic skeleton.'

'Right, don't touch anything.'

Willis hurried through the flat to the corridor, and called to the uniformed officers, 'Shift that crowd, even if you have to nick the lot of them, and radio Forensic.'

Ashworth had noticed that whenever Holly was angry, she abandoned any pretence of ladylike behaviour; as they entered Rutley police station, her stride lengthened, and a determined expression marred her attractive features. Indeed, Ashworth was finding it difficult to keep up with her as she marched along to the underground headquarters of the Special Unit.

She made straight for Inspector Derry's office, but found it empty, and moved on to the Operations Room. Flinging open the door, she found George sitting at a table with a thick ham sandwich in his hand.

'Russ Pearson,' she said, in a dull monotone.

The sandwich hovered at George's mouth, and he said, 'You know, don't you?'

'I know,' she confirmed, tartly. 'Where is he?'

'At Ambrose's betting shop. The boys are –'

But Holly was not listening; she was already making her

way back along the corridor. George took a bite from the sandwich, and looked at Ashworth.

'That girl's out of control,' he said. 'You'd better be able to do something about it.'

'I can control my staff, thank you,' Ashworth replied with dignity.

But for all his outward show of confidence, he was beginning to wonder whether that remark was true.

Lenny could smell freedom.

Even as he left the taxi outside the airport, and a gigantic jet took off with a roar over the nearby house tops, a massive sense of relief swept over him.

He had only twenty minutes in which to board the aeroplane which would carry him off to Spain, and so he hurried into the terminal with his single suitcase, and pushed his way through the crowded departure lounge.

It was then that he noticed a man standing at the ticket desk, scanning the crowd. Lenny was wary, and tried to dodge out of sight, but the man spotted him and straight away spoke urgently into a mobile radio.

Dropping the suitcase, Lenny turned around and ran, but there were now two policemen standing by the outer doors, effectively blocking his escape. Panic welled up in his throat, momentarily taking away his breath. What could he do now?

Women screamed and men called out irately, as Lenny pushed a path through them to the ascending escalator, and he was almost there, when a small child stumbled in front of him. Lenny steered to one side, trying to avoid her, but they collided, the child becoming entangled in his legs, causing him to trip and almost fall. The girl was crying as he straightened up and carried on running.

He bounded up the escalator, taking the steps two at a stride, and by the time he reached the top, Lenny was breathless from exertion and fear, but he kept on going, frightened to stop, and came face to face with a policeman wearing a crash helmet.

Turning sharply, Lenny ran back on to the moving stairs, slipping and sliding, his feet keeping up their precarious hold as he attempted to run down; but then more officers came into view below him, and Lenny, giving up the struggle, allowed the escalator to gently lift him to the upper floor, where he found himself staring along the barrel of a gun.

'Armed police, Lenny. Lie on the floor, and spread your arms and legs. Do it, Lenny, now.'

His mind was a mixture of confused terror and relief, and when he saw the man's finger tighten on the trigger, Lenny sank to his knees, and lay flat on his face, while dozens of officers swarmed around him.

Chapter 20

Holly had not spoken one word since they left Rutley police station, and in the Scorpio, she had sat morosely while Ashworth reminded her to fasten the seat belt.

He parked as close as he could to Ambrose's betting shop, and Holly was out of the car and picking her way through the maze of alleys before he had time to lock it. Activating the central locking device on the run, Ashworth hurried to catch up with her.

Turning into the alley in which the betting shop was situated, they caught sight of Russ Pearson, and straight away he held up his hands in surrender at the furious expression on Holly's face.

'I'm sorry, that's all I can say.'

'You put me through all that,' she snarled.

Pearson looked imploringly at Ashworth, and said, 'I couldn't take you into my confidence. Surely you can see that.'

'Yes, I can, son,' Ashworth said.

'How did you find out about me?'

'Bernie Williams mentioned that you were put into the team to find out who was passing information on to Ambrose.'

Pearson turned to Holly. 'When you saw me in the betting shop, I thought I'd blown it. Derry turned up thirty minutes after you'd left to pass on final details of the police plan. If you hadn't volunteered for that mission, Derry would just have walked in and out of the shop that Sunday night. You put a serious spoke in their wheel, believe me. Can you see now why I couldn't tell you what I was doing?'

'Yes,' Holly admitted grudgingly.

'So now will you leave it to us?' Pearson coaxed. 'Derry's in there, collecting his pay-off money.'

'No,' Holly said, her face determined. 'I've got something to settle with that bastard.'

Pearson sighed, and took hold of Ashworth's arm, leading him a few yards away. 'Look,' he said, 'get her away from here. You know Derry was screwing the arse off her, I suppose?'

Ashworth nodded. 'I guessed.'

'My officers are going to stop Derry when he comes out with the money. There is an up side to this: Derry's going to talk, you can take my word for that, and when he does it means we can get Ambrose for something, and he'll have to drop the charges against you. Just get Holly away before she messes the whole operation up.'

'Yes, all right, Russ.'

Holly was still where they had left her, fuming on the spot. 'Why did he do it? Why take money from Ambrose?'

'Because he'd divorced his old lady, and she was screwing him every which way for money,' Pearson told her, as he looked towards Ashworth, motioning for him to get her away.

'Come on, Holly,' he said.

'No, guv. There's something here that needs to be done.'

'There's nothing for you to do here,' Ashworth insisted, taking her arm. 'Now, I said, come on.'

'And I said, no, now just get off.'

She tried to break away, but his hold was tight, and his sheer strength and size were too much for her. She was still struggling and protesting when they reached the end of the alley and turned into a narrow passageway between two buildings. Unceremoniously, Ashworth pushed her on in front of him.

'Look, guv, this has got nothing to do with you,' she said, spinning round to face him.

'It has everything to do with me.'

'This is personal –'

'Holly, I went along with what you did at Bernie Williams's shop, because I could understand why you did it …'

She tried to push past him, but he shoved her back, and said sharply, 'You're going to listen to me, Holly, by God, you are.'

Recoiling, she adopted the classic fighting pose: legs spread wide, hands held high, poised for attack.

'You do, my girl, and it'll be the biggest mistake you've ever made,' he warned her solemnly.

For a few seconds she looked deeply into his angry eyes before averting her gaze and lowering her hands.

'Just leave it,' she shouted, turning her back on him like a petulant child.

'That's what I can't do,' he said, following her along the passageway. 'Your behaviour's getting out of control.'

'Bollocks! Derry's caused me some grief, and I've got a score to settle.'

'You caused yourself grief by jumping into bed with him. When are you ever going to learn?'

She turned to face him then, her pretty features distorted by rage. 'That's none of your business,' she spat.

'On most occasions, it's not, but this time, it is. Stop thinking about yourself for once. If we can nail Ambrose for paying money to a police officer, his case against us collapses.'

'And how would I mess that up?'

'You'd cloud the issue: one police officer attacking another.'

'He's got it coming.'

Ashworth's fragile patience finally snapped; he pointed a finger towards the alley, and yelled, 'Holly, go and sit in my car, and wait for me. Now, that's an order.'

He dug the car keys from his pocket and held them up. 'From now on, you do as I say.'

Holly's face flushed, and she seemed on the verge of

arguing, but then she snatched the keys, and ran past him towards the alleyway. And as her footsteps faded, Ashworth exhaled slowly, releasing his pent-up emotions.

The cell smelt of stale urine and rose-scented pot-pourri; and of the two, Lenny found the pot-pourri the more obnoxious. He was lying on the bed, staring up at the ceiling.

There came to him a jangling of keys outside the door, and he sat up expectantly on the bed. The heavy door creaked open, and a duty officer entered with a mug of tea and a packet of cigarettes.

'Here you go, Lenny,' he said.

'Cheers, mate.'

'I got your smokes in the canteen.'

'Cheers,' Lenny said again, as he tore the cellophane from the packet. 'Do you want one?'

Looking towards the open door, the officer shook his head.

'Better not, eh? I'll get put on a charge if I'm caught.'

Lenny lit a cigarette, and sat with his back against the wall.

'What's going to happen to me now?'

'Tomorrow morning, you'll be taken to Bridgetown in the Midlands. The police there want to talk to you.'

'Yeah, I thought they might,' he said philosophically.

'You all right in here?' the officer asked, on his way to the door.

'Yeah, great.'

The officer mistook the reply for sarcasm, and came back with, 'Well, our main suite was taken, and this was the only one available at such short notice. Sleep tight.'

The steel door slammed shut. Lenny wandered across to the small table, and flicked ash into an empty tobacco tin serving as an ashtray. Then he began to hum softly. For the first time since the murder he felt safe, and was even relishing the thought of a good night's sleep on the lumpy cell mattress.

Back at the car, Ashworth found Holly slouching in the passenger seat and glaring out of the side window, refusing to look at him. All the way to her flat, she remained silent while Ashworth related that Steve Derry had been arrested. The man had resisted initially and, in Ashworth's opinion, his fellow members of the Special Unit had used more than necessary force to subdue him. Hedley Ambrose, he went on to explain, would undoubtedly be charged with attempting to pervert the course of justice.

Bringing the Scorpio to a halt outside the flat, he said, 'Right, I take it I'll see you in the morning.'

'Yes,' she pouted. 'I'll stay here tonight, and go back to Bridgetown first thing. I suppose that's where we'll be based from now on?'

'Yes,' was his curt reply.

'Good,' she said, reaching for the door handle. 'I'll see you, then.'

He watched until she was safely inside and then, searching the radio stations, hoping to find some cheerful music, he started the drive home.

Two more bouquets, each carrying a similar message to the first, were delivered to Reginald Carter's home before he plucked up enough courage to visit Whopples and demand to know the identity of the sender. The staff did try to help, in fact they were most obliging. Yes, they remembered the customer, a tall, thin man, casually dressed, but as he always paid with cash, they had no idea of his name.

From the scant description, however, Carter was certain he knew the identity of the man, and his terror and alarm at that revelation overflowed into an unpleasant scene during which he tartly informed the startled staff that he had no wish to receive any further flowers, and if the man tried to place another order, they were to refuse it.

He left the shop still vulnerable, but feeling better. At least now there would be no more flowers. And no more messages.

Holly poured herself a large gin and tonic the moment she got into the flat, knocked it back quickly and poured another. Carrying it through into the bedroom, she took off her blouse and skirt, and studied her reflection in the dressing-table mirror.

'The trouble with you, Holly, is that your brains are in your knickers.'

Draining the glass, she returned to the kitchen for the gin bottle and a large pair of scissors, and put them in the bathroom. Then, with a determined stride, she fetched Steve Derry's red jacket from her wardrobe.

She sat uneasily on the side of the bath, for the gin was already taking effect, and after a hefty swig from the bottle, she picked up the scissors and attacked the jacket. Systematically, she cut the left sleeve into six-inch strips and threw them one by one down the lavatory bowl, activating the flush every now and again. And when all the pieces were gone, she took another drink, and started on the right sleeve.

Ashworth arrived home feeling tired, but when Sarah passed on the message that Lenny Spencer had been arrested, and would be delivered to Bridgetown by the Metropolitan Police the following morning, his spirits were lifted considerably, and he rang the station immediately to have the details verified. Good, he thought, at last it looked as if a conclusion would be reached on the Terence Wells murder case.

Sarah suggested a walk with the dog, and although it was the last thing he wanted to do, Ashworth agreed. As they trekked across green fields at the rear of their house, a light rain began to fall, strengthening the delicate scent of the grasses. They watched the dog frolicking about, racing after rabbits, and worrying a squirrel, as Ashworth told Sarah about his day, and she tut-tutted throughout the tale of Holly's exploits, as she always did.

'Is the girl that good, Jim?' she asked, with a definite edge to her voice.

'When her mind's on the job, yes.'

They stopped, and in the gathering dusk, Ashworth leant against a fence and took in the view, as he said, 'I just hope this Wells case is straightforward from now on. Josh, through no fault of his own, is not at his most efficient, and Holly will probably be sulking for a week.'

Sarah tutted again. 'I don't know, this preoccupation with sex.'

'She could be moving on. Rutley are about to offer her a job.'

'Really?' she said, trying to sound uninterested.

Sarah would never have dreamed of letting on, but secretly she welcomed the news. Her husband was an attractive, middle-aged man, and although she did not doubt for one minute that he was devoted to her ... well, when confronted by a pretty, shapely girl who was not overly selective in her choice of sexual partners, some middle-aged men were liable to do very silly things in an attempt to recapture their youth.

'Shall we go home and have a drink, dear?' she suggested.

'Ouch, that hurt, you twisting my arm like that,' he joked, with a grin.

They linked hands, and he called, 'Peanuts. Come on, girl, home.'

At the sound of his voice, the dog readily abandoned her attempt to carry part of a tree branch which was twice the size of herself, and trotted after her master with a wagging tail.

Reginald Carter spent the evening in the library at the rear of his house, which was just as well, for had he been looking out of the windows of his lounge, his fragile peace of mind would have been cruelly shattered on seeing the silver car passing by twice within a few minutes, before parking in the next road.

The driver got out of the car, and removed a carrier bag from the boot. He was a tall, thin man with a gaunt face, and his eyes darted nervously from left to right as he started towards Carter's house. Approaching the gates, he was caught in the headlights of a passing vehicle, and he ducked his head swiftly and stood rigid on the spot, but once inside the drive, his nervousness vanished. His tread was stealthy, not for fear of discovery – Carter knew who he was, and would know why he was there – but because he wanted his gift to have the maximum impact.

He slowed as he approached the front door, and removed an object from the carrier bag. He laid it gently on the top step, then crumpled the bag and stuffed it into his pocket as he hurried back towards the road.

Holly had despatched both sleeves and one jacket lapel to the sewers when the bathroom started to spin. One minute the washbasin was fixed firmly to the wall, and the next it was floating, turning over, forever moving.

She looked towards the gin bottle, which was now almost empty, and fell back into the bath, hitting her head against the wall, but safely cushioned against pain by the effects of the alcohol. She tried to rise, but her limbs refused to obey, and she fell back, slurring, 'Goodnight, lover,' and sank into a deep sleep.

Chapter 21

Although he had hardly been away, Ashworth was welcomed back heartily at Bridgetown police station, the next morning. Bridgetown did not welcome change, and as the chief inspector was a familiar figure, his absence for even a short time was met with disapproval. The attention made Ashworth feel good, and with the end of the Wells case hopefully in sight, he was in a bright, cheerful mood by the time he reached the CID office.

Holly, in contrast, felt like hell. Throughout the drive from Rutley, she had tried not to think about the amount of alcohol still in her bloodstream, and had driven carefully, praying that she would not be stopped. And by the time she reached the office, she felt as if she had spent the whole night fighting with Frank Bruno.

'Morning,' Ashworth's voice boomed, as she walked in.

Josh turned to give her a weak smile, and she smiled back, then winced when Ashworth loudly launched into an explanation about Lenny Spencer who was, even now, waiting to be interviewed. She acknowledged the information with a nod of the head, and went to sit with Josh at the computer.

'Hello, lover,' she said, with all the enthusiasm she could muster. 'How's Greg?'

'Dying.' He turned sad grey eyes in her direction, and added, 'He thinks he's getting better, but he's still losing weight, and the antibiotics aren't controlling his chest infection any more,'

'And what about you?'

'Worried to death about the results of the second test.'

Holly felt pure misery sweep over her as she deposited her shoulder bag by her chair, and when Ashworth banged the desk top with the flat of his hand, she felt as if he had hit her on the top of the head with a hammer.

'Right, Holly, let's go and interview Leonard Spencer, shall we? Oh, I forgot to ask how you are this morning.'

'I'm fine,' she said, with a smile which came out as a grimace. And when he disappeared into the corridor, she added quietly, 'Apart from the mother and father of all hangovers, and a sore arse where I fell in the bath.'

Suddenly his head came around the door. 'I was only being polite. I didn't want the sordid details.'

In spite of her delicate condition, Holly laughed and patted Josh's arm. 'From here on, it's just got to get better.'

'Not from where I'm sitting,' he said, with that sullen expression which was fast becoming a permanent fixture on his face.

Reginald Carter could see the milkman strolling along the drive, and he heard the clink of bottles as the man picked up the empties and deposited two full pints in their place. He was about to turn away from the window, when the man did a curious thing: he appeared to be staring closely at something near the front door, and then he backed away, almost losing his footing on the steps in his haste. That familiar unsettling feeling surfaced in Carter but then it subsided slightly when the milkman, almost at the gates, seemed to regain his composure and went on his way, whistling loudly.

Carter hurried into the hall and threw open the front door. On the top step lay a floral cross, made up solely of white lilies, and on one of the arms lay a small black-edged card with a simple handwritten message: 'Have a nice funeral.'

Lenny Spencer was sitting at the interview table under the watchful gaze of a uniformed officer. He was wearing a baggy red sweatshirt and blue jeans, and he seemed totally relaxed. When Ashworth entered with Holly, he smiled at them and lit a cigarette. Holly switched on the tape recorder, gave the required details, and then joined the chief inspector at the table.

'Leonard Spencer,' Ashworth began.

'Lenny. People call me Lenny.'

'Yes, Lenny.' We're investigating the death of Terence Wells on –'

'I killed him,' Lenny interjected confidently. 'I shot him.'

Ashworth cast a quizzical look at Holly, and then said, 'You're admitting that you murdered Terence Wells?'

'Yeah,' Lenny replied, with a shrug. 'No point in me denying it, is there? The London fuzz found the shooter at the place I'd been using. You'll match the bullet to it so, like I said, what's the point in me denying it?'

'Why did you do it?' Ashworth asked.

''Cause the geezer was begging for it,' Lenny said reasonably. 'See, I was a bouncer at the Nite On The Town. Wells used to collect the protection money. He was always swarming about, acting hard – know what I mean? Anyway, we had some trouble there one night: this geezer come at me with a broken bottle, and I had to put him and his mates outside. I thought I'd done pretty good an' all, I mean, there was about half a dozen of them, and I didn't get a mark on me. But Wells started taunting me about it, didn't he? Kept saying how he'd have cleared it up in half the time – stupid prat – and that just got right up my nose. Know what I mean?'

'And that's why you killed him?' Holly probed.

'Yeah, that's right,' Lenny said, smiling. 'See, Wells was always acting hard 'cause he'd got this gang, but on his own he'd have been about as much use as a piece of shit. But I started brooding about it, see, like I always do if I lose face. I've been in trouble with the law before 'cause of my brooding – only GBH though, things like that.'

'Minor offences,' Ashworth suggested, trying not to smile.

'That's right,' Lenny said. 'But you know how it is when you've got form, you've only got to give somebody a couple of slaps, and the law throws the book at you.'

It's an unfair world,' Ashworth sympathised.

'Yeah, ain't it just,' Lenny agreed.

'Tell us about Wells.'

'What?' he said, staring blankly at the chief inspector. 'Oh yeah, got you. Okay, well, I could feel it building inside me, see. I couldn't eat, couldn't sleep, couldn't do nothing, so I took to walking about, brooding, like. Do you know,' he added, in a conversational tone, 'I walked to the nick one night, and the nut-house – I was going in, see, to surrender myself before I did anything.'

'But you didn't go in?'

'No, I bought myself a shooter instead,' he said, completely matter-of-fact. 'And then I found out where the bastard was staying, and then I topped him.'

'Tell us about the night of the murder, Lenny.'

'Okay, well, I was walking about, brooding, like I said, and there was these voices inside my head –'

'No,' Ashworth interrupted, 'tell us about when you got to the house.'

'What? Oh yeah, right. I just went to the house, and broke in.'

'How did you get in, Lenny?' Holly asked. 'Did you break in through the front door?'

'What are you trying to trap me for?' he said, his eyes narrowing. 'I went in through the back door, didn't I? I saw the motor in the garage, and I went along the side passage, and broke in through the back door.'

'And what did you do then?' she queried.

'I went into this room with a table and chairs in it. There was an empty plate on the table, I remember that, like somebody had just finished their dinner. Anyway, there was nobody around, so I was just going to have a poke about upstairs when I heard this snoring coming from the other side of the wall. I thought, funny, 'cause I couldn't see no door, not at first, anyway. It was a funny room, bleedin' depressing, all dark panelling everywhere. Anyway, I found the door – it was one of them concealed things – and I opened it up and there was this room with hundreds of books around the walls. Wells was in a chair, with his back to me, and he was asleep, so I walked round and shot him.'

'Fair enough, Lenny,' Ashworth said. 'You've convinced us you were there.'

'Well, of course I was. I'm admitting it, ain't I?'

'Yes, but when you get a brief you might change your story. You might try to claim we beat the information out of you.'

Ashworth was about to conclude the interview, when Lenny said vehemently, 'No way, I intend to plead guilty, save everybody a lot of trouble.'

'Are you going to try for insanity?' Ashworth asked with a smile as he got to his feet.

'Here, I ain't bleedin' mental,' Lenny protested. 'I'm dangerous, see. I want to be locked away where I can't do no harm to nobody.'

Holly terminated the interview at the tape recorder, and Ashworth prepared to leave. 'Can we get you anything, Lenny?'

'A cup of char wouldn't come amiss.'

'Right,' he said, at the door.

'And perhaps a plate of biscuits?'

Ashworth nodded to the uniformed constable, and made to leave. 'All right.'

'Oh, and a bit of cake, if you've got any.'

'We'll see what we can do,' Ashworth said, closing the door.

In the corridor, he turned to Holly, and laughed. 'If

we'd stayed in there much longer, he would've requested a four course meal.'

'What do you think, guv?'

'He did it. There's no grounds for us to doubt that.'

'But surely an argument couldn't have been sufficient reason?'

'With the best will in the world, he's not the most intelligent of people, is he? The loss of face, the feudal thing, it could easily have preyed on his mind.'

Holly stared up at him. 'But there's something you're not happy about.'

'Yes. I thought he was going to try for insanity. He seems so eager to get himself locked away. Still, as I spend the majority of my life trying to prove guilt, when someone like Lenny comes along with an admission, well, if his story checks out, who am I to look a gift horse in the mouth? Come on, let's get back to the office.'

'Guv,' she called, to his striding figure.

'Yes?'

Keeping her voice low in the bustling corridor, she said, 'I'm sorry.'

'I take it you're referring to the débâcle of yesterday?'

She gave a slight nod of the head, obviously embarrassed.

'Right, with that out of the way, can we forget it? And tell me, what's all this about a sore posterior and a bath?'

'It's a long story, guv,' she laughed. 'And I can't remember most of it.'

'Ah.' He gave her a knowing wink. 'Then I think two paracetamol are called for to put you back on your feet.'

'I wish that's all it would take.'

'Holly,' he said, studying her closely.

'No lectures, guv, please. This time I've learned my lesson. From now on –'

'I'm going to be a good girl,' he finished for her.

She gave him a weak smile. 'This time I mean it.'

'Come on,' he said, taking her arm, and leading her along the corridor. 'Let's get some tea, tablets, and a book on moral behaviour.'

'I should be offended,' she protested mildly.

'You would be, if I wasn't so lovable,' he chortled.

The remainder of the day was spent extracting a formal statement from Lenny, and checking out his story.

Holly and Josh were despatched to the Nite On The Town, and there they gleaned that Terence Wells had indeed visited the club on a number of occasions, but everyone denied that protection money was ever handed over. However, it was agreed by all that Lenny Spencer was mentally unstable, and capable of anything. No one could recall the incident which he had spoken of, but as there had been hostilities between the two men for quite some time, there was little doubt that it had taken place.

All of this seemed to satisfy the thorough Chief Inspector Ashworth, and he was willing to deem the case closed.

Holly gave Josh a lift home, and on the way they bought a Chinese take-away meal for three. Holly was reluctant to spend the evening alone, and had been quick to accept Josh's invitation to dinner.

Greg greeted her sullenly, but she was too shocked by his emaciated appearance to notice. Josh fussed over him constantly like a mother hen, and when they were all seated at the table, nibbling the spare ribs, Josh told him about the arrest and confession of Lenny Spencer.

Greg thought about it for a long time. 'No,' he said, at last, 'it doesn't make any sense.'

'It doesn't fit in with your theory, you mean,' Josh corrected him.

'This Spencer's saying he killed Wells because of a dispute they'd had?'

'Yes,' Holly said. 'And it makes sense when you've met the man, believe me.'

'No,' Greg said stubbornly. 'Oh, does anybody want any wine?'

'Not for me,' Holly said. 'I'm just getting over a hang-over.'

'It's a light white,' he told her charmingly. 'It'll clear your head.'

Holly smiled across at him. 'Oh, go on, then.'

During the evening, they drank four bottles, and despite the fact that they were all complete emotional messes, they enjoyed themselves enormously. Greg played to perfection the part of the Chinese detective, Charlie Chan, and with arms folded, he sat cross-legged on the floor in the lounge, and went through various scenarios to do with the Wells case, with Josh reminding him all the time that the case was closed. And then he had them roaring with laughter, by bending forward and waggling a finger, saying, 'Case far from over, number one son, you mark my word – light?'

The wine was temporarily washing away their troubles, and they made the most of that pleasant interlude, until it was time for Holly to take a taxi home.

Two days later, Lenny was brought before the magistrates and formally remanded into the custody of a local prison to await trial for the murder of Terence Wells. As he was pleading guilty to the charge, the trial would be a swift affair, some time in the near future.

Lenny was born to be institutionalised and he soon settled into a routine at the remand wing. He was sharing a cell with two other prisoners, Jock and Roy, both of whom were awaiting trial for burglaries. On hearing that Lenny was facing a murder charge, they straight away treated him with a touching reverence, and the favoured top bunk was his for the asking.

His first full day on the wing was spent playing table tennis, working out in the gym, watching television, and dwelling on his future plans. After sentence when, hopefully, he would be transferred to a prison far away from the Midlands, he believed that before too long – and if he behaved himself – he would be allowed out on 'away days' – accompanied by a prison officer admittedly, but then, screws weren't such a bad breed; they knew a bloke needed sex.

After an evening meal of shepherd's pie, peas and broad beans – which he voted passable, but not the best prison nosh he had ever tasted – Lenny, returning to his cell, was strolling along the top causeway when he noticed a distinct lack of prison officers, but he thought nothing of it at the time.

He climbed into the top bunk and started to roll a cigarette, oblivious to the noise in the cell until it had ceased. When Roy stopped noisily turning the pages of his book, and when Jock stopped trying to get comfortable in the bunk below, Lenny ran his tongue along the edge of the cigarette paper, and looked up to see a large man standing in the doorway. He was dressed in a white T-shirt and black jeans, and his head was shaven.

Lenny, assuming that his notoriety had spread, grinned and said, 'Want a smoke, mate?'

The man ignored the offer, and said, 'Lenny Spencer?'

'Yeah, that's me.'

'Got a message for you, Lenny.'

There was something about the cold tone in the man's voice which sounded warning bells in Lenny's head, but he tried to appear nonchalant, as he said, 'What's that, then?'

The man pulled a finger across his throat, then pointed it at Lenny. 'You,' he said simply, before turning and walking away. For a few seconds, all was quiet in the cell.

'Who was that?' Lenny spluttered. 'Who the bleedin' hell was that?'

'I didn't see nobody,' Jock said, pushing himself up from the bunk.

'There was a bloke in the doorway. Didn't you see him?'

Lenny waited for a reply, but the two men were all of a sudden sorting busily through their lockers, unwilling to get involved.

'Here, what's going on?' Lenny demanded, swinging his feet off the bunk.

'Them boys run the prison,' Jock whispered. 'The tobacco, the drugs, the booze. If you've got the wrong side of them, you're in a wee spot of bother.'

Returning from the off-licence, Reginald Carter toured the house, as was now his habit, to check all of the doors and windows. Then, satisfied that everything was secure, he went into the library, cradling a bottle of scotch. Making himself comfortable in the leather chair, he removed the cap and placed the bottle on the small table by his side.

On top of everything else, he feared he had caught a summer cold, and he delved into his pocket for a handkerchief, coughed several times to clear his throat, and blew his nose, before pouring himself a liberal measure of the scotch. The drink would do him good, he told himself, and as he drained the glass a terrible tiredness swept over him, and he dropped off to sleep in the chair.

Holly was becoming a regular evening visitor at Josh's house, and her earlier reservations about Greg had melted away for, although he was prone to moods and could sometimes be withdrawn – understandable in the circumstances – he was also very good company, especially after a couple of drinks.

She had several worries though. It was all too obvious that Josh still thought a lot of his friend, a situation which could only lead to heartache, for Greg was now wasting away at a terrifying speed. And the pressure this was putting on Josh, coupled with the strain of waiting for the results of his own Aids test, was affecting his judgement where drink was concerned. But who was she to condemn? Her own alcohol consumption had soared, in the misguided belief that it would dull the pain in the aftermath of her affair with Steve Derry. Still, she had decided that it was time to pull herself together, and that morning she had told herself in no uncertain terms that although she might well be a dick-happy cow, she was not a lush, and did not intend to become one.

Now, as she sat in her car outside Josh's house, she was determined to lay off the booze; and anyway, they both appeared to be out, so she might not get the chance of a drink. Glancing at her watch, she saw that it was nine p.m. and was on the point of driving home when she saw Josh turning the corner and heading towards her. His hands were thrust deep into his pockets, and his shoulders were slumped. As he drew near, Holly got out of the car.

'Hi, lover,' she said, attempting to sound cheerful.

'Holly, I didn't know you were coming round tonight.'

'Just thought I'd pop in and see if you were ready to admit that you do fancy me after all.'

He laughed, but she could see that he was preoccupied.

'Where's Greg?' she asked.

'I don't know.' he told her, slipping his key in the lock. 'He's out. I've just been down to the weir-pool to see if he was there, but no luck.'

'The weir-pool? At this time of night?' She shuddered. 'That's spooky.'

In the kitchen, Josh said, 'He likes to sit there and watch the water cascading down. He says he finds it peaceful.'

Holly pulled out a chair and sat at the table, as Josh opened the fridge door, and said, 'Do you want a drink?'

'Josh, don't you think we're putting too much booze away?'

'Are you trying to tell me I'm drinking too much?'

'No,' she said, defensively. 'But, remember, I've had to take a taxi home for the last three nights.'

'Sorry, Hol, but I need to drink. It's all getting too much for me.'

He decided against a beer and reached instead for the vodka bottle.

'Oh, not the hard stuff, Josh.'

Suddenly he turned on her. '*You*, of all people, are trying to sort *me* out.'

The hurt registered in her eyes as she sat stock still, and then she got up.

'Oh God, I'm sorry, Hol, I didn't mean that.'

'No, it's fair comment, Josh, but I'm only trying to help.'

He half filled a glass with vodka, and topped it up with lime juice. 'I hurt so much,' he said. 'Just about every way I turn, there's hurt.'

Holly said nothing as he took a long drink, and when he had finished, grimacing at the sweet taste of the lime, her heart almost broke in two at the desperate look clouding his eyes.

'I love him, Hol.'

'I know,' she said softly.

'You don't understand,' he said, pouring another vodka. 'I don't want to love him, but I've got no control over it.'

He drank again, and then turned to her. '*He* left *me*, you know. I mean, he was the one messing around, and yet I couldn't bring myself to throw him out. In the end, he got fed up with me and left.'

Tossing back what was left in the glass, he reached again for the bottle, laughing bleakly. 'Do you know what my dad used to call me? The gutless wonder. I can still see him sneering when he said it. All my bloody life, I've been trying to prove it's not true. Do you know what that's like?' He gave her no time to answer, and went on, 'I hate Greg,

213

but I can't stop loving him. I'd still do anything he wanted me to. There was no need for him to stay here, you know. He doesn't give a stuff if he's passed it on to me. He just wants somebody to look after him, and after all he's put me through, I'm still willing to do it. God, that makes me feel so spineless.'

He lifted the glass to his lips again, spilling some of the vodka down his shirt.

'If you love somebody, Josh, you love them, there's nothing you can do about it.'

'I know. You just let them use you over and over and over again.'

He stared down into the glass, and murmured, 'He thinks he's getting better, but he's not, he's dying. The weight's falling off him, his chest's getting worse, and now he's got blue marks all over him.'

Staggering slightly, he waved the glass in Holly's face, and said, 'I'm watching him die, and do you know something? If I found out who'd passed it on to him, I'd kill the bastard.'

'Come on, Josh,' Holly said, taking the glass from his hand. 'I think it's time for bed.'

'I would, Hol, I'd take a knife –'

'Come on,' she repeated firmly, grabbing his arm.

'I'm capable of murder, you know. Over the last few weeks, I've realised that.'

'You're incapable of anything at the moment,' she said, leading him across the room.

'Wait,' he said loudly, stopping dead. 'Reports, I've got some reports for our files.'

'In the morning will do, Josh.'

'No,' he said, 'I always pride myself on doing my job.'

Breaking away from her, Josh wove an erratic path back to the kitchen cabinet, and at the third attempt, he managed to open the drawer and take out three sheets of paper. With a sigh, Holly walked over to him.

'Now,' he said, stabbing a finger at the papers. 'There's some handwritten amendments here, but they're only for our files. Do you understand that, Holly?'

'Yes,' she said patiently.

'Repeat it, then,' he insisted, swaying about and waving a finger at her.

'They're only for our files. Now, come on,' she said, taking his arm.

Chapter 22

The next day was hot and humid; it was the type of weather that made clothing sticky, and tempers short. By early evening the clouds were bubbling and building, and distant rolls of thunder echoed across the skies. Darkness fell prematurely as banks of black angry cloud obscured the sun, and for at least an hour a strange brooding silence prevailed over the streets of Bridgetown, with all residents unwilling to leave their homes for fear of the approaching storm.

Just when it seemed that the oxygen in the atmosphere was almost exhausted, the storm broke, starting with a bolt of forked lightning snaking from the heavens, and followed seconds later by thunder rolling across the sky. Rain began to fall heavily, large drops that pitter-pattered on the pavements.

The storm moved closer. More forked lightning illuminated the landscape, and sheet lightning lit up the sky, while thunder cracked overhead in a crescendo of sound and light. Torrential rain lashed the town, swiftly filling the gutters with water, ankle-deep.

At its height, the sound of the storm covered the quiet tinkling of breaking glass. A gloved hand stole through the shattered pane and felt around for the bolt securing the door. It slid back easily, and the door swung open, as a flash of lightning brought temporary daylight to the gardens and interior of Reginald Carter's house in Lilac Avenue. The intruder's shoes squelched, and his breath rasped, as he crossed the threshold.

Lenny was lying on his bunk when the storm broke, and it made a small part of him yearn for freedom, the freedom he had lost due to the incident at the large house in Lilac

Avenue. But he consoled himself with the thought of three good meals a day, and everything found for him for at least fifteen years.

The prison had been tense all day long. When hundreds of men, deprived of their liberty, are crammed into crowded cells in stifling hot conditions, it brings about a powder-keg atmosphere to the establishment, and most of the staff were breathing sighs of relief when cooler air followed in the wake of the storm.

Lenny was still perplexed by the threats being made to his health by the prison barons, and the only reason that came to mind was that he had joined the big league on a murder charge and, seeing him as some sort of threat, they wanted to warn him off. In view of this, he had decided to keep his head down, and stay out of bother; he didn't want trouble with anybody.

It was four o'clock the following afternoon before some of more curious residents in Lilac Avenue noticed that the two pints of milk, delivered that morning, were still on the step at number twenty-five; and although aware of the dwelling's recent violent history, they chose to assume that the owner had, once again, gone away on business and forgotten to cancel the milk. So no action was taken until the next morning.

It was the milkman who raised the alarm. After checking that the car was in the garage, he peered through the downstairs windows, and found nothing amiss, but nevertheless decided to risk appearing foolish, and set off back to his milk float with the intention of telephoning the police. He was returning the bottles intended for number twenty-five to one of the crates when a panda car went by, and he stepped out into the road and waved his arms wildly to attract the driver's attention.

Police Constable Alan Bennett listened to his story, all the while picturing his wife waiting for him to take their

217

boy to school. Determined to use another route home in future, he reached for his radio.

Josh was becoming more withdrawn and sullen with each passing hour. Ashworth had thought of offering the man leave, but decided against it. Instead, he avoided giving him duties which could be in any way taxing, and left him to himself.

Holly, back on home territory, and attracting more than her fair share of wolf whistles, now realised that she had mistaken a bruised ego for a broken heart, and even that, when closely examined, was in no way a disaster. Steve Derry might be every kind of louse, but he had gone to bed with her because he wanted to, rather than for any ulterior motive. It was small consolation, but it helped her to feel better about herself.

Ashworth was in reception, talking to Martin Dutton, when the call came through. Dutton replaced the receiver, and said, 'That was Central Control, Jim. They didn't know whether to alert us, or go to you.'

'What is it?' Ashworth asked.

'Carter's house in Lilac Avenue. The milk wasn't taken in yesterday, so the milkman reported it to us. Gordon Bennett's found a broken pane of glass in the back door again.'

'I'll take it,' Ashworth said, already moving away.

Dutton called after him, 'Jim, Gordon's got to get his lad to school. That wife of his gives him a hell of a time if he's late home.'

'Get a relief there, then.'

'It's not Gordon's fault, you know,' Dutton said, chuckling. 'He didn't realise happiness ended at the wedding reception.'

'You're a cynic, Martin,' Ashworth called, from the stairs.

'You show me a married man who isn't.'

Ashworth strode into CID, and said, 'Are you ready, Holly?'

She looked up at him, and grinned. 'You betcha, guv. What have you got in mind?'

He gave her a sideways glance which was not without humour, and then told her about the call from Reginald Carter's home.

Jumping to her feet, she grabbed her shoulder bag, and followed him out. All through this, Josh kept his gaze fixed on the computer screen, failing to acknowledge Ashworth's arrival, or his departure.

'Is that lad all right?' he asked Holly, as they headed for the stairs. 'I'm wondering if I should offer him leave.'

'He's going to need it soon. He reckons Greg's entering the final stages of his illness. Anyway, now I'm back, leave it with me, eh?'

'Yes, all right. I must say, you seem to be back to your old self.'

She sighed, and said, 'I'm beginning to realise that in life, guv, you've got to learn to roll with the punches, or you get your head bashed in.'

'Not how I would've put it, but I agree with the sentiment,' he said, as they left the station.

Lenny stumbled out of the shower, with one hand holding a towel around his middle, and the other pushing wet hair from his eyes. The room housed a row of six showers, open to view, and six lavatory cubicles. There was a urinal along one wall, and a wooden bench along another.

As Lenny sat on the bench, and lit a cigarette he had rolled earlier, the swing doors at the far end of the room burst open, and two prisoners walked in and stood either side of them.

'All right?' he called.

The way in which they laughed sent a chill running down Lenny's spine, and he got to his feet, quickly flicking

219

the cigarette into the urinal where it spluttered and died. Then, picking up his clothes, he made for the doors, but the two men blocked his way.

'Look, I don't want no trouble, see,' he said, feeling vulnerable and open to attack, with one hand cradling the clothes, and the other holding up the towel.

The man on his left – an evil-looking northerner – stepped forward.

'That's good, because there's some people who want to have a chat with you. Now, go and sit down,' he said, pointing to the bench.

Lenny obeyed meekly, and five long minutes passed before the doors opened again, this time letting in six men. Straight away, he spotted the large, shaven-headed man who had threatened him in his cell, and his bowels started up an uncomfortable rumble. They all stayed near the doors, and parted to make a path for an older man who was the last to enter. He was diminutive, his dull grey prison clothes too large, and he studied Lenny with gimlet blue eyes.

'Lenny,' he said, 'I'm Baz.'

'Look, mate, I don't want no trouble, honest. I'm just after a quiet life.'

'Thank God for that,' Baz said, laughing benignly, as he sat down. 'I've been dreading this, because I thought there might be some unpleasantness.'

The men by the doors guffawed, and Lenny looked on in confusion.

'Let me explain,' Baz began. 'We're a little upset about Terry Wells's demise, as they say.'

'Oh yeah?' Lenny said, the blood draining from his face.

'So what we want is a bit of information from you.'

'But I don't know nothing.'

'You disappoint me, Lenny. Now, I'm going to give you time to think it over, and when we meet again …'

'Tell me what you want to know, and I'll rack me brains, like.'

'You'll remember,' Baz assured him. 'I have complete faith in you.'

He stood up, and headed for the door with Lenny following behind, still clutching the towel, and saying, 'Look, let me walk along the corridor with you – yeah? Then you can give me some idea of what you want to know.'

'You'll come up with the answers, Lenny. As I said, I have complete faith in you.'

Lenny licked his dry lips as he watched the men part to allow Baz through, and then close ranks again.

'Look, mates, I'll tell you anything you want, right? I mean, there ain't no need for this.'

But they advanced on him, a circle of mocking faces, and he backed away, allowing the towel to drop to the floor. One of the men kicked it aside, as his back touched the warm condensation-soaked wall.

With all escape routes now blocked, Lenny – no stranger to fisticuffs – launched into attack, and he saw several smiles vanish as his fists crashed into flesh, but sheer weight of numbers inevitably overcame him. A galaxy of colours exploded before his eyes, and he slumped to the ground, where hard toe-caps sank into his body. And as blows rained upon him from all angles, sounds became distant, the smell of the urinal began to fade. Finally, the beating ended, and footsteps sounded around his head.

'You slipped in the shower, Lenny, remember that,' a voice seemed to call from the far distance.

'You bastards have done my bleedin' ribs,' Lenny complained through swollen lips.

'You slipped, Lenny,' the man said, aiming another vicious kick to his side.

'Okay, I slipped,' Lenny whimpered, writhing in agony.

He heard them shuffling towards the door, and rolled on to his back, gagging as blood trickled down his throat. And then everything faded away into a soothing blackness.

'We meet again, Gordon,' Ashworth called. 'Same time, same place.'

The young constable was staring at the house, and contemplating the prospect of another row with his wife, when Ashworth and Holly made their silent approach.

'Same as before, sir, break-in round the back.'

'Right, off you go, then. You're supposed to be off duty.'

'I should stay, sir.'

'You reported it in, we're attending. He looked towards the road, and said, 'Bobby Adams is here somewhere. Now, off you go. There's nothing more important than your marriage, son.'

'Thanks, sir,' Bennett said, smiling gratefully.

He started along the drive, and by the time he was passing Bobby Adams on the way up, Bennett had broken into a trot. Bobby came striding towards the chief inspector.

'Sorry I'm late, sir, I was just reassuring members of the public who were worried about such a large police presence in the avenue.

'Good man.'

Ashworth looked towards the house, and was wondering what horrors they might find behind its elegant façade, when Bobby announced, 'The break-in's round the back, sir.'

'Lead on then, Bobby,' he said, suppressing a smile.

They found that the rear garden had been badly neglected since their last visit: the grass was long, almost top-heavy with seed as it swayed in the wind, and crawling weeds snaked across the borders.

The kitchen door was open, and Ashworth led them towards it. Across the threshold, various sounds and smells came to him in the oppressive silence. He could hear

Chapter 23

Six stitches were needed in a cut above Lenny's right eye, and after these were inserted, the doctor carried out a thorough examination. His ribs were not broken, merely bruised severely, to match the rest of his body.

'You're okay, Lenny, no permanent damage,' the doctor said. 'It's lucky you're strong though. A beating like that could easily have killed you.'

'I slipped in the shower,' Lenny said, easing himself slowly to a sitting position on the couch. 'I told you, didn't I?'

The doctor cast him a suspicious glance. 'You don't get injuries like that slipping in the shower.'

'I got up, and then I fell down again.'

'Lenny, I'll have to report this to the Governor, but if you're not willing to say who did it, then no one can help you.'

'Come on, doc, talk some sense,' Lenny protested, fingering his rapidly closing eye. 'You know what it's like in here. If I grass on who did this, I'll be in more bother than I am now.'

The doctor shrugged resignedly. 'Is there anything I can do for you?'

'Yeah, keep me in hospital, out of harm's way.'

'It's quiet at the moment, so I suppose I could keep you in a few days for observation. It's not the answer though, is it?'

'Look, doc, I'm just thinking one day at a time – all right?'

'Okay, Lenny. Is there anything else?'

'I wouldn't mind a nice little nurse,' he said, trying to grin.

'You're beyond hope,' the doctor laughed, as he pulled

aside the curtain, and left the cubicle.

'Yeah, ain't I?'

Lenny winced as he climbed off the couch, muttering, 'You bastards, I'll have you one at a bleedin' time, I swear to God, I will.'

When he tried to stand, he doubled over in pain, and slumped into the wooden chair by the side of the couch.

'I don't know,' he moaned, 'I came in here to get away from them geezers.'

'The police surgeon pronounced him dead, did he? It must have been a close decision,' the pathologist, Alex Ferguson, joked, as he viewed the mutilated remains of Reginald Carter.

Ashworth did not share Ferguson's macabre sense of humour, and wanted to look away from the corpse, but found his eyes riveted to the multiple injuries decorating the man's flesh. Carter had been in bed at the time of the attack, and the whole of his naked torso was covered with gaping stab wounds; dried blood covered the bed, its white satin sheets drenched, and some of it had even jetted up to stain the ceiling.

'A small plastic skeleton was found on the body, I believe,' Ferguson said.

'That's right.' Ashworth held up a sealed plastic bag containing the item.

'How weird.'

The pathologist looked into the chief inspector's face, and said, with a fleeting smile, 'Is it the light in here, or are you green?'

Ashworth turned away from him, and his eye was caught by Holly, who was indicating her queasy state with a mimed retch, and inclining her head towards the landing.

'We'll leave you to it,' he said to Ferguson.

'Yes, all right. I should have something for you in about half an hour.'

Outside the room, the forensic team were coming and going in a flurry of activity, and Ashworth manoeuvred Holly around them as they descended the stairs.

'What is it with Ferguson?' she complained. 'He's usually so serious, but show him a dead body, and he comes to life.'

'How do you feel?' Ashworth asked.

'Really sick.'

'Me too. Shall we get some fresh air in the garden?'

On the way out, they met the police photographer, and after directing him to the scene of crime, they stepped out into the bright sunshine.

'What do you think, guv?'

'It was a particularly violent attack.'

'Yes, I'd say somebody didn't like Reginald Carter very much.'

'Revenge,' Ashworth said quietly.

'Revenge?'

'A very frenzied I'll-get-even-with-you attack.'

'Then we're looking for Brian Wells, aren't we? He must think his brother was murdered by Carter.'

'Or that Carter had his brother killed.'

'By Lenny Spencer, you mean?'

'That's my belief, yes. If you look at Lenny's record, he's a real hard case. He wouldn't normally admit to anything, but he was too quick to hold up his hands for the Wells killing. I believe he wanted to get out of circulation before Terry Well's friends caught up with him.'

'But what would Carter have gained by having Wells killed?'

'Nothing. I don't think Carter was involved. Think about it, Holly. Who, in all of this, has gained by effectively wiping out the Carter gang?'

'Bernie Williams,' she whispered.

'Exactly. Bernie had Terry Wells killed, which led to the collapse of Carter's empire. Don't forget, he gave us the name of the killer. And then he fed into Brian Wells's mind that Carter had killed his brother. Hence the chaos in there.' He jerked his thumb towards the house.

'Clever,' Holly remarked. 'Making sure that whatever happened, the Carter gang couldn't re-emerge.'

'That's only half of it. Who actually plotted Hedley Ambrose's downfall? Bernie Williams. It was he who told us that an officer was taking money from Ambrose. All right, I know you used a little gentle persuasion, but I think he would have told us sooner or later that Russ Pearson had been put in there to investigate it. Williams knew that, even if we went through the usual channels, we would've found out about Derry in the end, but he wanted things speeded up.'

'So he could take over the whole city?'

'That's how it looks to me. Whatever Ambrose is charged with, his activities are out in the open now, and every time he puts a foot wrong, the Rutley police will be able to jump on him.' Ashworth scowled. 'Mr Williams has been using us, I fear, and that makes me very angry.'

Further discussion was curtailed by Alex Ferguson, breezing his way through the back door.

'I'll give you what I've got. Cause of death, stab wounds,' he said needlessly. 'It looks like Carter was asleep, with just a single sheet covering him. The first two wounds were the fatal ones, straight through the heart. Then the sheet was thrown back, and the fun really started. I counted thirty-three stab wounds in all, to the chest, stomach, shoulders, and throat. The killer must have been getting tired towards the end – the wounds to the neck are quite shallow.'

Ashworth shuddered, and asked, 'Time of death?'

'About nine o'clock, on the night of the thunderstorm.'

'So Carter was in bed and asleep at nine?' Holly said. 'Isn't that a bit on the early side, especially during a violent storm?'

'Maybe the man was tired,' Ferguson shrugged. 'I did

find signs of what could be cancer, and that might explain it. I'll have to look into it, of course, and it'll probably take time, but I can't see it having any bearing on the case.'

'And that's it?' Ashworth said.

'More or less, for the moment. Forensic have come up with something: it seems the killer took a bath.'

'A bath?' Ashworth echoed.

'Yes, fully clothed, they think. He would have been covered in blood, obviously, so they reckon he hopped into the bath to clean himself up.'

'And afterwards, the fact that he was soaked to the skin wouldn't draw attention, because we had two hours of torrential rain. Leaving him time to get clear, and then dispose of his clothing,' Ashworth concluded.

'That's my guess.' Ferguson was suddenly serious. 'Jim, find this man quickly. He's very dangerous.'

'We've a good idea who he is, but we need to get the man who put him up to it.' And then, almost to himself, Ashworth added, 'Because Bernie Williams is as guilty of these two murders as the men who carried them out.'

'I'll leave you to it then. I'll let you have the reports as soon as I can.'

They walked with him along the side entrance, where they said their goodbyes.

'What now, guv?'

'A visit to Bernie Williams, I think.'

Dr Ferguson was pushing his way through the crowds lining the pavement outside the iron gates, when Ashworth and Holly headed the same way. Bobby Adams was doing a good job in keeping the onlookers off the drive. Most of them were neighbours who stood aside obligingly as Bobby cleared a path for the two detectives.

'Thank you, constable,' Ashworth said, as he unlocked the door to the Scorpio.

'Thank you, sir,' Bobby replied, standing to attention.

They were strapping on their seat belts, when Holly

said, 'If we find Brian Wells, guv, he's likely to have a cast-iron alibi.'

'I know, and even if we break that, we're going to have a devil of a job implicating Bernie Williams in the murder.' He shook his head, and sighed despairingly. 'He's the one we want, Holly. He orchestrated the whole thing, I just know it.'

As Ashworth started up the engine, he glanced back at the crowd.

'He's a good lad, that Bobby Adams. There's a lot more to him than most people think.'

Bernie Williams was not pleased to see them, and his expression was sour when they emerged, unannounced, at the top of the spiral staircase.

'You're no longer welcome here, Mr Ashworth,' he said.

'We're not looking for a welcome, Bernie, just some information,' Ashworth told him, as he stopped just short of the desk.

Holly remained by the door, and Williams flicked a look of disdain in her direction, before saying to the chief inspector, 'I have no information to give you.'

'Reginald Carter is dead,' Ashworth pronounced, watching the man closely for signs of shock. And when his face betrayed nothing, he said, 'You don't seem very surprised, Bernie.'

Williams merely shrugged.

'I'll have you,' Ashworth promised, with a snarl.

'For what?'

'I believe you had Terry Wells killed,' Ashworth said, learning across the desk. 'And then you planted the seed in his brother's mind that Carter had done it. You shopped Hedley Ambrose every which way, and now you've got a chance to take over the whole city.'

'Good theory,' Williams said, with a tight smile, 'but do you have any proof?'

The smile slipped from his face when he saw Holly dart

towards the desk, saying, 'We'll get it, don't worry.'

'We want Brian Wells's address … now,' Ashworth ordered.

'With pleasure,' he said, picking up a pen and a piece of paper. 'I'm always ready to help the police.'

He handed it across, saying, 'I don't know if he'll be there, but that's the last address I've got for him.'

'I'm going to put you behind bars, Bernie,' Ashworth said. 'You'll do time, I promise you.'

Williams maintained his look of injured innocence until they were out of sight, and when the shop bell signalled their exit, he smiled.

'What can you do to me, Mr Ashworth? I just stood and watched it happen … and helped it along in places.'

He snatched up the telephone receiver, and tapped out a number. 'Come on, come on …'

The connection was made. 'Ah, Brian, it's Bernie. The police are looking for you.'

He listened to the reply, then said quickly, 'No, don't try to leave the city. They'll be expecting that. I've given them your old address, so it should take them some time to find you. Now, if you could get a watertight alibi, it might be wise to let them catch up with you. After all, what can they prove?'

Bridgetown CID was a hive of activity. Holly was on the telephone to Special Unit – now headed by Russ Pearson until a suitable replacement for Steve Derry could be found – requesting that they apprehend Brian Wells. Josh had asked for an interview with Ashworth, and the moment she finished the call, Holly diplomatically left the office.

Josh pulled up a chair in front of Ashworth's desk, and sat fidgeting with his hands, ill at ease.

'I'd like to request some leave, guv,' he said.

'Request granted. This is to do with Greg, I take it?'

'Yes, guv, you see, in the last couple of days, his condition's worsened. I think he's losing his will to live.'

'I see. Josh, I can only say, I'm sorry. I know that sounds lame, but –'

'He's spending most of his time sitting by the weir. I'm really worried he's going to throw himself into the river.'

'Take as long as you need.'

'I don't think I'll need long,' Josh said, his eyes misting over. 'Perhaps a couple of weeks.'

'Do you want to go home now, son?'

Josh nodded. 'Yes, please. I'm sorry to leave you like this, guv, with the investigation just hotting up.'

'Don't think about it,' Ashworth told him.

Without another word, Josh collected his jacket, gave the chief inspector a wan smile and left the office.

Ashworth was giving considerable thought to the predicament in which he now found himself. The conclusion of an investigation was not the time to lose one of his team, and with Holly likely to be needed at Rutley again, his position would become impossible.

Holly bumped into Josh in the corridor, and sympathised when he told her what was happening.

'Look, I'll pop round tonight,' she said.

'No, don't, please. It's not going to be long now, and it's something I've got to face alone.'

He walked away without looking back, and she longed to run after him, to offer him some support but instead, when he disappeared down the stairs, she continued on to the office.

'Special Unit have been on the phone,' Ashworth informed her. 'They've had no luck with Brian Wells at the address Williams gave us. He hasn't been there for a couple of weeks.'

She digested the news, and then said, 'I've just seen Josh, and he explained about his leave. He's really cut up, isn't he?'

'Yes, but there's nothing we can do, and I think he'd resent us trying to interfere.'

Ashworth sat back in his chair. 'I've got a proposition to put to you, Holly.'

'Oh, really?' she said, flashing her cheeky grin. 'Go on, then.'

When she was leaving, fifteen minutes later, she paused in the doorway, and said, 'Are you sure about this?'

'Trust me,' he told her.

Holly was popular with the uniformed police officers. She was quite capable of taking a joke and, unlike some of her female colleagues, did not claim sexual harassment every time a blatant sexual innuendo was cast in her direction. She was also capable of holding her own, giving as good as she got, in any banter of an intimate nature.

When she pushed open the swing doors to the canteen, she saw half a dozen uniformed constables sharing a table, drinking tea and eating cakes. At the far end of the room, she could see Bobby Adams sitting alone, reading a book.

She was starting towards him, when one of the officers called her name, and she turned to see Scott Jacobs – a young police constable, who fancied himself as a gift from on high for all women – gesticulating for her to join them.

As she weaved her way between the tables, he said, with a wide grin, 'We've raffled you off, Holly.'

'I haven't got time to play, boys,' she said. 'Some of us have got work to do.'

'No, really,' Jacobs persisted. 'I've got the winning ticket. Now, what would you say to a night of passion with a man who was born to give women pleasure?'

'Well, I suppose my initial reaction would be to say, shove it.'

The group jeered, and beat their hands on the table.

'Think about it,' Scott called after her.

'Do you mind? I've just eaten,' she retorted.

Holly ignored the catcalls and juvenile laughter, and approached Bobby Adams's table.

'Hi, Bobby,' she smiled.

'Oh … hello.'

He started to get to his feet, but Holly said, 'Sit down, I want to have a word with you.'

'All right.'

He closed his book, and blushed when he caught her trying to read its title. 'It's poetry,' he explained. 'I like reading it.'

She smiled again, and sat down. 'Look, Bobby, the guv'nor asked me to have a word with you.'

'I didn't do anything wrong at the scene of crime, did I?' he asked, alarmed.

No, it's nothing like that. Josh Abraham has had to take some leave. He's got family problems. Anyway, there's a temporary post in CID, and the guv'nor wonders if you'd like it.'

'Me? Are you pulling my leg?'

His eyes strayed to the table occupied by his more outgoing colleagues, and he briefly wondered if they were behind this.

Holly followed his eyes, and his train of thought, and said, 'No, honestly, this comes from Jim Ashworth. He'd like to give you a try.'

'But I always thought he regarded me as an idiot.'

'What makes you think that? He's quite impressed with you. It'll be good experience, you know, look good on your record.' Bobby stared into his cup of tea, and said, 'All right, then.'

'Good. Turn up tomorrow morning in your best suit.' She held out her hand. 'Welcome aboard, Detective Constable Adams.'

He grabbed it, and laughed. 'Thanks.'

Chapter 24

Nothing happened until four thirty. Ashworth was out of the office at the time, so Holly took the call.

At five o'clock, when Ashworth sauntered in with a bored expression which told of an uneventful afternoon, she said, 'Special Unit have detained Brian Wells, guv.'

'Oh, good. With a bit of luck, we could have this wrapped up today.'

He glanced at his watch. 'You're not looking for an early night, are you?'

She shook her head.

'Right,' he said, settling behind his desk, and reaching for the telephone. 'Get Special Unit to bring Wells to us. Oh, did they search where he was staying?'

'I think so, guv. Russ Pearson phoned me as soon as they'd picked him up, but I think it's safe to assume that they know what they're doing.'

Ashworth did not share her faith in the Special Unit team, but he bit back any cutting remarks, and said, 'I'll get on to Forensic, and see if they've come up with anything.'

When Josh arrived home, he found Greg missing. After a frantic search across Bridgetown, he made his third visit to the weir-pool, and at last found him sitting at the water's edge, staring into its muddy depths.

Josh approached him carefully, well aware of his violent mood swings of the last few days. The storm had filled the river to its capacity, and water was tumbling over the weir in a frothing mass of foam which eddied as it hit the pool, before snaking away along the flood relief channel.

'Come home, Greg,' Josh shouted above the roar of the water.

Greg turned his face, which was now so haggard, he appeared to have aged twenty years in as many days.

'I'm watching the water,' he said, a distant look in his eyes, 'and wondering how far a body could travel before it's discovered.'

'Come home,' Josh implored. 'I've taken some leave, so I can look after you.'

Greg got to his feet with little effort for, surprisingly, he still had his strength.

'I read in the early evening paper about Carter's death,' he said.

'Let's go,' Josh urged, taking his arm.

They began to walk, the spray from the falling water making the air chill and damp.

Josh shivered.

It was six o'clock before Russ Pearson, together with another member of the Special Unit, delivered Brian Wells to Bridgetown police station. Ashworth waited with Holly on the back steps, and watched the white Orion pull into the car-park.

A smiling Pearson emerged from the driver's seat, and waved to them before opening the rear door of the car to let out his colleague and Brian Wells, who was a tall, gaunt man, in his fifties, and dressed in a stylish blue blazer and grey trousers. He straightened up and looked towards the building, as the two officers escorted him to the steps.

'This is Brian Wells,' Pearson announced.

Ashworth nodded to the man. 'I'm Chief Inspector Ashworth, and this is Detective Sergeant Bedford.'

Wells seemed uninterested, and all that showed on his thin face was contempt.

'Can we get this over with? I've things to do,' he said.

Ashworth signalled to a uniformed officer waiting by the doors.

'Take Mr Wells to interview room number one,' he ordered.

'Yes, sir.'

The officer stepped forward, and placed his hand lightly on Wells's arm.

'Take it off,' he warned, with a sneer. 'All of you had better believe I'm here of my own free will.'

Ashworth quickly intervened. 'Of course you are, sir. Now, if you'd like to follow the officer, I'll be along in a moment.'

They watched the man being led through the double doors, all the while uttering indistinct grumblings at the patient police constable. 'He's a nasty piece of work,' Ashworth commented.

'That's one way of putting it,' Pearson replied. 'I've got all the information for you.'

'Give it to Holly,' he said, starting up the steps.

'Chance would be a fine thing,' Pearson quipped.

Holly laughed. 'Okay, what have you got?'

'Not much,' he had to admit. 'Which is precisely what I expect you'll get out of Wells.'

'I'm not following.'

'We found him too easily. With his contacts he could have dropped out of sight for months. You can see what his attitude's like, and yet he didn't give us any trouble. In fact, he invited us in to search his flat without a warrant.'

'Perhaps he's got nothing to hide.'

Pearson gave a biting laugh. 'Do you know what that man's record's like? He's fifty-eight years old, and has one conviction for stealing a hundred cigarettes, forty years ago. Since then, he's made his living from crime. Take my word for it, that man's got a lot to hide.'

'Did the search come up with anything?'

'No. We took some things away: dirty glasses, ashtrays; we're keen to know who was there. Wells didn't protest, he gave us his permission without a fuss, but we didn't find a knife, or any suspect clothing.'

'Right, I'd better get in to my guv'nor,' Holly said, making for the doors.

'Keep in touch, eh?'

'Will do,' she called back.

Ashworth was waiting for her in the interview room, pacing the floor, while Brian Wells sat at the table watching him and toying impatiently with a cigarette lighter.

When she came in, the uniformed officer retired discreetly to the side of the door, and Ashworth cleared his throat.

'This is not a formal interview, Mr Wells,' he said, pulling out a chair to sit facing the man.

'Then what am I doing here? And what's Maigret doing on the door?'

'Don't you know why you're here?'

'No. Tell me.'

'Did you know that Reginald Carter has been found murdered?'

'Yes,' Wells said, holding Ashworth's gaze.

'But I don't suppose you know anything about it?' he asked, with heavy sarcasm.

Wells lit a cigarette, and blew smoke towards the ceiling. 'I know a lot about it.'

Holly gave Ashworth a surprised look as she joined him at the table, her chair scraping noisily on the floor.

'Would you like to tell us what you know?' she asked.

He looked at them all, and said quietly, 'I think I know why you want me to do that.'

'Yes?' Holly said expectantly.

Wells put out his cigarette, and paused. 'It's because you can't read,' he said, grinning broadly. 'It's in all the news-papers. That's where I got my information from.'

Ashworth let out a sound of exasperation, but when he spoke, his voice was normal. 'Very droll, sir. Now, I'll ask

237

you directly: Do you know anything about Carter's death?'

'Hardly knew the man.'

'Your brother was found dead at his house,' Ashworth reminded him.

'Terry's death cut me up at the time, but I'm over it now.'

'Where were you on the night of Carter's murder?'

'That was two nights ago?' He frowned, and thought for a while, then finally said, 'Don't know.'

This time, Ashworth's irritation manifested itself, and he banged hard on the table.

'Temper, temper,' Wells said, with a mocking smile. 'I don't know where I was, I have a busy social life.'

'It was the night of the storm,' Ashworth pressed. 'You must remember where you were then.'

'It wasn't as bad in Rutley,' Wells countered, 'and that's where I was.'

'You can't prove you weren't at Carter's house that night, can you?' Holly interjected.

Wells viewed her with total disdain. 'I don't have to prove I wasn't there. You have to prove I was.'

Ashworth sat back, and viewed Wells's grinning face through narrowed eyes. He said, 'I think you murdered Reginald Carter because you believed he had your brother killed.'

'I thought you'd got someone for Terry's murder – a toe rag named Lenny Spencer,' he said, his expression unchanged.

'But who paid Lenny Spencer?' Ashworth asked, trying a shot in the dark.

Wells shrugged. 'Ask him.'

'I've got enough to hold you on overnight.'

'Hold me then,' he said, yawning widely.

Ashworth managed to control his anger as he stood up and left the room, but when Holly followed him into the corridor, he struck the wall forcefully with the flat of his hand.

'What's happening?' he asked, rounding on her. 'We haven't got enough to hold him on, and he knows it.'

'Calm down, guv,' she said, in that matter-of-fact tone she had developed to deal with his tantrums. 'It is strange, though. If he got a brief in here, he could just walk out.'

'And yet he hasn't asked for one,' Ashworth said, pacing the corridor. 'Why?'

'He can't explain where he was, guv.'

'But then, like he said, he doesn't have to.'

'Look, guv, we're used to dealing with ordinary criminals, there's something here we don't understand. I'd like to ring Rutley, maybe Russ Pearson could put us wise.'

Back in the office, Holly dialled the number for Rutley police station, and requested to speak to Russ Pearson. He took some time to get to the telephone, and Holly's voice betrayed her irritation as she explained what had happened during the interview. She listened intently to his long-winded reply, and then replaced the receiver, smiling broadly.

'Well?' Ashworth asked.

'Russ said there's one thing we can be certain of: Wells is hiding something.'

'We'd already guessed that,' Ashworth said, perching on the edge of the desk. 'What else did he say?'

'He made a couple of remarks about us being country hicks, and not knowing how to deal with these people –'

'Holly, can we get on with it, please?'

'Hold on, guv, this is all relevant. Wells isn't saying anything, because he wants to know how much we've got first. Russ said criminals like Wells are masters at getting information, without the interviewers even realising they're giving it – forensic, the lot.'

'So, we were right, he is hiding something,' Ashworth muttered to himself.

'If we haven't got anything, then tomorrow we'll just

have to let him go. But Russ says, if we make it look like there's the slightest chance we could send the case to the CPS, then Wells'll come up with a cast-iron alibi, and if it's a weak case to start with –'

'It'll collapse,' Ashworth concluded.

'Exactly. That's how these criminals operate.'

'But why doesn't he just come up with his alibi? If we couldn't break it, then a good brief would have him out of here in minutes.'

'Because for his alibi to count for anything, it has to be from somebody outside his circle, and the only way he can bring that about is by instilling the fear of God into that person. Now, if he gave us his alibi too soon, we'd have more time to persuade that person to withdraw it.'

Ashworth suddenly looked hopeful. 'If we forced an alibi out of him, then we could still do that.'

'It's a remote chance, guv. It's also possible that Forensic might come up with something. Anyway, Russ says that's how these people evade detection, by being ultra-careful.'

Ashworth stalked across to the window, and glared down at the town. 'So, we know he's done something, but we don't know what, and we have little chance of proving it anyway.'

'We're asking the wrong questions. We should be asking what car he drives.'

'Where would that get us?'

'If it turned out to be silver, like the one outside Carter's house …'

Ashworth's expression was one of high scepticism.

'I know,' she said, 'I'm clutching at straws, but we've got to find something. I want a chance to work on that alibi.'

'Bleedin' hell.'

Lenny turned over in the hard hospital bed, and pulled the sheets high up around his head, but the snores of his fellow patients easily penetrated the thin material and, still muttering, he was left to toss and turn.

The real source of his annoyance was not so much his noisy companions, but the fear that he would very shortly be released back into the remand wing. His reputation as a hard man was not unfounded, and although his beating had been severe, Lenny was quickly recovering, the bruises around his ribs already turning an ugly violet blue, the pain beginning to fade.

Lenny was enough of an actor to put on a show when his dressings were changed, but the doctor's expression was becoming ominous, however much he groaned. And the situation was worsened by an outbreak of gastro-enteritis. He felt, with some justification, that his current run of bad luck was set to continue for, try as he might, he seemed unable to contract the illness, meaning that sooner rather than later, he would be discharged back to his cell, for his bed was badly needed. And the prison grapevine was humming with the news that, once he was out, the barons were going to organise a football match – with Lenny's head as the ball.

'Bleedin' Nora,' he moaned. 'How am I gonna get out of this?'

'Shut up,' somebody shouted from along the ward. 'Talking to yourself – you oughta be in the nut-house, you.'

'Button it,' Lenny yelled back, 'or you'll have more than guts-ache to worry about.'

Rutley police forensic department had finally come up with something, and when the news came through the next morning, it was much welcomed in Bridgetown CID.

Bobby Adams turned up smartly dressed and ready for his first assignment, and was standing rigidly to attention.

'Sit down, Bobby,' Ashworth said, pointing to one of two chairs in front of his desk. 'And relax, son.'

Bobby took the chair, and Holly eased herself into the

other, favouring the shy officer with a reassuring smile.

'This is our morning meeting,' Ashworth explained. 'Right, Holly, carry on.'

Flicking through the file, she began, 'As you know, I was talking to Russ Pearson again this morning and, among other things, he informed me that Brian Wells doesn't own a car as such. It seems that when these characters need a vehicle, they drop in on the car dealer who's paying them protection and borrow one. I'd like to take Bobby and have a chat with the dealer.'

'To what end?'

'I'd like to locate the car Wells was driving at the time of the murder. If we can get hold of it and go over it with a fine-tooth comb –'

'We haven't got the power to do that.'

'Not if it belonged to Wells, but if the dealer lets us take it, gives us permission –'

'Why would he do that?'

She gave a tight smile, and said, 'Because his arm's being twisted. Oh, it's all right, guv, it's nothing that could backfire on us, and we do need a break, badly.'

Ashworth considered this. 'It's nothing that could land us in any trouble?'

'No, it'll just be friendly persuasion, that's all.'

'Right, how long is this going to take you?'

'The journey to Rutley and back should take about two hours. Then there's the visits to Forensic, and the car dealer … about five hours, guv.'

'It's half nine, now. That means you'll be back here at half two. You'd better get moving, we can only hold Wells until seven p.m.'

Holly motioned to Bobby, and they stood up, as she said, 'Are you going to see Wells this morning, guv?'

'No, I'll let him sweat, leave him to wonder what we've got.'

Chapter 25

Jodie Summerland was expecting a knock at the front door, but she still jumped when it came. She made her way cautiously to the hall of the high-rise flat, a tall, slim, dark-haired girl, with a face that life had hardened beyond its twenty-two years. Her clothes, a leather mini-skirt that hardly reached her thighs, and a tight white top, suggested that she sold her favours for hard cash.

As soon as she opened the door, the two men waiting there pushed her aside as if she were no more than the dirt they plainly thought she was. Jodie watched as Don and his companion – Bernie Williams's loyal henchmen – marched into the flat, and then she followed.

'Me and Geoff just called in to remind you how things are,' Don said, smiling. ' 'Cause the police might be calling round today.'

'I know,' Jodie replied, 'I've been told enough times.'

'Tut, tut,' Don said. 'You're not being polite, Jodie.'

He grabbed the startled girl by the hair, and pulled her into the kitchen. She went willingly, knowing that any struggle or protest would simply make matters worse. Smiling grimly, Don pushed her against the wall, and stood before her.

He thrust his hand under her skirt, and dug his nails viciously into her flesh. 'Now, if the police come round and ask where Brian was when Reggie Carter got done, you just tell them he had his dick up here all night.'

'All right,' she said, grimacing with pain as he pressed harder.

''Cause if you don't …'

He nodded for Geoff to pass him a half-full bottle of milk, and then he smashed it on the edge of the worktop, showering the floor with broken glass and the sour-smelling liquid.

' 'Cause if you don't, I'm gonna shove this up you …'

'Don't. Oh God, don't,' she cried, when the broken bottle was placed between her legs, the sharp jagged edges piercing her pants.

'And then I'm gonna turn it round.'

He pushed his leering face close to hers, and she could smell his fetid breath, could feel a trickle of blood oozing from where the bottle had punctured her skin.

'Leave me alone, Don, please,' she begged. 'You know I'm going to do what you tell me.'

He applied more pressure to the bottle, enjoying her screams, and then he released her, and tossed it on to the floor where it smashed.

'There, Jodie, we all know where we stand now, don't we?'

The men sauntered to the door, and then Don stopped. 'Clean this place up, Jodie,' he said, pointing to the mess on the floor. 'You can't bring punters into a shit-hole like this.'

She heard their laughter in the corridor as their foot-steps faded away.

Holly quickly discovered that Bobby Adams was no great conversationalist. He had hardly spoken a word since their departure from Bridgetown; he simply stared straight ahead through the windscreen of Holly's Micra. She was a sympathetic person by nature, but she couldn't see how Ashworth would turn this shy young man into a detective constable.

The journey had taken longer than expected, on account of a hold-up on the motorway where a lorry had overturned. And Holly fretted still further when they had difficulty in finding the garage. The point had been reached where she was now swearing at fellow motorists who committed even minor transgressions, and finally, an embarrassed Bobby Adams, consulting the A-Z, pointed towards a side street.

'There it is,' he said.

'But which one?' she snapped.

With infuriating slowness, he consulted the map again. 'Third on the left.'

As she turned into it, Holly looked at her watch. It was eleven thirty. Time was passing.

The salesman was out of the office before the Micra had even pulled to a halt on the forecourt. He came towards them as they got out of the car, smiling and straightening his tie.

'Don't think I'm pushing you in any way,' he said, 'but I'm in the office if you need any help.'

'Cut the sales pitch,' Holly said, as she produced her warrant card. 'DS Bedford, Bridgetown nick, and this is DC Adams.'

'Oh yes?' the man asked, his poise vanishing as swiftly as his posh accent.

Holly snapped the warrant card shut. 'Are you the owner – Barry Tew?'

'Yes. Look, what's this all about?'

'Brian Wells comes in here and takes one of your cars whenever he feels like it – is that right?'

'Mr Wells is a valued customer,' Tew said, looking decidedly worried.

'Bullshit. You're paying him protection money.'

Bobby's mouth was hanging open, and his disbelieving eyes were wide, as Barry Tew protested, 'You've got no right to come here, shouting the odds about.'

'Shut up, I haven't got time,' Holly muttered.

The angry man glanced at Bobby, and said, 'You can't treat me like this. I'm not a kid. I've had it up once or twice.'

'So have I,' Holly replied, 'and it's very pleasurable, but that's not what we've come to talk about. Now, give.'

And if I don't?'

'If you don't, I'll have to search your office.'

Tew looked away, and said, 'What do you want?'

'Has Wells been driving a small metallic-silver car recently?' The man laughed, and indicated the hundred or so cars on the large forecourt. 'Look, a third of these are metallic-silver. It's a popular colour.'

'Was Wells driving a metallic-silver car three days ago?' she persisted.

'Yes,' Tew said. 'The Renault.'

Holly followed his pointing finger, and smiled. 'A small silver-grey Renault. Let's take a look at it, shall we?'

They picked their way towards it through the rows of vehicles.

'Has anyone driven it since Wells?'

'No,' Tew said.

'We'd like to take a look inside.'

'I'll get the keys then.'

'No, we want to take it to Rutley nick, give it the once-over there.'

Her words stopped him in his tracks. 'But you can't just take one of my cars.'

'I'm asking your permission. Now, stop messing me about.'

'And if I don't?' he blustered.

'I've got a message for you from Russ Pearson of the Special Unit,' she said, calmly. 'He's giving you an hour to get the bent MOT certificates off your premises.'

She watched the high colour disappear from Tew's cheeks, and said, 'That's if you let us have the car. If you don't, you're nicked.'

'Okay, okay,' he said resignedly. 'You lot are getting worse.'

'So's crime,' Holly called to his retreating back, and then she turned to Bobby. 'Radio Russ Pearson, and tell him to get a tow truck over here.'

'What was all that about?' he asked, confusion written all over his face.

Holly sighed impatiently. 'Look, the Special Unit sometimes has to use rather unorthodox methods to get things done. They'll often turn a blind eye to minor offences, let them ride, knowing full well that if they ever need information or a favour, they've got something to twist arms with. He who squeals loudest, is he who has something to hide – remember that.'

'I thought we had to be polite to the public, you know, helpful,' Bobby said, even more confused. 'I didn't think CID would be like this.'

'We haven't got time for all that, Bobby, just make the call.'

Shaking her head, she watched him walk away, and thought: There's not a Father Christmas either, boy. You've got a lot to learn.

Lenny lay back on the couch, and hoped that his wince was convincing when the doctor touched his ribs.

'They're still giving me gyp, doc.'

The doctor stood back. 'Lenny, I can't keep you in here any longer, I need the bed.'

'Just another night, doc,' Lenny wheedled. 'What do you say, eh?'

'I can't do it, Lenny.'

'Think it through, doc. When I get out there I'm going to get badly damaged, and I'll only have to come back in again. Ain't it better to keep me here till you ain't so busy?'

'Go to the Governor, Lenny.'

'I can't do that.'

The doctor was about to remonstrate, but then he had second thoughts and relented. 'All right,' he said –'I need the bed, but you can stay on the hospital wing. You'll just have to sleep on this couch tonight.'

Lenny beamed. 'I owe you one, doc – all right?'

'Sooner or later, you've got to do something, Lenny. If you stay in here for much longer, your friends are going to come in looking for you.'

'I know, but don't you worry, doc, I'm working on it. If I can get some money in from outside, I might be able to buy them off. Or maybe I'll get lucky,' he added with a wink, 'and we'll have a bleedin' earthquake or something.'

Ashworth glanced at the wall clock. It was one fifteen.

'Come on, Holly, come on,' he muttered, tapping his fingers on the desk.

There was a knock on the door, and Martin Dutton popped his head round.

'Brian Wells is getting restless,' he said. 'He's saying either interview him now, and tell him what you've got, or he wants to be released.'

'Stall him, Martin.'

'He's getting more confident by the minute. He's making my lads' lives hell, boasting you've got nothing, and going on about what a crowd of tossers we all are.'

'I said, stall him, Martin.'

'Jim, I pacified him as best I could. I even sent out for a Chinese take-away for his lunch, but you've got to do something.'

'Martin,' Ashworth barked, 'stall him.'

Dutton, interpreting the warning signs, withdrew rapidly, just as Ashworth sprang from his seat.

'Come on, Holly,' he kept on saying, as he paced the office, unable to keep still.

Holly glanced at the clock on the dashboard of her Micra. It was two thirty, and she was caught in heavy traffic, so Bridgetown was still an hour's drive away.

'Get out the fucking way,' she shouted, as a Ford Escort pulled out into the middle lane, blocking her path. She smashed her palm on the horn and kept it there, letting out a string of expletives which threw doubt on the driver's parentage and sexuality amongst other things, until he finally pulled back into the inside lane.

Bobby gripped the sides of his seat, and swallowed nervously as he watched the needle of the speedometer edge past seventy, and continue to climb towards eighty miles an hour. With considerable skill, Holly switched to the busy fast lane to skirt around a coach laden with tourists, only to find herself stuck behind a Jaguar which was keeping to the seventy miles an hour speed limit. For a few seconds she fumed, and then she turned on Bobby.

'What is this? All Prats day?'

Bobby shrugged and closed his eyes and ears as Holly once again leant on the horn.

Ashworth was livid by the time they arrived back in the office at four p.m.

'Where the hell have you been?' he demanded, the second they walked through the door.

'Don't start, guv,' Holly said, in much the same tone of voice. 'I'm up to here, all right?'

'We would have been earlier, sir,' Bobby cut in, 'but we got stopped by the Rutley police for speeding.'

'Why didn't you just explain the urgency?'

'Holly told them to go and play with themselves –'

'Oh, shut up, Bobby,' she shouted. 'Look, guv, the traffic was hell, and I was wound up. They pulled us over, tried to give us some verbal, I gave them some back, and they held us up for nearly half an hour.'

Ashworth looked ready to yell, and Holly appeared set to retaliate, but then they both laughed, defusing some of the tension.

'What have you got, then?' Ashworth asked.

Holly passed him a large white envelope. 'That's for you, from Forensic. And we found out from the car dealer that Wells was using a silver Renault at the time of the murder. Rutley police are going over it now.'

'Come with me, Bobby,' Ashworth said. 'Let's interview Wells.'

'It's that alibi we need, guv,' Holly shouted after him.

'If he ever decides to part with it,' Ashworth called back.

Holly closed the door, and threw her shoulder bag in the direction of her desk.

'Holly told them to go and play with themselves, sir,' she said, mimicking Bobby's voice. 'God, boy, you you're really getting on my tits.'

There was purpose in Ashworth's step as they marched into the interview room. Brian Wells, sitting at the table, looked up as they entered.

'And about time,' he said. 'I'm not staying here much longer, you know.'

Ashworth acknowledged the constable at the door, and instructed Bobby to set the tape recorder, taking his seat before Wells as the instrument clicked on, and Bobby intoned, 'Interview with Brian Wells, at …' He looked at his watch. '… at four fifteen.' Four fifteen. Ashworth's stomach turned over. Less than three hours to go before they had to release the man.

'I'm not staying here much longer,' Wells said.

'I heard you the first time,' Ashworth snapped. 'Now, I've got something to show you, Mr Wells.'

He took the white envelope from his jacket pocket, and opened up the flap with his thumb, then slowly turning it upside down, he allowed the contents to drop out on to the table. Wells stared down at the small polythene bag which contained a tiny white plastic skeleton, and as he did so, Ashworth watched him closely.

'Is that it?' Wells asked, amusement colouring his voice.

'That's it,' Ashworth confirmed. 'Found in an ashtray at the flat where you were picked up. It has two sets of finger-prints on it – yours, and Bernie William's.'

'So?' Wells said, with a shrug.

'It's identical to one found on the body of Reginald Carter.'

Wells looked away then, but kept his tone light. 'Bernie used to play with that thing, used to roll it around in his hand like it was a dice. I remember he tossed it on the table the last time he was at the flat, and I picked it up and put it in the ashtray.'

'We found a lot of fingerprints on the glasses that were taken away,' Ashworth said.

'I had some friends in,' the man said, ill at ease now. 'You wouldn't know what friends are, though, would you?'

'We also found the car you borrowed,' Ashworth said quickly, with a small smile. 'The silver Renault.'

Wells's eyes narrowed, and for an instant his face held a truly murderous expression, but then he checked himself, and said, 'What are you doing with that?'

'We're having it checked over at Rutley police station. They're going over it with a fine-tooth comb.'

'That won't do you any good,' Wells scowled.

'We'll see.'

'It won't do you any good, because I've remembered where I was the night Carter got killed.'

'Tell me, then.'

'I was in Flat 444, Carmen Rise, Rutley, with a woman called Jodie Summerland.'

Ashworth wrote those details down on the back of the white envelope. 'All evening?'

'From six p.m. till ten the next morning,' Wells said, grinning broadly. 'Ask Jodie.'

'We shall, Mr Wells, we shall.'

Ashworth motioned for Bobby to terminate the interview at the tape recorder. The time was now four thirty.

'This Jodie Summerland …' he said. 'Is she a prostitute?'

'Yes, but she'll verify that I was there, and that's all that matters to you.

'Oh, no,' Ashworth said, 'it's all that matters to you.'

Bobby could hardly keep abreast of Ashworth as he strode back to CID. Holly was at her desk when they entered the office.

'We've got it,' he told her. 'Jodie Summerland, Flat 444, Carmen Rise, Rutley. Get on the phone and tell Russ Pearson to get round there.'

'Guv,' Holly said, getting to her feet, 'is this girl a pro?'

'I believe so, Holly, just get on the phone.'

'Hold on, guv, the Special Unit go into everything as if it's World War Three. They're just going to alienate the girl.'

Ashworth was growing impatient, and as he pointed to the telephone, Holly said, 'No, listen, the Special Unit will only succeed if they can frighten the girl more than Wells's people can.'

'What are you suggesting, then?'

'Let me have a word with her.'

At that moment, Martin Dutton poked his head round the door. 'Wells is getting agitated, Jim. He's asking for a brief.'

'He's worried, guv,' Holly said, grinning. 'He wants to get out of here, so he can go to ground.'

'How long will it take you to get there?' he asked her.

'It could take me up to two hours in rush-hour traffic.'

'Jim …' Dutton called from the doorway.

'Hold on a minute, Martin,' Ashworth scowled. Turning back to Holly, he said, 'That'll give you less than half an hour with the girl.'

'It's the only chance we've got, guv. Have you got enough to hold Wells on?'

'Just about, if his brief's not too bright. Go on, then, Holly. God knows what Newton's going to say when he sees the petrol expenses.'

She snatched up her bag and car keys from the desk and ran to the door, pushing past the dispirited Dutton.

'Jim …' he said, again.

Holly's high heels sounded as she raced along the corridor, and Ashworth turned to the sergeant. 'Please, Martin, just stall him. I need two hours, that's all.'

'But I've been trying to tell you, he wants Percy Watkins,' Dutton said. 'And I know for a fact he's in court today, because some of my lads are giving evidence against one of his clients. He won't be free until six at the earliest.'

Ashworth breathed a sigh of relief, and said, 'Martin, I could kiss you.'

Dutton laughed. 'I'll give that a miss, Jim, if you don't mind.'

Chapter 26

It was six twenty-five, and Holly felt as if she had been running since first light that morning.

'Better take the stairs,' Pearson advised, as they entered Carmen Rise. 'Everybody pisses in the lift.'

'I don't care if it's knee-deep in there,' she said. 'I'm in a hurry.'

'So be it,' he said, pressing the button.

By the time they reached the twelfth floor, Holly was gagging, and she hurried out of the lift and along the corridor, gulping in the stale air.

Pearson stopped at flat number 444, and rapped on the door, saying, 'Let me do the talking.'

Jodie opened it up an inch, and said, 'Yeah?' Her voice held a mixture of boredom and feigned surprise.

'Hello, Jodie,' Pearson said, with a smile. 'How's business?'

'You hanging about won't improve it.'

Pearson laughed, and pushed past her.

'Here, what's your game?' she shouted indignantly.

'Hi, Jodie,' Holly said, following Pearson through to the surprisingly neat living-room.

Jodie slammed the front door.

'You've got no right, you know.'

'We just want to ask you a couple of questions,' Holly said politely.

'And who are you?' she asked, eyeing Holly with suspicion.

'Leave it,' Pearson said. 'Brian Wells claims he was with you on the night of the storm.'

'Yeah, he was. He got here at six o'clock, and left at ten the next morning.'

'Have it up all that time, did he?'

'He got here at six o'clock, and left –'

'Cut the crap,' Pearson said. 'If you don't co-operate with us, I'll have you nicked every time you step outside the front door.'

'Big deal,' she yelled. 'Now, get out.'

Holly pulled Pearson to one side, and whispered, 'Leave her with me … please?'

With obvious reluctance, he made his way out of the room.

'Hi, I'm Holly Bedford, Bridgetown CID.'

'Oh yeah?' Jodie said, highly uninterested.

Holly took a good look at the girl, as the front door slammed behind Pearson. 'Do you want to see my warrant card?'

'No need for that. I'm just a piece of shit everybody does what they want with.'

Back in Bridgetown, Ashworth was startled out of his thoughts by the ringing of the telephone.

'Ashworth,' he barked.

'Sorry, Jim,' Martin Dutton said. 'I know you're still waiting for Holly, but Percy Watkins is in reception.'

Ashworth exhaled sharply, and rubbed at his aching forehead. 'Take him down to the interview room, Martin. By the longest possible route.'

The time was six thirty-five.

'Can I sit down?' Holly asked.

'If you want.'

Holly made herself comfortable on the settee, and asked, 'What are you doing here, Jodie?'

Immediately, the girl rounded on her. 'What is this? The heavy mob can't get anything out of me, so they've sent you in to be nice. Well, just get out of my life.'

'Stop being so bloody stupid. Look, you complain about the way people use you, but when I try to treat you half

255

decent, you do this get-out-of-my-life act.'

Jodie was astonished by the outburst, and seemed to view Holly in a new light as she settled in an armchair, retrieving a packet of cigarettes from the floor.

'Do you want one?'

'Okay.'

After accepting a light, Holly said, 'You've got a slight accent. Is it Lancashire?'

Jodie shook her head. 'No, Yorkshire.'

'And you've got some education, too,' Holly ventured. 'What are you doing here?'

'You lot down here don't know you're born,' the girl snorted. 'I've got five O levels, and three As, and until I left Leeds three years ago, I was working in a lollipop factory, taking home fifty pounds a week, for forty hours.'

'So you came down here on the game?'

'No, I didn't,' she said, bitterly. 'I met a girl named Lucy at the DHSS. Anyway, she let me stop at her place, because I hadn't got anywhere to sleep. At the end of the first week, she brought two guys back, and I ended up in bed with one of them, and afterwards he gives me fifty quid. Then, before I know it, I'm on the game, making six hundred quid a week.'

Holly hadn't smoked for a long time, and the cigarette was making her feel dizzy, but not wanting to break the link she had formed with the girl, she persevered with it. 'I think I've got the picture. I suppose Lucy introduced you to somebody she said was going to look after you.'

Jodie nodded.

'And that was Brian Wells?'

'Yeah, him and Bernie Williams.'

'And pretty soon, they were taking most of what you earned?' Again the girl nodded.

'And they're in complete control of you?'

'Oh no,' Jodie said vehemently. 'They don't control me.

After all, I'm a nothing, a nobody. They don't control me, they bloody own me, don't they?'

Percy Watkins came out of the interview room looking perplexed, and Ashworth was waiting for him in the corridor. The two men knew each other well, and were on good terms.

'What's all this about, Jim? Plastic skeletons? Cars being looked at by Forensic? You're being a bit naughty here.'

'Wells is here of his own free will.'

'No,' Watkins corrected him. 'He was, but now he wants to leave. Have you got any sort of case against him?'

Ashworth's shoulders slumped. 'We're checking his alibi – if that holds up, then, no.'

'Then you'll have to release him,' Watkins said, consulting his watch. 'It's ten to seven, Jim. If you haven't broken his alibi by now, you're not going to.'

'Give me the ten minutes,' Ashworth pleaded. 'Just as a favour.'

'Jim, I'm quoting the rules here, not granting favours. Now, you've either got enough to charge him with, or at least to apply to hold and question him for a further period, otherwise you've got to release him. What's it going to be?'

Ashworth turned away. 'We'll release him.'

'Good.'

'Percy, I need to know where he's staying. Officially, he's of no fixed abode.'

'Are you trying to delay me, Jim?' The solicitor attempted to hide a smile.

'Yes.'

Holly glanced at her watch. It was ten to seven. Time was running out, but her desire to break the alibi was now vying with her concern for the girl. Jodie was in a hopeless situation.

'What did you want out of life?'

'Life?' Jodie reflected. 'Believe it or not, I wanted to be an air hostess. It was something exciting, and …'

'And challenging?' Holly suggested.

'Yeah, challenging.'

All of a sudden the girl's face was animated, and without the dull flatness in her eyes, and the sullen line of her mouth, she was really quite pretty.

'I'd have liked to end every day feeling I'd achieved something, you know? Perhaps have a nice flat, and a car.'

'Did you want a boyfriend, or a husband?'

'No, I didn't want to be tied down. I enjoyed my freedom too much. Perhaps I'd have had two cats for company, and just led a peaceful life.'

'Why don't you leave all this behind you? Just walk away from it.'

'You don't walk away from that lot,' Jodie said, with a hollow laugh. 'They won't let you. I've seen girls scarred for life. Wherever I went, they'd come and fetch me back.'

'Brian Wells wasn't here that night, was he?' Holly asked softly.

'No, of course he wasn't.'

'Then say so.'

The hopeless expression returned to Jodie's face, and Holly said, 'You could be done for perjury …'

'Perjury?' Jodie said, with a look of incredulity. 'You think I'm frightened of that? Look at this.'

She got to her feet, and without the slightest embarrassment, she pushed down her briefs and pointed to the ugly deep cuts around her vagina where the broken bottle had dug into her flesh.

Holly shuddered at the mass of congealed blood. 'Did Brian Wells's men do that to you?'

'Yeah, it was just a little reminder that I do what they tell me.' Gingerly pulling up her briefs, Jodie crossed to the window, and stared down at the pavement far below.

'Sometimes, Holly, I could throw myself out of this window,' she murmured, tears streaming down her face. 'You don't know these people.'

Ashworth waited with Bobby outside the interview room. When the door opened, Brian Wells came out, followed by his solicitor.

'Mr Wells will supply you with an address where he'll be staying,' Percy Watkins informed the chief inspector.

'You'd got no right to keep me here for so long,' the man protested.

'Mr Wells,' Ashworth began politely, 'may I remind you that you came here of your own free will. When you requested the presence of your solicitor, you were given immediate access to a telephone. I believe my behaviour throughout has been perfectly correct. Thank you for your help, sir. Detective Constable Adams will escort you to the duty officer where your personal effects will be returned to you.'

'We're breaking the gangs,' Holly said encouragingly.

'You might be, but you haven't broken Bernie Williams or Brian Wells yet, have you?'

'No, but if you don't alibi Wells, we could.'

'I can't take that chance, Holly. Can't you see that?'

'But it is a chance, Jodie, and it's got to beat throwing yourself out of the window.'

'I can't do it,' she insisted, the tears brimming again as she turned away.

'Look at me, Jodie. All those things you want are out there, but you've got to have the guts to get yourself out of this mess and go for them.'

'But they'd get me.'

'They might not be about. Anyway, we'd protect you.'

'You couldn't protect me all the time.'

'I'd do all I could to help, I promise you that.'

For a few moments, the girl hovered on the brink of submission, but then the hardness crept back into her features. 'No, you wouldn't, you'd get what you wanted by promising me everything, and then you'd desert me.'

'I wouldn't desert you, Jodie.'

'Can you guarantee my safety?'

'No, I can't, you'd be taking a risk. I'd do everything I could, but to be honest, there're no guarantees.'

'It's one way out ... Oh God, Holly, I'm so frightened.'

'It's your choice, Jodie. You can lie down and let that scum treat you like a piece of shit, kick you, push you around ...' She paused. 'Or you can get up, girl, and give the bastards some of it back.'

She studied Holly's face, her expression betraying the turmoil within her.

'Your choice,' Holly whispered. 'Your life.'

Chapter 27

Lenny Spencer spent the day wandering aimlessly around the ward, hoping to catch the stomach bug. And in the evening, he was sitting on the couch in his cubicle, when the curtains rustled. Lenny caught his breath, expecting half a dozen heavies to rush in and overwhelm him, but instead, a small hatchet-faced man of around fifty nervously sidled in.

'You Lenny Spencer?' he asked.

'Who wants to know?'

'Look, I got a message for you, from the boys waiting outside.' All at once, Lenny vaulted from the couch and strode across to the man. Grabbing him by the front of his shirt, he hauled him into the cubicle, and slammed him up against the wall.

'Right, I've been waiting to get one of you on your own.'

'Leave it out,' he spluttered. 'I'm just like you – I have to do what I'm told, or I get a duffin' up.'

Aware that the man was trembling, Lenny eased his grip, and said, 'What's the message, then?'

'They said, if you don't come out tomorrow, they're coming in for you.'

'Oh yeah? Well, you tell them I'll come out, and there'd better be a lot of them waiting,' Lenny replied with much bravado, as he heaved the man away from the wall. 'Now, piss off.'

The man gulped as he looked back, and then he scurried away.

Lenny hitched himself up on the couch and, running a nervous hand through his hair, he glanced around the tiny cubicle in despair.

'Lenny Spencer, this is your life. Oh God, what a bleedin' mess.'

Brian Wells was pocketing the last of his belongings. He opened up his wallet, and checked the contents before slipping it into the inside pocket of his jacket, and then the duty sergeant asked him to sign the release document.

'Thank you for coming in to help us, sir,' Bobby said diplomatically.

Wells scrawled his signature, and scowled. 'It's been my pleasure.'

'Then you're really going to enjoy tonight,' Ashworth said loudly from the doorway.

All eyes turned to him, and there was a tight smile on his lips as he said, 'Your alibi has collapsed, Mr Wells. Jodie Summerland says you were not with her on the night of Reginald Carter's murder. So, there are a few more questions to be asked.'

'The little scrubber,' Wells spat, before quickly regaining his composure. 'Forty years I've been running rings round you lot,' he said, glaring at the chief inspector, 'and you get me like this.'

Feeling for the moment that he had the advantage, Ashworth left Brian Wells to simmer in the interview room while he went back to CID. He was in a self-congratulatory mood, aware that the conclusion to the case was almost in sight. As far as he was concerned, the murderers of both Terence Wells and Reginald Carter were now in custody, and a celebratory cup of tea was in order. After a detour to the canteen, he sat at his desk, savouring the drink, and put a belated call through to Sarah, informing her that he would be late home.

Ashworth drank slowly, and when the tea was finished, he tossed the plastic cup into the wastepaper basket, and rose to his feet. It was time to interview Brian Wells.

His steps were jaunty as he made his way, with Bobby Adams, to interview room number one, and he paused outside the door briefly, getting straight in his mind the questions he wanted to ask. Inside the room, the uniformed constable nodded respectfully to the chief inspector as he strode to the table where a dejected Brian Wells sat with head bowed.

'Brian, are you ready to talk to me?'

The man nodded, and Bobby activated the tape recorder, as Ashworth took a seat, saying, 'Tell me about Reginald Carter.'

'I'm not holding my hand up for that,' Wells said. 'I know nothing about it.'

That was not the answer Ashworth had expected, and he stared at the man, completely nonplussed, as Bobby settled in beside him.

The chief inspector remained silent, so Bobby pushed aside his shyness, and said, 'What are you holding your hand up to?'

Wells considered them, and in a barely audible whisper, he said, 'Armed robbery. In Bath, on the day and night you're talking about. A security van. There were five of us. We got away with three hundred thousand pounds.'

'Why are you telling us this story?' Bobby asked, grinning cynically. 'So we won't be able to tie you in with Carter's murder?'

'Don't talk like a prat,' Wells said, in the same dull monotone. 'As soon as you said you'd got the car we'd used, I knew I was in lumber.'

'What difference would that make?'

'It's the cars that get most thieves caught on robberies, isn't it? If you nick one for the job, you have to burn it, destroy the clues. And then there's always a chance you'll be seen switching to another one.'

He laughed, a self-mocking sound. 'We thought our method was foolproof: borrow one from a used car sales lot, change the number plates, do the job, then return it. I mean, that's about the last place you lot would look for a car that'd been used in a robbery, and in a couple of days, it could be sold. But when you told me the Special Unit were going over it, I knew I was in trouble, because our fingerprints were all over it, fibres from our clothes; we even counted the banknotes on the back seat. I knew by the time those bastards had finished with it, they'd compare what they'd found with serious crimes all over the country. That's why I was so keen to get out of here, before you got their report.'

'I see,' Ashworth said. 'No doubt Special Unit will want to see you.' 'No doubt,' Wells said, shrugging resignedly.

Ashworth pushed himself up from the chair, eager to get out of the room, while Bobby crossed to the tape recorder, and terminated the interview, then turned to face Wells.

'Brian,' he said, 'You know who killed Carter, don't you?' Wells made no comment.

'You know why he was killed, don't you?'

'Maybe I do, but telling you isn't going to help me, is it?'

Bobby seemed on the point of pursuing this until Ashworth signalled that they should leave the room, and as the door closed on Wells, he said, 'He does know something, sir.'

'Perhaps he does, Bobby, but he's not going to tell us.' He glanced at the young detective, and smiled. 'You did some good work in there, son.'

Reddening a little, he said, 'I've been keeping quiet and watching interview techniques and what have you, sir, and I think I'm ready now.'

'Good,' Ashworth said, 'but we're back to square one, son.'

'I'm all right, doc,' Lenny said, following the doctor through the hospital ward.

'You're not, Lenny, you should go to the Governor.'

'That wouldn't do no good.'

'Come on, I'll take you back to the remand wing.

There's a shortage of warders at the moment.'

'Look on the bright side, doc, I could be back with you in an hour,' he said, laughing feebly. 'Just keep the operating theatre open.'

In spite of the fact that Lenny's remark could be true, the doctor chortled as he led him through a maze of passages. Three doors had to be unlocked for them before they arrived at the remand wing, and as the last one was opened, Lenny peered through the bars to see the majority of prisoners out of their cells, awaiting his arrival. Nothing enlivened a prisoner's day so much as seeing one of their fellows beaten to a pulp.

'Thanks for walking me home, doc.'

Attempting a swagger, Lenny passed through the doorway, and when it closed behind him, the key turning loudly in the lock, he sauntered forward.

'Lenny.'

The voice stopped him in his tracks, and he turned with a sigh.

'Yeah?'

'You've got visitors,' the warder announced.

His face broke into a smile. 'Visitors?'

'You want to see them?'

'Yeah, why not?'

'Don't you want to know who they are?'

'I couldn't care less,' Lenny replied, scanning the corridor crowded with expectant faces.

When Lenny saw Ashworth and Bobby waiting in the visitors' room, he glanced up at the ceiling, and breathed, 'Oh God.'

'Do you want me to leave him with you?' the warder asked.

'Thank you,' Ashworth said.

'I'll be just outside the door, then.'

'Sit down, Lenny,' Ashworth ordered lightly.

He sat, his eyes flitting about the room, determined to avoid the chief inspector's piercing gaze.

'Been in the wars, have we?' Ashworth remarked.

Lenny fingered the stitches above his eye, and said, 'I fell over, didn't I?'

'Nasty,' Ashworth said, with a smile. 'We've had the report from Forensic. The bullet that killed Terence Wells was fired from the gun found in your possession.'

'I could have told you that,' Lenny said. 'I was the other end of it, wasn't I? Pulling the trigger.'

'And I didn't know, until I saw the report today, that this was also found at the same time.'

Ashworth leant across, and placed before him the polythene bag containing the small skeleton. A startled expression flashed across Lenny's face.

'Never seen it before,' he mumbled.

'But it's got your fingerprints on it, Lenny. Tell us about it.'

'I've got nothing to tell. I've admitted I killed Wells – what more do you want?'

'Lenny, you're going to get thirty years for this. If you keep claiming you had an argument –'

'I ain't going to live for thirty years, am I?'

Ashworth exhaled loudly, and Bobby cleared his throat. 'Sir, could I have a word with Lenny?'

'Yes, detective constable, go ahead.'

Bobby took a packet of Benson and Hedges from his pocket, and said, 'Why did you own up to killing Terry Wells?'

'Because I done it,' Lenny answered, reaching for the proffered cigarette.

Taking his time, Bobby lit his own, and held out the flame for Lenny. 'But it doesn't make any sense. I've been studying your record: six years ago you were caught beating somebody around the head with a claw hammer, and yet you pleaded not guilty.'

'He had it coming, didn't he? He'd been mouthing off about me.'

'You've always pleaded not guilty in the past,' Bobby said. 'I think you wanted to get in here, away from Terry Wells's friends.'

Lenny lowered his eyes, and concentrated on the ashtray.

'I'm right, aren't I? Only it hasn't worked out.'

'You could say that,' Lenny said, looking up briefly.

'They beat you up because you killed Wells.'

'Oh no, this wasn't a beating-up I got. These geezers want to ask me some questions, see, and they just give me a little slapping about so I don't waste no time when they ask them.'

'But don't you think that's odd, Lenny? Why should they want to ask you questions?'

Lenny frowned. 'Dunno, I never thought about it. I was getting me head kicked in at the time.'

'You were paid to kill Wells, weren't you? These people want to know who hired you.'

Lenny shook his head vigorously, but his 'No' was unconvincing.

Bobby allowed a few seconds to tick away, and then he crushed his cigarette in the ashtray. 'Say we offered to have you segregated.'

'Segregated?'

'Solitary confinement. A cell of your own, away from the other inmates. You wouldn't have to mix with any of them.'

'Could you fix that?'

Bobby gave him a confident leave-it-with-me wink, then turned to Ashworth, and whispered, 'Could I, sir?'

'Yes,' he whispered back. 'Keep going. You're doing well.'

'It can be arranged, Lenny, but you'll have to co-operate with us. Now, you were paid …'

'Yeah, all right, I was paid,' he said. 'That's how I got into this bleedin' mess. I was drinking in the Cross Keys a few weeks back when this broke comes up to me and says, are you interested in doing a hit, Lenny? –'cause we've heard you're a useful boy. Well, I was a bit chuffed, so I said, how much? And he said, thirty grand. I mean, thirty grand – nowadays you can get somebody topped for ten, so I was even more chuffed 'cause that meant it was somebody important.'

'Look, Lenny,' Ashworth cut in, 'fascinating as your career structure is –'

'Hold on, that's what I'm coming to. I ballsed it up, didn't I?'

For a few seconds there was a stunned silence, and then Bobby said, 'How did you balls it up?'

'I shot the wrong geezer, didn't I?'

Chapter 28

Holly had managed only a few hours' sleep on Russ Pearson's settee, and was therefore stiff and bad-tempered as she viewed the crowded motorway from the slip-road.

The previous evening, as soon as news came through that Brian Wells had been charged with the robbery at Bath, and that four other men, including Bernie Williams, were being interviewed in connection with the crime, she stayed true to her word and offered to drive Jodie Summerland back to Leeds.

Jodie readily agreed, unable to believe that the gang leaders would be out of circulation for the foreseeable future. Holly secretly feared that minor members of the gang might seek revenge against the girl, but they were unlikely to pursue her as far as Yorkshire.

Russ Pearson went along too, and witnessed a tearful reunion. Jodie's parents begged them to stay for refreshments, but they declined and arrived back in Rutley at five a.m.

Holly, now heading for Bridgetown, forced her way aggressively into the inside lane.

'You shot the wrong person?' Ashworth could hardly believe his ears. 'What do you mean, you went to the wrong address?'

'No, I ain't that stupid,' Lenny said. 'I went to the right place all right, saw the Merc in the garage, so I broke in like I told you before. I went into the room with all them books, and the geezer was snoring his head off. Well, I didn't think, did I? I mean, I could only see the back of the chair, so I walked round, and I shot him.'

'Hold on, hold on. Who were you paid to kill?'

'Some bloke named Reggie Carter.'

'Reggie Carter?' Ashworth echoed.

'Yeah. I'd never heard of him. Anyway, when I saw I'd wasted Terry Wells, I knew I was in big trouble.'

'And you were supposed to leave the skeleton on the body?'

'Yeah.'

'Who put the money up?'

'Honest to God, I don't know. You know how these things get done, through a broker. The only bloke I saw was the messenger in the pub. He gave me half the money, and I had to buy the gun.'

'I believe you, Lenny,' Ashworth said. 'So, you only collected half the money?'

'No, I hung around till the news broke. The reports just said a body had been found in Lilac Avenue, so the broker must have decided I'd done the job. I picked up the rest of the money from the bloke in the pub, and scarpered to London.'

'Give DC Adams a description of that man, Lenny,' Ashworth said, standing up. 'I'll go and see the Governor about your solitary confinement.'

Ashworth walked along the passage with his mind in overdrive. So, someone wanted Reginald Carter dead, and all this time the murder of Terence Wells had sent them along so many false trails, leaving Carter vulnerable to his fatal attack.

It was a long drive back to the station, and Ashworth was silent for most of the journey as various people flashed through his mind.

Bernie Williams. Terence Wells's two brothers, working in Germany.

And the plastic skeletons kept edging back into his thoughts. One was found at each of the murder scenes; he was sure they were the key to this mystery.

Back in CID, it seemed that Bobby was having similar

thoughts, for as he sat at Josh's desk, looking through the reports, he said, 'Sir, Terry Wells's other brothers – I know it says here they work in Germany, but I'd like to check their whereabouts at the time of Carter's murder.'

Ashworth lowered himself wearily into his chair. 'No doubt you're working along the same lines as I am: Bernie Williams paid to have Carter killed, and when that went wrong, he made the best of a bad job and told the Wells boys that Carter had killed their brother.'

'Thirty thousand pounds is a lot of money to find, but Williams would have no trouble putting it together. And he'd probably think we wouldn't even look at the two brothers working abroad.'

'It's a long shot, but check it out.'

At the door, Bobby almost collided with a uniformed officer. He said, 'Pathologist's report on Reginald Carter, sir,' and placed a large brown envelope on Ashworth's desk.

'Thank you, constable.'

When he was alone, Ashworth picked up the envelope. 'I don't want to know when or how, I want to know why,' he said, withdrawing the document.

His eyes glided over the typewritten lines, and as he flicked through the pages, his expression remained passive until he came to the final paragraph, which he read again and again. Dropping the report on to his desk, Ashworth walked to the glass wall and stared down at the car-park, where his Scorpio stood alone, the spaces either side – allocated to Holly and Josh – empty.

He stood deep in thought for a long time and then picked up the office file on the Terence Wells case from where Bobby had left it on Josh's desk.

'I now know why,' he muttered to himself.

With much haste, he dialled the forensic department, requesting to see the small cards delivered with the flowers to Carter's home, and the plastic skeletons found on

Carter's body, and in Brian Wells's flat. The items were brought to him immediately, and he studied them for some time, occasionally glancing at the file and the pathologist's report.

Finally, he sat back, and said, 'Yes, I know why, and I think I know who.'

Ashworth disliked driving, and the long haul to and from the remand prison had already exhausted his patience, so having to journey to Rutley did not improve his temper. The motorway was crowded, and the day was stuffy, the heat inside the car insufferable, and by the time he pulled up at Rutley police station, his shirt was sticking to his back.

Taking a few deep breaths to compose himself, Ashworth collected his jacket from the back seat and made his way to the station building. Russ Pearson, looking rather pleased with himself, was waiting in reception.

'Chief inspector,' he said, 'Bernie Williams and Brian Wells have been charged with the robbery at Bath. They're looking at nine years apiece.'

'I'm going to put Bernie Williams away for life,' Ashworth replied shortly.

'I've got him in the interview room, as you requested.' The room was air-conditioned, and a wonderfully cool blast hit Ashworth as he stood on the threshold and glared at Williams sitting at the table. The man responded with a look of pure hatred, before turning away.

'The feeling's mutual,' Ashworth assured him, as he took the tiny bagged skeleton from his pocket and tossed it on to the table. 'Your fingerprints are on it.'

'So what?' Williams shrugged. 'You can buy them in any joke shop.'

Ashworth placed his hands on the desk, and leant across. 'Only you didn't buy them in a joke shop, you were given two or three, and one was to be left on Reginald Carter's dead body.'

Williams looked up at him, his eyes challenging.

'You were the broker, weren't you? Someone paid you thousands of pounds to have Carter killed. You were even willing to turn your own hit man in because you knew Lenny wouldn't dare name you. Terry Wells's people were already after him, and you were too, for bungling the job. Lenny was really in a no-win situation.'

'Spencer's a cretin. I had word passed to him that if he kept quiet about me, I'd overlook the little matter of him killing the wrong person. So, he talked, did he?'

Ashworth shook his head slowly. 'No, he didn't have to. Information I've received has made me realise the significance of the skeleton. Now, I want to know who paid to have Carter killed.'

Williams smiled, and said, 'Can't you find out?'

'I could, but it would be easier if you told me.'

'I may yet have the last laugh, Mr Ashworth,' Williams said, his smile becoming a wicked grin, 'because this involves one of your own people.'

The tiny coffin rolled down the steep concrete banks of the weir-pool and, through his tears, Josh watched as it hit the water and sprang open. A small plastic skeleton spilled out and spun around in the circling current, before meeting the main flow and bobbing away downstream. The coffin followed, quickly filling up with water, until it disappeared from the surface.

Josh's cheeks were wet as he stared across at Greg sitting beside him on the damp grass, his eyes heavy, the lids closing against the strong sunlight.

'Josh, please let me die with some dignity,' he slurred. 'No one need ever know then.'

Taking up the empty aspirin box lying beside his friend, Josh suddenly scrambled to his feet and hurled it into the weir.

'Thank you for what you've done,' Greg murmured. 'I

love you. I always have.'

Fresh tears stung Josh's eyes, and he walked away sharply.

'I love you, Josh. Thank you.'

But he was not listening. He began to run, his feet pounding the ground, faster and faster until he collapsed on to his knees, fighting to get oxygen from the oppressive atmosphere. His hair was damp with perspiration, and his clothes clung uncomfortably, but even so he struggled to his feet, and ran on.

Holly passed Bobby Adams in the corridor outside CID.

'Is the guv'nor in?' she asked, sipping a cup of tea from the vending machine.

'No,' Bobby said, without stopping. 'He's gone to Rutley, and I'm checking something out.'

'Oh, good.'

She pulled a face and entered the office, craving a shower and a few hours' sleep on a soft mattress. She settled behind her desk to drink her tea and happened to glance at Ashworth's desk, straight away noticing the chaos there, the pathologist's report and the files scattered about, the florist's cards spread across the blotter.

Her curiosity was aroused, and she walked across, first picking up the pathologist's report. She flicked through it, scanning the pages without taking in fully the information contained there, and then dropped it back on the desk and went to finish the tea. Her tired brain finally made the connection as she drained the cup, and she hurriedly went back to the report, turning to the last page and the final paragraph, which read:

There were several swellings on the neck and armpits which I at first attributed to the early stages of cancer, but on investigation this proved not to be the case. After performing various tests, and conducting an extensive examination of the anal regions, I am of the conclusion that Reginald Carter was a practising homosexual, in the first stages of Acquired Immune Deficiency Syndrome (Aids). When he contracted the virus is impossible to say, for it is known …

The report slipped from Holly's fingers, and landed with a soft rustle on the desk.

'My God,' she muttered. 'Someone with a silver car was watching Carter

In her mind's eye, she saw Josh's silver Nissan. And she remembered that night at his house, when he had drunkenly forced the reports with handwritten amendments upon her – he had said if he could find out who had given Greg the virus, he would kill the bastard.

'I'd take a knife …' he had said.

She saw again vividly Carter's ravaged body.

Her hand was trembling as she picked up the florist's cards to compare the writing with the amendments on the report. It was an exact match.

'Jesus Christ, Josh, what have you done?'

She grabbed her bag and dashed from the office, leaving the door open behind her.

Rational thought had no place in Holly's mind as she drove to Josh's house. All that registered was the fact that he was in trouble, and she must help him.

Still dazed, she steered the Micra into his road and saw Ashworth's Scorpio parked outside his house. She pulled up sharply behind it, and without bothering to switch off the engine, she scrambled from the car, leaving the door swinging on its hinges.

Ashworth grabbed her arm. 'Holly,' he said, alarmed by her glazed eyes.

She tried to push past him, but he held on to her,

refusing to loosen his grip.

'Get off me,' she shouted, trying to break free. 'Josh's in trouble. He's murdered Carter. The silver car – it was Josh's. The handwriting on the report's the same as on the cards –'

'Holly, stop it,' he yelled.

But she continued to babble, continued to struggle, and finally Ashworth took hold of her shoulders and shook her forcefully.

'Listen to me,' he said, 'Greg used Josh's car while you were in Rutley. Greg did the reports. It was Greg's handwriting.' Very slowly, Holly came to her senses, and her bewildered eyes focused on his face.

'Do you understand me?'

'Oh, thank God, guv.'

She fell against him then, her head resting on his shoulder, and Ashworth held her close while her tears of relief flowed freely.

'Now, pull yourself together,' he said. 'Josh's front door is wide open. We have to go in there.'

Ashworth proceeded with great caution, unsure of what they would find inside. Holly still looked stunned, but was now able to think clearly, and she followed behind, swearing softly as she wiped away the mascara running down her cheeks.

In the hall, they heard sounds from the kitchen, and Ashworth slowly pushed open the door. Josh was sitting at the table, a glass of vodka in his hand, his hair dishevelled, his eyes red and swollen.

He looked up at them, and studied their faces. 'You know, don't you?'

Ashworth nodded and moved forward, his huge bulk seeming to fill the tiny room. Sensing that Josh was treading an emotional tightrope, with the alcohol acting as a further irritant, he moved slowly, easing himself into

276

a chair at the table.

'We understand, Josh,' he murmured gently.

'No, you don't, nobody does,' Josh replied, his voice little more than a whisper. 'Do you know, guv, when I was about sixteen, before I even knew I was gay, I used to cry at the sad films on the telly – I couldn't help it – and my dad used to say: If you're going to behave like a big Jessie, get up to your room where nobody can see you. So I'd run up the stairs with him shouting: Go on, you gutless wonder …'

Ashworth crouched before him. 'Listen to me, Josh, I need to know about Greg and Carter.'

Josh snorted, and took a long drink.

'Tell me,' he urged.

Josh sat back and closed his eyes.

'Greg met Carter just over a year ago in London,' he began hesitantly. 'They spent the night together at a hotel. When Greg woke up, Carter was gone, and on the bedside table was a small coffin. Inside was a tiny skeleton and a note saying: Welcome to the Aids Club. Carter knew he was HIV, you see, and he was deliberately passing it around.'

Josh opened his eyes. 'Greg took the tests, and found he was positive. He developed full-blown Aids almost immediately. He sold everything he had, the house his parents left him, his car, everything. He eventually traced Carter to Bridgetown, and took to hanging around the pubs and clubs in Rutley until somebody introduced him to Bernie Williams, who said he could get Carter killed for sixty thousand pounds. Greg paid the money, but when Lenny Spencer made a mess of the job, he went back to Williams and asked for it back. Williams just laughed. So, Greg came here, and started to watch Carter. He said it all just built up in his mind, and he broke into the house and stabbed him. He said he couldn't stop.'

Picking up his empty glass, Josh stared into it, his mouth a bitter line.

'Greg used me. He knew he couldn't have passed the

virus on to me – that was just an excuse. He said he was leaving me everything, but it was all gone, he hadn't got any money. He needed somewhere to stay, and he needed to know what the police were doing … he used me.'

Ashworth took the glass from Josh's hand, and placed it on the table.

'When did you find out about all this?'

He said nothing, his face a total blank.

'It's important, Josh. Bernie Williams thinks he can tie you in with this. He's claiming you knew what was going on.'

'Greg told me about half an hour ago. He'd taken some tablets, enough to kill himself. All he could do was beg me to let him die in peace. He told me he loved me.'

His voice cracked, and he shook his head angrily.

'Where was this?' Ashworth asked, an urgency in his tone.

'At the weir.'

'Holly, get a mobile and ambulance there. Quickly.'

She was moving to obey the order, when Josh's harsh voice brought her to a halt.

'You think I ran away, don't you? The gutless wonder. That's what you both think, isn't it? Well, sorry to disappoint you, guv, but I did my job. I called the ambulance, and the station. I did my bloody job.'

'Oh, Josh.'

Ashworth reached out a hand to touch his shoulder, but Josh recoiled from it and moved back in his chair, hugging himself.

He said, 'I don't want anybody near me, ever again. Please, go.'

Ashworth straightened up, and led Holly from the kitchen, but before he closed the door, he looked back to where Josh was slumped in the chair. He seemed about to speak, but changed his mind and moved out into the hall.

'Holly …' he said, his voice gruff.

'It's all right, guv, I'm not leaving him. I'll go back and try to talk him through it.'

In the street, Ashworth sighed, and said, 'I'm sure he won't resent your presence … just mine.'

'He doesn't resent you, guv.'

He stood still, staring along the road.

'Perhaps if the opportunity presents itself,' he said, stiffly, 'you could tell the lad I'm proud of him.'

And then, without waiting for a reply, Ashworth walked to his car and drove away.